Evan Knowlson was sitting in one of the plaid chairs in front of the fireplace. A small lamp disguised as a candle was lit on the table by the chair; its light beamed down on a cup of creamy liquid beside a plate of tiny cookies shaped and decorated to look like wreaths. It took Susan a few moments to realize that he must be dead; no one could live with a hole the size of the one he had in his right temple.

"Susan? Why is it taking you so long? Are you okay?" Kelly appeared behind her.

Susan heard her gasp, but then there was almost a full minute of silence before the other woman spoke.

"I told you he would come back, didn't I . . .?"

Also by Valerie Wolzien
Published by Fawcett Books:

MURDER AT THE PTA LUNCHEON
THE FORTIETH BIRTHDAY BODY

WE WISH YOU A MERRY MURDER

VALERIE WOLZIEN

FAWCETT GOLD MEDAL • NEW YORK

For my parents

A Fawcett Gold Medal Book
Published by Ballantine Books
Copyright © 1991 by Valerie Wolzien

Library of Congress Catalog Card Number: 91-92197

ISBN 0-449-14723-1

Manufactured in the United States of America

First Edition: December 1991

ONE

"WHAT I REALLY HATE IS BUYING GIFTS FOR TEACHERS. Between the teachers at her day school, and her piano teacher, and the prima donna who runs her ballet classes, I don't have time to shop for presents for the family."

"And the gymnastic instructor, and their tutors . . . I know exactly what you mean. Tell me, do you really like this dress, or is it too tailored?"

"I bought a dozen rolls of imported paper at a fabulous shop up on the Cape and now I can't remember where I put the damn things. And this year was going to be different. This year I was going to get organized."

"What I hate more than anything is helping the kids buy gifts for his ex-wife. I know she's their mother, but that doesn't mean they have to buy her the most expensive thing in the store. Last year—"

"Do you think it's a little long? Not that it couldn't be shortened easily, but I wonder if it would drape as well if it were hemmed."

"Of course, we had to get rid of all the poinsettias before

the cat poisoned herself again, and I don't know what the house is going to look like without them."

"Kathleen, will you stop listening to everyone else's conversation and tell me what you think about this dress?" Susan Henshaw, an attractive brunette in her early forties, urged the woman with whom she was sharing a large dressing room in one of the most expensive dress shops in Connecticut. "I know the paisley—"

"It looks fine, but there's a green dress out there . . . It's a size eight, but it looks big. I'll get it for you." Kathleen Gordon pushed aside the heavy canvas curtain and vanished down the plushly carpeted corridor back to the selling floor.

"Next year, I'm going to St. Bart's and forgetting about Christmas!" announced a harassed-looking woman, glancing into the cubicle Kathleen had just left. "Susan! I didn't know you were here! Good to see you. We're looking forward to your open house. My husband wants to know if Jed's going to make his famous Ivy League Punch again."

"We wouldn't know how to celebrate Christmas without it," Susan answered. As soon as the other woman took off, heading in the same direction Kathleen had taken, Susan pulled a large notebook from her handbag and, finding a clean sheet of paper and pen, she wrote: "Find crystal punch bowls."

She was still staring at those four words, sucking on the end of her pen, when Kathleen returned, a sweep of jade silk across her arm.

Susan frowned at the material. "I think that's more your color than mine. Probably more your size, too," she added, glancing up at the stunning blond.

"Try it on," Kathleen urged.

"I don't think it's going to fit," Susan said, her voice muffled as she pulled the dress she had been wearing over her head.

"So what will it hurt to try . . ." Kathleen began, and then stopped. "Damn it. I sound like my mother."

"If she's anything like mine, she'll be thrilled to hear it," Susan answered, smoothing the silk down over her hips.

"That reminds me, I wanted to stop at the drugstore and buy some gardenia-scented soap. She might like that. I can hang up the paisley, if you don't want it."

"Take it. I think you were right about this one," Susan said, swirling before the mirror. "It's lovely, isn't it?"

"Perfect," agreed Kathleen, looking down at the clothing she held.

"I was talking about the dress I'm wearing," Susan said.

Kathleen looked up and smiled. "I'm sorry. I was just wondering what I've forgotten. My mother's visit is starting to make me crazy—and she hasn't even arrived yet."

"Your mother, my mother-in-law—we're going to be nervous wrecks by the New Year. Maybe we should take the first plane out of here. We could go someplace warm and sip rum punch instead of eggnog."

"Good idea. When do we leave?"

"I'd say now, but what will I do about the fifty couples we invited to a holiday open house next week?" Susan asked, taking a last look at herself in the mirror.

"If they have enough of Jed's punch, they won't even miss you."

"Now there's an idea." Susan laughed. "Let me pay for this and we can go to the drugstore. I can look at stuff for Chrissy there while you shop. I think her Christmas wish list this year was drawn up by the editors of *Vogue* magazine. It ranges from expensive makeup to expensive clothing; it's dreadful."

"She's fifteen years old, Sue. Remember how we were at that age?"

"Well, maybe . . . But I think I was influenced more by *Seventeen* magazine than *Vogue*." She stopped to fasten two buttons on the shoulder of her sweater. "Our latest crisis is what to buy Seth St. John for Christmas."

"Then they're still dating?" Kathleen said, walking out of the dressing room in front of her friend.

"Yes, and this is the first time Chrissy has ever given or gotten a present from a boy. She's so young and so vulnerable . . ."

"Susan, are you talking about your daughter?" the woman whose cat's eating habits were interfering with her holiday decorating scheme asked from behind her.

"Barbara!" Susan exclaimed, turning and looking into the face of her daughter's boyfriend's mother.

"You will never believe what Seth just bought Chrissy. She'll be so thrilled," Barbara St. John gushed enthusiastically, brushing her abundant red hair over her shoulder and licking glossy burnished lips.

"What?" Susan asked, suspecting that she wasn't going to get an answer.

"I'm sworn to secrecy. But I can tell you that it's perfect. She'll love it. Look at the time! I'm going to be late. See you at Evan's party!" In a swirl of mink, she trotted between long racks of party dresses, leaving a rainbow of silk, brocade, and beaded chiffon shimmering in her wake.

"I . . ." Susan started to speak before realizing that she was standing at the counter alone. "Kathleen?"

"Over here," came the reply from behind a mannequin wrapped in a beaded black velvet cape.

"Find something interesting? Something you can't live without?" Susan asked, following the sound of her friend's voice to the men's department, where, as usual, Kathleen's remarkable good looks had attracted all the men in sight. What a way to get sales help during the holiday rush. "Is that for you?" she asked, as Kathleen held a beige sweater up in front of her chest.

"No. I was thinking about Jerry. Do you think he'd like it?"

"It's hand knit from a combination of hand-spun and hand-dyed silk and alpaca yarns," the salesperson quickly informed them.

Susan glanced at the dangling price tag. "Wow. Those hands must belong to some union. It's pretty expensive. Does Jerry need a new sweater? Weren't you going to knit one for him?"

"I must have been crazy to even think about it. I signed up for a class at the knitting shop in Darien, spent over a hundred dollars for yarn, and then remembered that I've never been able to do any sort of handwork."

"Not really?"

"Really. My lowest grade in junior high was home economics. My knitting and sewing were a disaster. When I was a rookie cop and hardly making enough money to live on, I still had to pay someone to hem my uniforms—or send them home to my mother. Why I thought living in the suburbs would change all that . . ." She looked at the sweater doubtfully. "I'll think about it," she halfheartedly assured the salesman, handing it back to him.

"We better get going if we're going to stop at the drugstore. I'd hate to be late for Kelly's party," Susan said, signing the credit-card form and collecting her package. "Maybe you should have tried knitting something simpler for your first project. Like a scarf."

"I once crocheted a scarf for my mother for Christmas. I got the pattern out of one of those magazine articles titled 'One Hundred Christmas Gifts to Make for Less than Ten Dollars.'"

"And?" Susan prompted.

"It was so ugly, my mother never wore it."

"Your own mother?"

"Especially my own mother."

"Kathleen . . ." Susan began a sentence not knowing how she planned on ending it.

"In a few days you'll meet her," Kathleen said. "Then you'll understand."

TWO

THE LARGE, WHITE CAPE COD COTTAGE LOOKED LIKE AN illustration in an advertisement urging people to spend Christmas in Connecticut, to experience Christmas "as it once was." If, of course, Christmas once was suburban and wealthy.

"What a beautiful wreath. I don't think I've ever seen one so lush."

"You're probably going to see dozens more. Kelly has always taken her Christmas decorating very seriously. Although this year . . ." Susan left the thought unfinished, pushing open the evergreen-laden gate and passing into the front yard of the pristine house.

"Wow." Kathleen stopped so abruptly that Susan plowed right into her.

"Oh, no. I'll bet I've crushed my cookies." Susan gently

shook the large basket she was carrying. "I should have baked something a little less delicate." She looked over Kathleen's shoulder. "It is beautiful, isn't it? It looks like a Christmas card."

And it did. The rambling house, with its dormers peeking out of the slate roof, its numerous windows, each made up of tiny panes of glass through which dozens of candles were gleaming, was surrounded by a forest of small evergreens, all trained or trimmed into the traditional Christmas–tree shape. Wreaths, bearing fluttering gold bows, hung atop windows and on either side of the gleaming red front door. A layer of snow shimmered on the trees and edges of the roof, and blanketed the now-dead lawn; it also made walking up the artistically curving, cobblestone path particularly hazardous.

"I feel a little like a drunken sailor," Kathleen commented as she slipped on a large, smooth rock.

"Be careful. I once twisted my ankle on this walk and it was only raining that day."

"You'd think Kelly would get rid of this health hazard now that Evan isn't around anymore," came a voice from behind the two women.

"You make it sound as though he's dead," Susan answered, turning to find out who was there.

"For her, he is. Not that she'll ever admit it," came the reply.

"Jennifer, I haven't seen you since your trip. How was St. Thomas?" Susan asked, recognizing a neighbor who was awkwardly holding a large cardboard box out in front of her.

"Fabulous. I got a tan and did all my Christmas shopping in the same week." The woman slid on the walk. "Damn it! I know this is going to distress Kelly, but I'm not going to break a leg just so that she can have the perfect entrance to the perfect home." She stepped off the cobblestones and on to the snow-covered lawn. Kathleen and Susan followed suit.

"Do you think it will really upset Kelly?" Kathleen quietly asked. Susan knew Kelly much better than she did.

But the front door opened, and she got her answer without anyone speaking.

"Merry Christmas! I was watching from the window and I saw you leave the cobblestones first, Jen! But it's Christmas and I forgive you all! Come in. Come in."

"Merry Christmas, Kelly." Jennifer entered and kissed Kelly Knowlson. An attractive woman in her mid-forties, Kelly was clinging to the look prescribed in the late fifties—fluffy hair pulled back by a headband and wearing a kilt and matching cashmere twin set. "I'm sorry I messed up your picture-perfect entrance, but I thought you'd appreciate me not killing myself on the way to your party. Bloodying up the walk and all that."

"You look wonderful—so tan," Kelly said. Susan noticed that she didn't assure Jennifer that walking on the grass was allowed. "Are these your cookies?" she asked, taking the large box from her friend's hands.

"Yes. Are you going to spread them out in the dining room?"

"Don't I always? Why don't I go ahead, while you put your coats and everything back in the cloakroom? Susan, you and Kathleen just leave your cookies there on the table and I'll come back for them. I don't want to spill Jennifer's precious cargo."

"Cloakroom?" Kathleen repeated, a little incredulously.

"Follow Jennifer," Susan suggested, putting down her basket next to Kathleen's large box and then hurrying down the hallway and through an open Dutch door.

"Why . . . it *is* a cloakroom," Kathleen was saying, looking around the square windowless room. The walls were white and had three walnut bands running around them. Sit-

uated at foot intervals along the wood were walnut pegs—
long enough to hold the heaviest fur and smooth enough not
to snag the most delicate scarf. "I've never seen anything
like this in a private home."

"You've never been to Kelly's before?" Jennifer asked,
fluffing out her hair before the mirror provided.

"No. She left Hancock about the time I arrived. And, in
the last few months since her return, I've only seen her around
the club. We were assigned to the same paddleball team this
fall."

"Then prepare yourself. Kelly's house is a monument to
compulsive behavior," Jennifer said on her way out of the
room.

"Compulsive behavior?" Kathleen repeated.

"Kelly is something of a perfectionist." Susan suggested
an alternate term. "You must have seen a little of it, if you
played on her team."

"Well, she certainly worked hard to win, but we all did.
And I don't see what that has to do with her house."

"You will," Susan assured her. "Follow me."

"Where are we supposed to meet?" Kathleen asked,
thinking about the size of the house.

"The living room."

"How do you know?"

"Because we always meet in the living room," Susan answered.

Kathleen decided not to ask any more questions.

Their progress to the front of the house was impeded by
the arrival of the rest of the guests. Moving into the hallway,
Susan and Kathleen were surrounded by a dozen women,
busily removing their coats and greeting each other. They
were swept up in the atmosphere of geniality that begins any
party, and it wasn't until most of the women were seated on
the deep, comfortable couches and chairs, that Kathleen had
a chance to look around.

"This place is perfect for a Christmas party," she said aloud.

"It certainly has the right color scheme," agreed another woman.

The living room was large and long. It had been divided into three seating areas: one before an elegant enameled brick fireplace in the center of the room, one around the grand piano that filled the farthest end, and one near the entrance. There were five couches and more chairs than Kathleen could count; they were all upholstered in various plaids and prints, chosen for their color scheme of muted dark greens and ruby red. Pictures on the walls were mainly watercolors of rural snow scenes, elaborate gold frames proclaiming their expense despite the homey subject. Each artwork was draped with evergreen boughs and holly berries. Dozens of shiny brass candle holders sat on tables and on the mantel; matching sconces hung at appropriate intervals on the walls. The candles were all bayberry and all lit, as was the fireplace. Any empty corners or tabletops displayed brilliant red poinsettias or copper bowls of paperwhites, just coming into bloom.

"I think the narcissus are an innovation," Kathleen heard someone say.

"Never. Nothing changes except the type of cookies we choose to bring. We must have just missed them other years," another contradicted.

"Nothing except the guest list; this is the first of Kelly's cookie-exchange parties in the past few years that Rebecca's missed."

"Shh! She might hear you!"

Susan smiled at this conversation, but didn't get involved. She was going to forget town gossip and intrigue and have a nice time. As nothing else was said on the subject, she decided that everyone else must feel the same.

Kathleen thought that they were all waiting for something,

but didn't know what until Kelly made her entrance. She carried a large silver tray, which she placed on the coffee table before the fire, then sat down in a wing chair that seemed to have been saved for her. She pushed back the tortoiseshell headband she wore and smiled at everybody.

"I always think of my party as the beginning of the holiday season here in Hancock," she announced.

"We all missed it when you were away last year," someone nearby stated, and a cloud passed over Kelly's face.

"We won't think about that," she insisted. "We're here to have fun. How about some eggnog?"

"It's a little early in the day for me—" Kathleen began.

"It's never too early for eggnog. Heavens, it's practically breakfast," Kelly said, clearly disagreeing. "Milk, sugar, eggs . . . All that's missing is some bacon or toast."

"Well . . ."

"It's not alcoholic," Susan whispered in Kathleen's ear. "Kelly doesn't drink."

"Oh."

"Why don't we all go into the kitchen and get some lunch?" Kelly suggested. "After all, we should have something nourishing before we get to the goodies, shouldn't we?"

So, almost immediately after sitting down, they were all getting up and walking to the kitchen. Kathleen, amazed, followed the crowd.

The kitchen matched the rest of the house. The color scheme was, of course, blue and white. Baskets and a king's ransom of copper pans hung from exposed rafters. Candles glowed, flowers blossomed, and, in the middle of the room, sat a gigantic antique trestle table, originally designed to seat a dozen hungry farmers, loaded with loaves of homemade bread and two varieties of muffins, three pots of steaming soup, and fruit salads with creamy dressing. With cries that signaled the abandoning of their diets for the holiday season, the ladies dug in.

"I didn't know Kelly had any children," Kathleen whispered to Susan as they made their way, plates brimming with food, back to the living room.

"She doesn't. Are you thinking about that gigantic table?"

"That, and the size of the house. There must be at least four bedrooms upstairs," Kathleen guessed, glancing toward the wide stairway, treads stenciled with different animal silhouettes, that led up to the second floor.

"Only three. Although two of them have sitting rooms attached. And there are three full baths. Kelly and Evan had this house built to very specific requirements. They did an incredible amount of entertaining. Not just this type of thing, but having people out from the city for weekends. I assume his business required it."

"And she loved it."

"That she does," Susan replied, finding a seat with a small table nearby. She balanced her food in one hand while moving a pot of flowers and a Lalique ashtray to make a place to set it down. "Or did," she said, correcting her last statement. "This is the first party she's given since the divorce. But it's the same as it always was."

"And that's just the way it should be. Why should she give up anything that she loved just because Evan decided to run off and marry another woman?" asked a woman whose striking clothing set off her elegant, prematurely gray chignon.

"Well, maybe." Susan didn't agree, but didn't think this was the time to talk about it. "Elizabeth, do you know Kathleen Gordon?"

"Of course. We met at one or two Christmas parties last year, and at the Labor Day extravaganza at the club. Although I was suffering from such bad jet lag the first week of September that I don't even remember the picnic. But Derek said it was important that we go," answered Elizabeth

Stevenson, looking around vaguely. "Don't you think Kelly is doing well?" she asked, changing the subject.

"Yes."

"You know, a lot of people said she should sell the house after Evan left, but Kelly wouldn't consider it. And she was right. There's no reason to change your life-style just because your husband leaves you."

"But to have your ex-husband and his new wife living in a house right behind yours . . ." started a voice from across the room.

"Evan can choose where he wants to live; that shouldn't change where Kelly wants to live," Elizabeth replied.

"Evan lives . . . ? I didn't realize . . ." Kathleen began, looking at Susan. But Elizabeth wasn't finished.

"There is no reason for Kelly to move. This house is as much Kelly's as it was Evan's—more even because she's the one who stayed home and took care of it. I told her—" Elizabeth stopped suddenly as Kelly entered the room. "Great party," she declared. "Better than ever."

There was an echo of appreciation from around the room.

"You always have the best food . . ."

"I love the bean soup . . ."

". . . the recipe, if it isn't too hard to make."

"These nutmeg muffins have always been my favorite."

"Evan used to say—"

There was a sudden silence.

"Oh, Kelly," the woman who had mentioned the name of her ex-husband moaned. "I didn't mean to—"

"You haven't done anything," Kelly protested, looking around the room at her guests. "I hate the fact that no one talks to me about Evan. Everyone acts as though he's dead. But he's not. He's just left for a while. And I—" she paused and looked around again, this time over the heads of the people, at the walls and furnishings"—and I am waiting for him to get over his silliness and come back where he belongs.''

"Good for you!" Elizabeth cheered.

But Susan felt the tension and was relieved when a voice called out from the hallway.

"Merry Christmas! I'm sorry I'm so late. I couldn't find a box big enough to put ten dozen cookies in, and then I couldn't find my car keys!"

"But you're here now." Kelly moved toward the late arrival with a broad smile on her face, and Susan wondered if their hostess was relieved that the conversation had to end.

After thinking it over a moment, Susan figured she just had to be. Evan Knowlson had left his wife a year ago, remarrying as soon as the divorce was final. Certainly his decision to build a new home right behind his old one—and then move in with his new family—was odd, but Kelly's apparent belief that the divorce was merely a temporary aberration made little sense.

New Year's resolution number one, Susan thought: help Kelly build a new future for herself.

THREE

Susan strode through the mudroom that separated her house from the garage, stepping over ski boots and wet running shoes, cheerfully humming a Christmas carol. Then she arrived in the kitchen, a room that displayed all the mess of a large-scale baking binge. She sighed and flung her coat over one of the chairs surrounding the table where her family would eat that night—if she ever cleaned it of its coating of wire cooling racks and crumbs. "Chad, turn that record down!" she yelled toward the study, where, experience told her, she would find her twelve-year-old son sitting in close proximity to her husband's expensive sound system.

"It's a tape, not a record, Mom."

Susan spun around to find the boy behind her; he was yanking off a parka, lift tickets dangling from the zipper pull.

"Chad, if you were outside, who's in the den?"

"No one. I just left the tape playing. Don't worry. It won't hurt it any."

"That wasn't what was worrying me. It's too loud, Chad,

and I like to know if there's anyone in the house when I come home—"

"Hi, Mom." Her fifteen-year-old daughter entered the room. "Where have you been? I was looking for you. Can I sleep over at Cindy's house tonight? Her mom and dad are going to be home. . . . You can check."

"I trust you, Chrissy. I don't have to check up on you. Chad, go out to the study and turn off that damn music. Please," she added a little tardily. She turned to her daughter. "But, Chrissy, your father wanted to pick out the Christmas tree tonight. You know we usually do it earlier than this. He doesn't want to put it off for another day."

"You can go without me," Chrissy suggested, putting her finger in the cookie crumbs on the table, then licking off those that had adhered. "Is there anything to eat? Lunch at school today was disgusting; I haven't had anything since breakfast but two Mars bars."

"Chrissy! You shouldn't eat like that. Let me make you a snack. A salad or a grilled cheese sandwich."

"I thought," Chad said, having disregarded his mother's instructions about the music, "that you were going to a party to exchange Christmas cookies."

"There's a big white box in the trunk of the car and it's full of cookies," his mother said, answering the implied, but unspoken question. "You may get it, but please don't open it. Just bring it inside."

"Okay. You don't have to yell."

"If I don't yell, you won't hear me over that music," she said to her son's back, the promise of cookies being a strong enough motivation to get him moving.

"I'll go turn it off, Mom. And I'll call Cindy and tell her that you said it was okay for me to come over at the same time." Chrissy disappeared in the opposite direction from her brother.

"I didn't say that, Chrissy," her mother disagreed. "Don't

call her and tell her anything. We have to talk first. And please come back here; I don't want to spend the rest of the day yelling all over the house.''

''This thing is really heavy. Is it all cookies?'' Chad had returned, a large smile on his face.

''Yes. Put it down carefully.''

''Where?''

Susan took a good look around her kitchen and sighed. ''Is it too heavy for you to hold just a few more seconds?'' she asked, picking up a sponge with one hand and grabbing three heavy black cookie sheets with the other. ''I'll clear enough space right away.''

''I can wait. Especially if I get an extra cookie or two,'' her son said.

''How many were you planning to have?'' his mother asked, dumping the cookie sheets in an already full sink and quickly sweeping the residue off the counter. ''Put it there and prepare yourself. I think you're going to like what you see.'' And she opened the box.

''Wow!'' Chad said, filling both his hands with the sweets.

''Chad, I think—''

''Oh, come on, Mom. It's almost Christmas.''

''But—''

''I called Cindy and told her I couldn't come over,'' Chrissy announced, reentering the room and slamming the kitchen door behind her. ''Her parents don't make her do dumb things like pick out Christmas trees. They understand that their children grow out of these things.''

Susan sighed. ''Would you like a cookie?''

Chrissy took a quick glance in the large box. Susan did, too. There were small candy canes made by winding bicolored dough together, diamond-shaped jewels of fruitcake, springerle with designs of flowers and birds pressed into them, little meringue mushrooms, tiny green spritz trees and wreaths, pecan crescents dusted with confectioner's sugar, gingerbread angels, and more.

"Wonderful," Susan said enthusiastically.

"No chocolate chip? Why doesn't anyone make anything I like?" Chrissy wailed, turning to the refrigerator and taking out a bottle of diet chocolate soda. "I'll be in my room," she announced before leaving.

Susan was grinding her teeth as the phone rang. She didn't bother to reach for it, however; with one teenager and one preteen in the house, calls for her rarely got through.

This time was the exception.

"Mom! Telephone!" came the wail from the second floor of the house.

"Hello?" Susan picked up the phone, but continued to clean her kitchen. "Oh, hello," she said as the caller identified herself. "I'm so glad you called back, but could you hang on for just one moment?" She held the receiver against her shoulder and spoke to her son. "This is private, Chad. Take those cookies and leave me alone for a few minutes, will you?"

"Sure," he said, grinning. "Is it a present for me?"

"It won't be for anybody, unless you leave the room."

He vanished. She hoped he wasn't heading for an extension. But, if he was, it was his own surprise that he would ruin. She returned to her caller.

The person on the line was, in fact, a representative of the phone company, calling to schedule a time to come to the Henshaws and install two new lines; both Chrissy and Chad were getting private phones in their rooms for Christmas. Susan couldn't wait. Not only would it clear up this line for her, but she could ignore incoming calls on their phones when they weren't home. In the past year or so, she had begun to feel like an unpaid message service. She scheduled an appointment for a time when both kids would be out of the house, then Susan hung up and continued her cleaning.

Much to her surprise, the next call was for her also. Years of housekeeping had taught her to talk on the phone while doing almost everything; she kept filling her dishwasher.

"Kathleen. Anything wrong?" she asked, thinking that maybe her friend had left something in her car after being dropped off at home.

"No, I'm just standing here cleaning—"

"Your kitchen," Susan finished for her. "Me, too. It's another Hancock Christmas tradition: cleaning up the mess from the cookie exchange. One of those irritating things you forget from year to year, like vacuuming up the needles under the Christmas tree. Or paying all the bills in January."

"Your kitchen must be something. I just made spritz cookies and I'm sitting in the middle of a disaster area. Those cream horns with two kinds of filling were really impressive; they must have taken hours! I've never seen anything like them."

"I spent last night making the horns from the puff pastry, then I got up at five this morning to stir the almond and the pistachio fillings and then squeeze them into the horns. I barely had time to put on makeup and change for shopping. And now this place is such a mess I can't believe it!"

"They were wonderful," Kathleen said. "I mean, they really stood out—and that selection of cookies was something. I was a little embarrassed that my recipe was so ordinary."

"Well, maybe some of us get a little competitive about this type of thing," Susan admitted.

Kathleen was glad Susan couldn't see her smile. "I don't want to interrupt your cleaning . . ."

"You're not." Susan pulled open the door to her trash compactor and threw in a couple of empty heavy cream containers and wrappers from pounds of sweet butter. "How did you like Kelly's house?"

"Lovely, but I keep thinking that it's a little big for just one person."

"Only if you think about it as merely a place to live. Kelly considers that house her lifework, her creation."

"I gather that's what Elizabeth was saying."

"Yes, and she's right about the house. I think Kelly would rather die than move out."

"Can she afford to keep it? After all, she doesn't work—and Evan can't be supporting her the way he was when they were married, can he?"

"I don't know. Kelly said he was very generous in his divorce settlement. But who knows what that means."

"Especially since she never says anything negative about him," Kathleen agreed. "Which is the reason I'm calling, by the way."

"Kelly's attitude toward Evan?"

"She asked me to have lunch with her tomorrow."

"So?"

"Well, she said that she had something to talk to me about. Something important."

"And, with Kelly, the only thing important is her ex-husband?" Susan suggested.

"That's what I was thinking. So I thought it might be helpful if I knew more about her. I wasn't just calling to gossip."

Susan, who knew Kathleen well, had never thought that she would.

"Susan, do you know if a private investigator got involved in the Knowlsons' divorce?" Kathleen was asking.

"I don't think so. You mean to collect evidence of adultery?"

"That, or just to check out their financial situation or something. I'm asking because I wondered if she wanted to see me about something professional. Maybe Kelly thinks that my business is more than just home security."

"Well, isn't it?" Susan asked, thinking of the murder investigation Kathleen had been involved with after leaving the police force, marrying a widower, and setting up what was supposed to be a home security business here in the suburbs.

"Not officially . . . not really." Kathleen dodged the issue. "But that house already has a very elaborate burglar and fire alarm system, so I don't think she could be interested in talking to me about that."

"Well, I can tell you what I know about the divorce, but it isn't much. I guess it happened before you came to town."

"All I know is that Evan left Kelly, they got a divorce, and he married Rebecca early last spring."

"Well, it's a long story. The first thing I knew about it, Barbara St. John called me one morning around Thanksgiving and asked if I had heard anything about Evan moving out of Kelly's house."

"And you hadn't?"

"No, and you know Barbara. She acted as if she were terribly, terribly concerned about Kelly, but you got the feeling that she was enjoying it."

"You're saying that she likes gossiping."

Susan thought that Barbara could use some interests in life besides her one son, her husband, and her house. "The next thing I knew, Kelly had gone home to her mother out West somewhere, and, when she returned, she filed for a divorce."

"Without waiting to see if Evan came back? Without waiting to see if he changed his mind?"

"It does seem a little strange, doesn't it? Especially if you consider what she was saying today. Why get a divorce if you're expecting him to come back?" Susan said.

"And she made that very clear."

"Maybe she wasn't thinking straight at the time. She was devastated when he left. When she went to visit her mother we were all relieved. I thought she was going to have a breakdown.''

"And how long was she gone?"

"I don't remember exactly. Two months at the most. Through the Christmas holidays and New Year's. And when she came back, she immediately went to a lawyer and filed for a divorce. It went through in record time. Just a few months.''

"And Evan married Rebecca right away," Kathleen said.

"Well, they had been living together since he'd moved out. It didn't surprise anyone.''

"Not even Kelly?"

"I don't know. Until today she's just avoided the whole topic. Now it turns out that she's keeping the home fires burning until he returns—at least that's what it looked like to me this afternoon," Susan said. "But I don't know if that's why she's calling you. Or what she thinks you could do about the whole situation. She has a lawyer, of course.''

Kathleen was silent for a moment. "Does she always give a cookie-exchange party at Christmastime?" she asked finally.

"Every year we've lived in Hancock—except for last year.''

"And it's always the same?"

"Almost identical. Oh, the guest list changes a little . . .''

"Like Rebecca not coming this year," Kathleen said, thinking of the comment that had been made.

"Yes." Susan laughed. "And things get a little more elaborate each year. At first, we just had tea and coffee and cookies. Then she added lunch. And, of course, like the rest of us, she's added more and more decorations each year. Although Kelly's additions are typical of her and not like the rest of ours—at least not like mine.''

"Meaning?"

"Well, we've collected ornaments made by the kids in

school each year, and decorations like the centerpiece that my mother-in-law crocheted out of gold thread. Things that have become a tradition.'' And some things that we hate, but can't get rid of, she added to herself.

''And there's nothing like that at Kelly's house, is what you're saying,'' Kathleen suggested.

''Exactly what I'm saying. Everything was picked to go perfectly with everything else. Even the objects with sentimental value. Their Christmas tree is decorated with wonderful copper ornaments that they bought on a trip to Mexico. They could have been made for that house, they blend in so well. We brought back ornaments from a trip, too. Plastic Mickey Mouses from Disney World. You don't need to see both trees to tell the difference.''

''I'm sure yours is very homey,'' Kathleen assured her.

''That's one word for it,'' Susan agreed, getting an urge to go up to the attic and peek into the large box of ornaments stored there. Her favorite was a pair of tiny mittens that someone had made for Chad when he was two or three, and that pretty pink angel. There was also a large orange dinosaur . . .

''Oh, no. Jerry just pulled into the driveway and I haven't even thought about dinner,'' Kathleen said. ''Well, I guess it's the inn again. Thank goodness their food is so good.''

Susan once again marveled at how sane Kathleen's approach to housekeeping was; when Jed got home before she was ready for him, she was inclined to panic.

''Mom, Dad's home, and he's carrying a huge box!'' her daughter called into the kitchen.

''Jed's here, too. They must have traveled from the station together. I have to hang up, Kath. Call me tomorrow. I'm dying to know what Kelly wants. Unless it's against your professional ethics to say anything.''

''*Professional ethics?* You must think I have a real job or something. But I'll call tomorrow. 'Bye.''

" 'Bye.'' Susan turned to greet her husband.

"Hi, hon.'' He leaned across the counter and just missed kissing her cheek.

"Hi. I thought Chrissy said something about a package.''

"Chrissy should learn to keep her mouth shut at Christmastime,'' her husband said, throwing his coat over hers and looking around the room. "Is this going to be one of your gourmet dinners? I missed lunch and I'm starved.''

"This mess is from the cookie party over at Kelly's,'' Susan said apologetically. "How do you feel about taking the whole family to the Hancock Inn? Or I could pull something from the freezer and microwave it?''

"We always go out to dinner before we pick out the Christmas tree,'' Chrissy said, entering the room with her brother close on her heels. "We always go down to Tony's, and Chad and I always get a pepperoni pizza with extra cheese, and you and Dad always have linguini with white clam sauce.''

"Always?''

"That's right,'' her brother agreed.

"I don't even like white clam sauce,'' their father said, a grin on his face.

"Okay. You can have the red clam sauce,'' Chrissy agreed, without a bit of humor. "We'd better go get dressed, Chad. It's going to be cold in the tree lot. I think I'll wear leg warmers. It would be nice if I had some that were tie-dyed,'' she added, with a look to see if her parents were getting the message.

"Tie-dyed leg warmers?'' Susan repeated, aware that there was a pair made up of the unlikely combination of pink, green, and purple in her daughter's size—locked in the trunk of her car waiting to be wrapped and placed under the Christmas tree.

"Bloomingdale's has them,'' Chrissy assured her, and hustled her brother out of the room.

"She was just telling me what a horrible thing it is to have to go pick out the tree with her parents, and here she is defending tradition with her last breath," Susan said.

"Adolescence," was Jed's reply. "Do we always go to Tony's for dinner?"

"We did last year."

"Actually red clam sauce sounds good. And maybe some garlic bread and a big green salad. I think I'll go put on warmer clothes, too. I thought I saw a flake of snow on the way home from the station."

Susan smiled. She loved snow. "It's wonderful that we're having a white Christmas," she called up the stairs to her family, and went to find a cord for tying the tree on top of her husband's Mercedes.

FOUR

THERE WERE FOUR OR FIVE PLACES THAT SOLD CHRISTMAS trees in Hancock. Susan and her family were at the largest of them.

"Where are Chad and Chrissy?" Susan asked, walking beside her husband down the long row of evergreens.

"I think these are just a bit too tall," was Jed's garlicky

reply as he raised his arm in the air next to an unnaturally symmetrical balsam. "Maybe something around the corner . . ." He drifted away from his wife into the forest of rootless evergreens.

Susan, who knew that one of her husband's favorite moments in the year was stretching up to measure a tree to fit the high ceiling in their living room, followed slowly.

"These damn treetops are dripping water down my neck. Would you please hurry up and pick out a tree so we can go home and have a drink?"

Susan heard a voice she thought she recognized.

"If you didn't want to come with me . . ."

That voice she was sure she recognized.

"You know I didn't. I am completely unnecessary for this job. You don't like any of the trees I pick out. You don't ask me if I like the one that you pick out. You don't even trust the way I tie the tree to the top of the station wagon. I don't know why we go through this every year. My family used to hike into the woods—and the woods in the winter in Wisconsin can be pretty raw—and my father would cut down the tree with us boys helping. My mother and my sister would bring hot chocolate and pfeffernusse that they had made that afternoon and we would eat and drink as we pulled the tree through the snow on a homemade sled. And that was less goddamn work than this is! And a hell of a lot more fun!" the voice continued angrily.

"And the tree was probably a scrawny thing only a few feet tall. I cannot live with a tree like that. What would our neighbors think? Christmas is important to me," his wife insisted, turning the corner of the line of trees—and running into Susan. "Oh, my goodness, look who's here, hon," she said, her voice turning to milk and honey. "I didn't see you before. Picking out a Christmas tree?"

"What else would she be doing here?" But his voice had

changed, too, and Jeffrey St. John greeted Susan with a kiss on the cheek.

"We're having our traditional picking-out-the-tree argument," Barbara admitted to Susan, with a laugh.

"There are so many trees here . . . It's hard to agree on just one," was Susan's tactful reply.

Barbara seemed to give up any pretense of marital harmony and changed the subject. "What did you think about Kelly today? Wasn't that just amazing? I couldn't believe it. I was talking to Rebecca before dinner and she thinks that Kelly has finally gone off the deep end."

"I was a little surprised," Susan admitted, not really wanting to hear what Evan's second wife thought about her predecessor. "But I've lost my family and I'd better find them."

"We really have to do something about Kelly." Barbara was unwilling to drop the subject. "I'll call you tomorrow and we'll talk."

"Fine," Susan said, starting to move away. "Good to see you, Jeffrey." She picked up her pace and hurried after her family, trying to ignore the argument that she was leaving behind.

"We found the perfect tree!"

"It is, Mom. It is absolutely, totally, completely, the most perfect tree we've ever had. Really."

"Also the most expensive," Jed said.

Her family was at the back of the lot; the children were displaying joyful faces, her husband smiling a bit ruefully. They stood in front of a large blue spruce, around which Chrissy had placed one proprietary arm.

"I found it," her son announced.

"The moment I saw it, I knew we had to have it," his sister said quickly.

"And I'm going to pay for it," Jed contributed.

"We've never had a blue spruce before," Susan said, "but

it certainly is beautiful. And I think it will match the Wedgwood blue stripe in the curtains. It's wonderful! Shall I go get one of the men who works here to carry it to the car?''

"I can do that," Chad boasted. And, with his father helping, he did.

"It certainly is nice to have such resourceful children," Susan said, regretting the comment almost immediately. Chrissy objected to almost all personal comments these days, even good ones. But, for once, her daughter didn't seem to mind. In fact, she smiled at her mother. Susan wondered for a moment if Christmas was a cure for puberty. But only for a moment.

"I saw Mr. and Mrs. St. John. They didn't make Seth come along with them, just like I said," Chrissy informed her in the voice she had adopted since turning fifteen.

Susan just sighed and followed her family back to the car.

An ice storm was beginning by the time the Henshaws drove into their garage.

"Whew! Looks like we just made it," Jed commented as the automatic garage door closed behind them. "It's going to be a nasty night."

"Is that the phone?" Susan asked, opening the car door. "I'll go get it." She hurried off, leaving the rest of her family to remove the tree from the car and put it in a pail of water. She was off the phone by the time they finished. As they entered the kitchen, Susan was just hanging up.

"That," she announced, "was your mother. She's not coming next Friday. She's coming tomorrow."

"Tomorrow?"

"Her plane gets in at Kennedy at nine A.M. She says she has a lot to bring through customs, so we don't have to be there until nine-thirty or so."

"We?"

"When you talked with her Thanksgiving Day, you seem

to have given her the impression that the entire family would meet her in New York."

"Dad! How could you?" his daughter cried. "No one around here has any respect for my time."

"Adam and I have plans to go to a movie tomorrow afternoon. I have to be back for that," his son practically wailed.

Susan looked at her husband. "I think I'd better go clean the guest room. I thought I had all week to do this . . ." She left the room before finishing her thought.

Jed turned to his children. "Your grandmother hasn't seen you for almost a year. She has been overseas for the last month, and she is going to be tired from traveling and jet lag. I think the least we can do is all go to the airport together and greet her."

"You three will have to go without me." His wife had come back into the room, her arms draped full of sheets. "I have more to do up there than I remembered." She headed for the laundry room, muttering to herself.

"Did she say something about fruitcake?" Chad asked, watching her go.

"Who knows? Anyway, you kids are to be up and ready to go to the airport with me at seven A.M. Dressed and ready—and no shirts with skulls on them, Chad. Now go up to bed. And don't forget to set your alarm clocks. I have to help your mother."

Chrissy rolled her eyes up toward the ceiling, and Chad mumbled something under his breath, but they left the room together.

Jed hurried to the basement. He found Susan standing in front of the washing machine, apparently listening to it hum. "Susan? Are you all right? I know this is a shock to you, but we'll be ready in time. Mom doesn't expect—"

"Do we have any Dry Sack in the house?" she asked, still staring at the machine. "Isn't that what your mother drinks?"

"Yes, and if we don't have any, I can shop tomorrow

afternoon. I have to order the liquor for the party next Friday, and I'll pick up some sherry at the same time. Why don't you come to bed, Sue? It will take hours for us to get out to Kennedy and back—especially if this storm continues; you'll have plenty of time to do everything while we're gone.''

"I . . . what the . . . ?" The lights suddenly went out. A less enterprising woman would have flung herself into her husband's arms at finding herself alone with him in the dark; Susan turned the other way and headed for the circuit breaker box underneath the cellar stairs.

"I don't think that's going to do any good," Jed said, following her.

Susan picked up the flashlight that lived under the metal box and, turning it on, peered at the switches. "Everything seems to be okay."

"Let's go upstairs. I'd guess this is the result of the storm; branches or trees on the power lines. The first thing to do is find out if it's just our house or the whole neighborhood."

"All the lights are out!" Chrissy met them at the top of the stairs, a lit candle in her hand.

"Where's Chad?" his mother asked.

"He's already asleep. I checked in his room on the way down. What are we going to do? Will the furnace go out? One of the girls in my geometry class has a house in Maine and the power was out for three days and all the pipes froze and burst. Is that going to happen to us?" Susan thought she sounded thrilled by the possibility.

"No, that is not going to happen, Chrissy. Go into my study and get the gas fire going. I'm going to call the power company." Jed looked out the front door. "Looks like the whole street is out. Susan . . ."

"I'll light candles in the hall and get out blankets and pillows. Chrissy may as well get some sleep on the couch in your study."

"Great." Jed headed toward the kitchen and the phone.

But, when he got to the study, he found Chrissy alone. "Where's your mother?" he asked, peering into the wavering shadows that candles and the fireplace cast about the room.

"Upstairs."

"She's probably checking on Chad. We may have to bring him down here if his room gets too chilly. The power company said that the whole circuit is out and they don't know how long it will take to get the lights back on." He headed over to the bar set up in the corner of and poured himself a large Chivas. Respectful of the storm, he slipped into his favorite chair and sipped his drink neat, not opening the freezer for ice.

There was a nice feeling in the room. Susan began decorating her house the week after Thanksgiving and a pinecone wreath hung over the mantel and red and green ribbons were tied around the candlesticks. The smell of bayberry mixed with the aroma of the Scotch, and Jed was almost asleep when he heard a high-pitched *whirr*ing over his head. Groggily he considered the layout of his home: the noise was coming from the guest room.

And where was Susan?

Moments later he found her kneeling on the floor under the antique sleigh bed that adorned their guest room, a battery-run Dustbuster whirring away in her hand.

FIVE

"ALL I KNOW IS THAT SHE'S BEEN TELLING ME FOR YEARS that she's allergic to dust, so I wasn't going to leave any little fur balls under the bed," Susan said into the phone. She paused to listen. "To be honest, I've spent so much time cleaning that I haven't even thought about a hostess gift for the Knowlsons tomorrow. A bottle of wine, I suppose. Maybe champagne. Although when I'm going to get a chance to pick it up . . . You will? Are you sure you have the time with your own mother arriving tomorrow? . . .

"Well, it would be a big help. I also need to get to the fish market, and there's a huge order to be picked up at the cheese store and the bakery. I called early this morning for emergency guest supplies. Thank goodness the power's back on." Susan reached across the kitchen counter and turned off the radio. "Then all I have to do is finish moving the presents out of the guest room closet, and Jed's mom can move right in. I was going to spend today and tomorrow morning cooking things to put in the freezer for our party Friday night. I suppose I'll have to go ahead with that, except that now I have to provide dinner and breakfast suitable for company as well. . . . No, we have to eat here. Going out to dinner means that we're 'making a fuss' over her visit, and she doesn't like that. So instead of paying a restaurant to make a fuss, I get to pretend that I can whip together a gourmet meal in a few minutes flat. No, I don't know why she changed her plans. She said something about wanting us to meet someone, but that doesn't explain anything to me. All I know is that she's arriving one week early, and I'm going to go crazy. Great. See you then.'' She hung up on Kathleen, running her hand through her hair in a distracted manner and pressing the button on top of the Mr. Coffee machine.

"Oh, God,'' she said as the water bubbled away. "I look terrible.'' After glancing around the room, Susan headed upstairs to shower and change. They couldn't possibly make the long journey back from Kennedy in less than two hours.

It was almost noon when she heard the telltale whine of the electric garage door opener. And she was on the phone again.

"Listen, Liz, I have to hang up. The family has arrived. But call me if anything changes. 'Bye . . .

"Claire! You're looking wonderful!'' She rushed across the kitchen to greet her guest. Susan had always assumed that her husband got his good looks from his father, who had died before they met. Jed's mother was a petite woman, with hair the nondescript color that hair turns before it becomes gray and hips that tended to display everything she had ever eaten. But the woman standing before her, while still short, had hips that matched the rest of her, and her hair, instead of turning to gray, appeared to have made a miraculous transformation to a soft shade of beige.

"Good to see you, Susan— Why, look at this. We're wearing the same slacks!''

Susan looked down and compared. They were indeed wearing identical salt-and-pepper tweed slacks; and it looked as if hers were at least two sizes larger than the older woman's.

"Chad and I will take your luggage up to the guest room, Mom," Jed announced, appearing in the doorway behind his mother. He kissed his wife on the cheek in passing. "What a trip."

"Lots of traffic?" Susan asked.

"Lots of ice."

"You should have seen us slide off the road. Zip!" Chad demonstrated the movement with a wave of his free arm.

"Jed . . . ?" Susan started.

"That must have been on the way *to* the airport. Everything was fine on the drive home." Claire seemed to think Susan was more concerned for her mother-in-law's safety than she was about Jed's or the children's.

"Everything's okay, hon. Just let me get these bags upstairs. Mom brought a lot of big boxes as well as her usual luggage. I guess it must be Christmas. When everything is in the house, I'll come back and tell you all about it. How about some coffee?"

"Already made," she told his back.

"Is something burning in the oven?" her daughter asked casually, walking right past it.

"I hope not!" Susan dashed over and opened the door for a peek. "I'm making a new recipe for something called a chicken melon. I thought it would be good for dinner tonight," she explained.

"Chicken is good. Low calorie and very little natural salt." Her mother-in-law beamed her approval.

Susan thought of the heavy cream, ham, and pistachio nuts she had spent the morning with and decided to say nothing to enlighten her. "It comes out in an hour, and it's supposed to be eaten at room temperature. Now how about some lunch? You all didn't eat at the airport, did you?"

"Never. Do you know what the food is like in places like

that? Fried garbage. I had two adequate meals on the plane, though. I've discovered that if you order the salt-free meal for diabetics the food is almost healthy. But I am just a slight bit hungry. Maybe a small snack. I'll go upstairs to freshen up first.''

As she left the room, the front doorbell began to chime. Susan rushed out to see who was there.

''Am I in time? I had to wait in line for the oysters. And I hope you've made room in your freezer for six pounds of frozen shrimp.'' Kathleen was at the door, her arms full of large white plastic bags.

''Is that all?''

''There's another bag from the fish shop in the backseat of the car. And the cheese store filled the trunk.''

''I'll call Chad—'' Susan began.

''For what?'' Chad asked, appearing behind her.

''Would you please help get things in from Kathleen's car?'' his mother asked.

''What sort of things?''

''Well, Brie and oysters,'' she answered, naming two of his favorites. ''We're having oyster stew for lunch.''

''Great. This year I don't have to wait until Christmas Eve for it.'' He dashed out the front door just as Susan noticed that he wasn't wearing any shoes.

''Chad!'' she called him back.

''Do you always let him go outside in his stocking feet in this weather?''

Her mother-in-law was right behind her. Susan opened her mouth, but nothing came out.

''You must be Mrs. Henshaw,'' Kathleen said, coming to her friend's rescue. ''I'm Kathleen Gordon. Susan's friend.''

''Oh, yes. You're the cop, aren't you? And you married that nice Jerry Gordon. His first wife was such a sweet woman. A home economics major I seem to remember. I was so sorry to hear about her death in that auto accident.

You and Jerry have been married for a few years, haven't you?"

"Yes." Kathleen shook her hand. "It's nice to meet you. We'll have a chance to talk more at the Knowlsons' party tomorrow. I hope you're going; Jerry will be happy to see you, too, I'm sure. I think I'd better get this stuff to the kitchen now."

Susan was relieved to see Kathleen smile sincerely as she left the hallway. "I'll just go show her where to put everything. When Chad comes in, will you ask him to please put some shoes on before he makes another trip?" She grabbed Kathleen in front of the refrigerator. "I'm sorry about that. I don't *think* she means to be the least tactful person in the world."

"Wait till you meet my mother! Where do you want all this shrimp?"

"The freezer in the basement. The bottom two shelves are empty," Susan said, and, taking her cue, Kathleen started for the basement.

"Are there two full wheels of Brie?" Her cold-footed son appeared behind them, his arms full of bags.

"Yes, and they're for the party Friday night; don't bend them." Susan grabbed for the wooden disk closest to her. "They might split, and then they won't look as nice. I'm going to put all of this in the basement, Chad. You go upstairs and put on your shoes before going outside again."

"I thought you wanted me to help right away," he explained.

"It wasn't necessary to be that fast," she said. "And change your socks before putting on your shoes. Those are wet."

"I know that. I'm wearing them."

If her mother-in-law hadn't appeared in the kitchen, Susan would have had more to say on the subject.

"Is there anything I can do?"

"Would you help Chad put the cheeses on the top shelf of the basement refrigerator? And, if he brought any crackers in that batch, they can be left on the counter."

"Of course, Chad and I will arrange everything." She vanished down the steps as Kathleen reappeared.

"I'm going to be late meeting Kelly for lunch if I stop first at the liquor store. Would it be okay if I picked up your order there later in the afternoon?"

"Why don't I do it?" Jed offered, entering the room. "I have to go to the hardware store and buy a large bolt for our tree stand—one seems to have vanished over the summer— and the liquor store is nearby. Besides, I can take Mom. She was wondering what changes have taken place downtown; this is as good a time as any to see everything."

"You're sure?" Kathleen asked. "I have the time to do it."

"I'm sure," Jed assured her. "And—" he put his arm around his wife's waist "—it will give you a chance to be alone. It can't be easy to have unexpected company right now. I know you were planning a day in the kitchen."

Susan smiled up at him. "Just go around to the back door of the liquor store and load up the car from there. And, if you're going to the hardware store, would you check and see if we have any extra little lights for the tree? I think we ran out last year."

"Good idea. I also want to get a few cases of those fake logs to have around in case we have electric problems again."

"You better save some room for your mother in the car."

"She can hang on to the ski rack."

"How about eating lunch first? I can have it ready in about five minutes."

"Fine. I'll get the last of the stuff from Kathleen's car and gather up everyone and meet you in the kitchen."

"We're eating in the dining room."

"Then I'll drag everyone in there."

Susan turned to Kathleen. "Call me. I'm dying to know what Kelly wants. I had a very odd conversation with Elizabeth Stevenson this morning."

"About Kelly?"

"Yes, but nothing urgent. We can talk later. Right now I think I'd better get the cream warming for the oysters."

"Sounds good. I wonder what Kelly is cooking up. She invited me to eat there. Probably leftovers from yesterday's party."

"Maybe," Susan said, doubting that Kelly had ever served leftovers in her life—at least not in public.

"I'll call later. Enjoy." Kathleen waved good-bye, and Susan hurriedly pulled a pint of cream from the refrigerator and poured it into a heavy copper saucepan. Setting it over a low fire, she continued her preparations, dousing a large salad with olive oil and sherry vinegar. In the promised time, she entered the dining room, a large tureen in her hands.

The table was set with her second-best china and green and white linen napkins. A large centerpiece of holly, mixed evergreens, and reindeer moss adorned the table. Someone had come through the room and lit the half-dozen votive candles in white ceramic holders that were set before each place. So where was her family?

Right behind her. And, according to Chrissy, starving.

"Where is your grandmother?" Susan asked, putting the stew before her seat at the table. There were also five blue and white Canton china soup bowls waiting to be filled with the buttery brew.

"She's standing in front of the microwave." It was Chad who answered her. "Should I go get her?"

"No, I'll—Oh, there you are. Were you looking for something?" Susan asked, wondering what her mother-in-law was carrying.

"No, I was just getting my lunch." She looked around at

the food on the table and smiled. "Didn't I tell you? I'm on Dr. Barr's Diet Plan. I don't eat anything that isn't in one of these little bags." She pointed to the cellophane package sitting on the plastic plate she was carrying. "I have a whole carton of them upstairs; they're like a miracle. They don't have to be refrigerated, they are totally nutritious, and almost calorie free." She smiled broadly at her daughter-in-law. "You should try one."

SIX

BIRCH LOGS BLAZED IN THE FIREPLACE OF THE HENSHAWS' living room as Susan and Kathleen relaxed on the couch, sipping from goblets of wine.

"She thinks someone is *what*?" Susan was so surprised by Kathleen's last statement that she almost broke the stem of her glass.

"She thinks someone is trying to kill her."

"She's crazy."

"Maybe she is, but that doesn't mean that she's wrong."

"You don't think someone is trying to kill her?"

"No, but I think she thinks someone is trying to kill her.

She's certainly upset. She was very nervous when she was telling me about it.''

''Did she say who she thought was trying to kill her?''

''No, but I think it's Evan.''

''Kathleen, are you crazy?'' Susan asked, pouring another glass of wine out for her friend.

''No, and it's just a guess.''

''You'd better explain.''

''Well, Kelly told me that she thinks someone is trying to kill her, and that's pretty much all she would say. So I started to ask questions about who she thought wanted to kill her, and she didn't answer until I suggested that Evan had something to do with the way she felt. She got very, very excited— and denied even connecting him with this. So my guess is that she suspects Evan. But it's just a guess.'' Kathleen leaned back in her chair and sipped the ruby-colored liquid. Her eyes wandered around the room. ''You're really ready for the holiday, aren't you? Everything looks beautiful. Did you make the swags over the windows?''

''The florist wired together the greens, and I added those tiny stars. Pretty, aren't they? I found them at Bloomingdale's right after Thanksgiving. But you're changing the subject. How does Kelly think this person is trying to kill her? She hasn't seen anyone sneaking around her house with a gun, has she?''

''Poison, sabotaging her car, making a pool of ice right outside her back door that was supposed to cause her to fall down some cement steps,'' Kathleen answered. ''Which, translated, means that she got a bad case of food poisoning or the flu and was sick to her stomach for over a week, that the brakes on her BMW gave out as she was backing down the driveway, and that this year, for the first time, ice is forming every night on the flagstone steps from her kitchen down to the garage. They're all things that happened, but she's convinced that they're part of some sort of plot to kill her instead of unrelated accidents.''

''Well, it seems to me that if someone in town was trying to kill her, it would be Rebecca.'' Susan reached around behind her and rearranged some pinecones in a blue and white bowl.

''Why Rebecca? She's the winner, after all. If you look at Evan as the prize in some sort of contest, that is.''

''Because of this obsession Kelly has over not changing her life any. Remember I told you that Elizabeth called this morning? Well, she says that Kelly is planning to go to all the traditional Christmas and New Year's parties in town— all except Evan's, of course.''

''So what?'' Kathleen asked. ''She was invited, wasn't she?''

''Of course she was invited. We've all invited her; she's our friend and neighbor. But no one expected her to accept. And she's going alone—at least her RSVPs were for one person, as far as Liz could find out.''

''Do you think that if Kelly goes to these parties alone, it's going to embarrass Evan and Rebecca?''

''Yes.''

''Then maybe he has good reason to want to hurt Kelly; maybe he's protecting his new wife.''

''You think Evan really could be a murderer?'' Susan, who had promised herself that one glass of burgundy would be her limit, poured out another.

''No. But I suppose it's possible that he's trying to scare her.''

''Into leaving town?''

''Or just leaving him alone?'' Kathleen suggested.

''Well, that's possible. Elizabeth also said that Kelly calls Evan over the slightest little thing.''

''Like?''

''Like which company they used to plow out the driveway

in the winter, and whether the warranty has run out on the refrigerator. Evidently all things she used to take care of herself when they were married.'' Susan passed Kathleen a slightly scorched spinach turnover. They were eating the rejects from her afternoon's baking.

''Thanks. Has Kelly become helpless now that she and Evan are divorced?''

''That's what Liz claims,'' Susan said.

''And Liz is worried about her?'' Kathleen asked.

''Very. They've always been good friends. It's logical that Kelly would turn to Liz in a crisis.''

''But evidently Kelly didn't tell Liz about the attempts on her life—or what she considers to be the attempts on her life.''

''That's right!'' Susan exclaimed. ''What do you think that means?''

''It may mean nothing. It might not even be true. It's possible that Liz knows all about it and just didn't tell you.''

Susan sipped her wine and thought for a moment. ''Why did Kelly tell you?''

''She wants to hire me to protect her.''

''Heavens! What did you tell her?''

''That I would think about it and talk to her Monday morning. I checked out her security system, just to make her feel more comfortable. Not that she has anything to worry about: that house is nearly a fortress. The alarms were put in when it was built and they were the best. It would be very difficult for anyone to break in there undetected.''

''But are you thinking of hiring yourself out as a guard or something?'' Susan asked, amazed.

''No. It's not something I'm qualified to do, and it isn't anything I want to do. But she seemed so desperate that I didn't want to turn her down immediately. Maybe I can think of something that will help her.'' Kathleen sipped her wine and stared into the fire.

"What she needs is a psychiatrist," Susan said.

"Have you tried to suggest that?" Kathleen asked, not disagreeing.

"Not recently. I suggested it last winter—before Kelly left town—and almost got my head bitten off. You'd have thought I was saying that the woman was a raving maniac."

"Maybe someone she's closer to—maybe Liz—could suggest it?"

"Not a chance. Liz doesn't believe in psychiatry."

"That's not possible. You don't have to believe in ghosts, or leprechauns, or things like that, but you have to believe in psychiatrists. Some of our neighbors are psychiatrists."

"Maybe what I should say is that she doesn't believe in psychiatrists treating people she knows. I asked her if she had suggested a psychiatrist to Kelly, and Liz said that she was sure that Kelly had enough friends to take care of her."

"Well, if Liz thinks that a friend—no matter how well intentioned—can take the place of a trained therapist, then you're right. She doesn't believe in psychiatrists." Kathleen paused. "But we have two possibilities here: either Kelly needs professional help . . . or else someone is really trying to harm her."

Susan sighed and looked at her friend. "Do you want another glass of wine?"

It was all she could think of to say.

"Susan, we're home!"

"It's Jed!" Susan grabbed the now-empty wine bottle and slid it behind the basket of logs beside the fireplace. "And his mother," she explained.

"Well, we got everything on the list and then some." The woman she had just mentioned entered the living room, shaking out her coat as she walked. "The town certainly has changed in the past two years. I almost didn't recognize it."

"It has, hasn't it?" Susan leapt to her feet. "I'd better help Jed get everything out of the car."

"He and Chad said for you to stay inside and they would do it all."

"Well, isn't that nice? Let me hang up your coat and get you something to drink," Susan offered, noticing that, while she had hidden the bottle, the empty glasses were shining in the firelight.

"Of course." Claire Henshaw handed her coat to Susan. "I'd love some carrot juice," she added, sitting down next to Kathleen.

In that moment, Susan realized she'd learned the true meaning of stopping in her tracks. "I don't think we have any carrot juice."

Her mother-in-law leapt to her feet in a way that made Susan think maybe there was something to all this healthy eating. Susan certainly wasn't feeling all that energetic—or steady, for that matter.

"We can solve that problem right now," she proclaimed. "Jeddy, you go right up to my room and bring down the big box sitting on the floor of the closet. Just open the door and you'll know the one . . . It's wrapped in bright green paper and has a big white bow. And, Susan, you must have carrots in the kitchen. Right?"

"Yes, of course," Susan answered, wondering if there was any food in the world that she didn't have in her over-stuffed kitchen these days.

"Bring all that you have out here with a tray and some clean glasses and we'll solve this problem right now."

Susan entered the kitchen to find her son leaning against the counter, doubled over with not-so-silent laughter.

"What's going on?" she asked Chrissy, pulling open the hydrator drawer in her refrigerator and removing two cellophane bags of carrots. "What's so funny?"

"Every time she calls him *Jeddy*, Chad cracks up," Chrissy explained. "It is a little silly, Mom."

"It's sometimes hard for parents to realize that their children are all grown up," Susan commented, smiling.

"That's right. Like making me have a midnight curfew on weekends," Chrissy said, picking up the cue her mother had unwittingly offered.

"Not now, Chrissy," Susan ordered, and hurried back to the living room. She had a horrible feeling that she knew what was coming.

"We waited so that you could be the one to open it," Claire said, beaming at the large box that had displaced one of Susan's carefully arranged displays of winter greens and cones on the large marble coffee table in the middle of the room.

"Oh," Susan said, putting down the vegetables. "But it isn't Christmas for more than a week."

"But we'll get so much use out of it while I'm here. I can show you all of my favorite concoctions— But I mustn't give the surprise away. Open it."

Susan knelt down and accepted the inevitable—a full week of fresh vegetable juice.

"It's the deluxe model. You can decide just how much pulp you want to retain in the juice. See? With the knob down here."

Susan looked at the bottom of the large chrome machine and, sure enough, there was a bright red circle labeled ROUGHAGE REGULATOR. She smiled up at her husband's mother and took a deep breath. "It's wonderful. Thank you so much. And how nice that you're here to show us how it works."

"Get ready to drink the best carrot juice you've ever had. Jeddy, hand me those carrots that your wife left there by the door. Thanks." She accepted the carrots and began breaking them and stuffing them into a tube in the top of the appliance. "You're going to love this, Jeddy. You know how you used to love a glass of V-8 juice before dinner? We used to call it your little cocktail, remember? Well, this is even better.''

Susan knew that Jed now preferred his cocktails with a little more punch but, after all, this was his mother. He deserved to be her first victim. ''I forgot the glasses. I'll go get them.''

''Don't worry. We can use the ones in the bar,'' Jed suggested, heading across the room to the large French wardrobe that had been altered to serve that purpose.

''Good idea. Where are the kids? They should have their vegetables, too.''

''Why don't we serve them theirs with dinner? Then we can have a nice chat now and they can get their vitamins later,'' Susan said, wanting time to remind them to mind their manners when presented with glasses of bright orange liquid.

''I have to get home and start Jerry's supper,'' Kathleen said, declining the glass that Jed offered her. ''I've interrupted your reunion. Don't get up. I can see my way to the door.''

''You don't know where I put your coat. I'd better get it for you,'' Susan said quickly, and followed her friend from the room.

''I don't know where my coat is?'' Kathleen whispered, pointing to where it lay across a chair near the front door.

''I wanted to talk to you for a sec,'' Susan whispered back, and pulled her away from the entrance to the living room.

''Kath, if there is something going on at Kelly's house, then Evan must be responsible. He's the only person who knows how that security system works.''

''No, that's not true. There must be diagrams of the initial installation around somewhere. Whoever got hold of them would know all about it.''

''So it could be Rebecca!'' Susan thought she might be catching on to something.

"Maybe, but I think you have other things to worry about," Kathleen replied, nodding her head toward the living room.

"It will be interesting to talk to Evan at his party," Susan said, unwilling to change the subject.

"I'm sure you're right," Kathleen agreed, pulling her coat over her shoulders. It's going to be an interesting party."

SEVEN

SOMETIMES DECORATING THE CHRISTMAS TREE IS AN ACTIVity that brings a family closer together. And sometimes not.

"Is it possible to be allergic to whatever kind of tree this is? Chrissy is getting red splotches all over her face. Ugly, red splotches," Chad elaborated, grinning at his sister. She, in turn, shrieked and raced to the hall to look in the mirror.

"Chad." His father's voice had a warning ring to it. "Decorating the Christmas tree is supposed to be a family time together. You are not to tease your sister."

"What did I say? She's just upset because Seth didn't call last night," Chad said, defending himself as he looked through a large cardboard box.

"I am not!" Chrissy reappeared in the room, screaming as she went.

"Chrissy! Tone it down! Your grandmother is asleep upstairs," her father ordered, leaning back so far that he almost toppled off the ladder he was standing on. Trying to regain his balance, he dropped the string of lights he had been holding. "Damn."

"Jed! And in front of the children."

He knew without looking that it was his mother; his wife had been known to say worse despite their offspring's whereabouts. "Hi, Mom. Sleep well?"

"Grandma, do you think I have a rash on my left cheek?" Chrissy turned to what she considered the most pressing business at hand.

"Come over to the window where the light is better . . . Well, maybe a slight one. I have some aloe cream upstairs that will help soothe it. It's made especially by Dr. Barr's company—and they don't use any unnatural ingredients."

"It was something natural that gave her the rash, Mother." Jed had stepped down to the floor and was trying to untangle the string of lights he had just dropped.

"I thought everything was put away perfectly last year," Susan said, entering the room as the two other females left, a large tray in her hands.

"That's what we always think and it's never true. Remember last year we left for Aspen on December twenty-sixth. We were in a hurry when we took down the tree."

"You mean *I* was in a hurry." Susan smiled at her husband. "I always take down the tree. Sorry I made such a mess of it. Want a doughnut? I just made them."

"Your homemade nutmeg doughnuts? Wow!" Chad was at her side in seconds. "It really *is* Christmas." He smiled happily as he munched a sugary circle.

"Could you please use a napkin?" Susan looked down at the Oriental carpet on her living room floor as she spoke. It was covered with spruce needles, tiny twigs, and golden specks of tinsel. She knew it would be worse before the morning was over.

"I need a glass of milk," Chad said, grabbing another doughnut and leaving the room.

"I'm thinking about calling Kelly to see how she is this morning," Susan said to her husband, picking up a tiny silver train engine and holding it up to catch the light. "We bought this for Chad when he was just a baby. Remember?"

Jed, who had traded the lights for a doughnut and some coffee from the pot that accompanied them on the platter, came over and put his arm around his wife. "Sure do. Someone could do a family history looking at the ornaments we've collected. There's even a little brass Old Faithful ornament from that year we went to Yellowstone."

"Do you think I should bother Kelly?" Susan returned to her first thought.

"Good idea. She could probably use some moral support today. Evan and Rebecca giving the same party that she and Evan used to give is going to be hard on her. These doughnuts are better than ever, Sue. But I don't know what Mom is going to say when she sees them. These are probably not included on Dr. Barr's famous diet." He chuckled gently as he spoke and reached for another doughnut.

"I know, but I thought and thought about this in bed last night. It's Christmas, and these are our traditions. If your mother decides that they're not for her, fine. But I'm not going to change the traditions of this family just because she's changed her life-style."

"I knew you were thinking about something besides me in bed last night." Jed kissed his wife on the top of her head.

She pulled away and looked up at him. "Jed, your mother is right next door in the guest room."

She continued, "I'm going to call Kelly before she goes out to church or someplace else. I can do it while stirring fudge.'' She gave her husband an absentminded smile, then headed for the kitchen.

Jed didn't respond. He was so busy trying to figure out exactly how long his mother's visit was to be that he stepped right on the tree lights. ''Damn.''

''I sure hope Grandma doesn't hear you saying that,'' Chad, returning to the room, said kiddingly.

''How about helping me with these lights,'' his father asked.

''You don't think we should wait for Chrissy and Mom?''

''Putting lights on the Christmas tree has somehow become the man's job in this house,'' Jed answered, climbing back up the ladder. ''Once we're finished, your mother and sister will come in and tell us how we should have done it. It's a holiday tradition.''

They chuckled together amiably and got down to work.

Susan also had her work cut out for her in the kitchen. Her fudge was starting to stick to the porcelain insert in her copper double boiler and she didn't want to interrupt Kelly, but she had to get off the line before she could reach a whisk that would fit into the sides of the pan.

''. . . I'm almost sure he's missing the cookies that I make. Rebecca isn't much of a cook you know. I used to spend hours and hours making the cookies that Evan likes best. Why it takes a whole day just to make the little tarts shaped like Christmas trees. And that recipe only makes a few dozen. And my *Bûche de Noël*—we were given that recipe by an old woman in Paris. Her family has been baking them for decades. Maybe even centuries. Now you know Rebecca isn't going to make almond paste from scratch, or meringue mushrooms with cocoa spores, or caramelize a sugar net to go over the whole thing. Is she?''

Susan stopped stirring. ''You do all that by hand?''

''Of course. I always did it for Evan. We honeymooned in

France, you know, so it seemed appropriate. Besides, who could I get to do it for me?''

Who indeed?

"But think of what you can do now with the time that you used to spend in the kitchen," Susan said, giving up on the spoon. She put down the receiver and dashed across the kitchen to the drawer where she kept her whisks.

She was back to the phone to hear, ". . . this year as well."

"Wait a second, I was getting something and missed a few words." Susan had missed more than a few words; the fudge had turned into a grainy mess. She shoved the pan off the burner and sat down at her kitchen table to listen more carefully. "Why don't you repeat everything?"

"I was answering your comment about using all that time for something else. What I've been telling you is that I don't have extra time. I'm doing everything Evan and I did, but without Evan. Actually I have less time than usual. Do you know how long it took me to put all those candles in the windows? And Evan used to roast and peel all the chestnuts for the marron glacé, and that took me hours to do!"

"Is your mother coming out for the holidays?" Susan asked, picking up a mug of coffee from the table where she had left it half an hour ago and absentmindedly taking a sip. Ugh.

"No, my mother never comes East for Christmas."

"Then, Kelly, who are you doing all this for?"

"For Evan. Susan, when he comes back to me he'll want everything to be the way that it was, won't he?"

Susan almost choked on her coffee, thinking that Kathleen must be wrong. Kelly wouldn't be cooking up a storm for a man who she thought was trying to kill her.

"I have to run, Sue. I have a very busy day ahead of me. I'll give you a call tomorrow morning, okay? Maybe we can go shopping together. There are still a few things I have to find."

"Great. Call anytime. Even if you just need someone to listen—Kelly?" Susan realized she had been talking to herself; Kelly had hung up.

Susan got up and went over to the sink, pulling out the garbage pail hidden beneath it. She had planned to scrape the burned fudge into it but, instead, she dumped everything in the sink and stood quietly in the middle of the room. Kelly was filling her life by preparing treats for a man who had left her and married another woman. Was this sane behavior? And what could she do about it? Susan shook her head despairingly and left the room. . . .

"Hi. That's perfect timing. What do you think of the lights?" Jed got down from the ladder and displayed the tree, now shimmering with ten strings of tiny white lights.

"It looks wonderful," she astounded him by answering.

"Hey, she likes it,' Chad cheered. "Let's put on the tinsel."

"I think we'd better wait for your sister to start that," his father answered. "Why don't you go call her? Tell her we need her presence. Rash and all."

"I'm here. What do you need me for?" Chrissy entered the room, followed by her grandmother.

"For—" Chad began.

"Those lights are going to need rearranging," Jed's mother announced from the doorway. "Who ever put them on so unevenly?"

EIGHT

Everyone was having a wonderful time at the Knowlsons' party—except for Rebecca Knowlson.

"I hate that woman. She's going to drive me crazy. You're her friend. Couldn't you talk her into moving out of town?"

"Rebecca . . ." Susan smiled, trying to pacify her hostess, a tall, thin woman whose red hair was cut in a fashionable angular style.

"How do you expect me to feel? Every time I turn around, she's calling on the phone or popping up in my path. I swear she knows half an hour before I run out of milk so she can beat me to the checkout line at the Grand Union. But this afternoon was the last straw. I can't believe what she did." She adjusted large silver cuff bracelets as she spoke.

"What?"

"Tell her, Rebecca. She'll die." This from Barbara St. John, who had taken a break from the party and joined Susan and Rebecca in the kitchen. Evidently she had heard the story before.

"Well . . ." Rebecca Knowlson paused, whether for dramatic effect or to make sure they weren't overheard, Susan couldn't tell. "Well," she repeated, "this afternoon, about an hour before the party was to start, Kelly appeared at our front door carrying a large wooden bowl of salad."

"Carrying *what*?" Susan thought she hadn't heard correctly.

"A gigantic salad bowl, brimming with lettuce, and herbs, and flowers, and things. You know how she is—always trying to be such an original cook. That damn salad had daffodils in it!"

"Surely not," Susan protested.

"Tell her what you did with it!" Barbara urged.

"I threw it at her."

Susan gasped. "You didn't!"

"I did." Rebecca started to smile for the first time since beginning her story. "You should have seen her: salad dressing oozing down the lapels of that blond ranch mink ski jacket Evan bought her the last year they were married. I hope I ruined it." She stopped and appeared to reconsider. "Of course, it didn't do much for my front steps, either. It was too cold to pour water over them; I didn't want to turn them into a miniskating rink. So I sent one of the boys out to sweep up as much of the muck as possible. I asked the man we hired to tend bar to do it, but he refused. Can you imagine?"

"But why did she bring the salad?" Susan asked, finally understanding what had been sticking to her shoes all evening.

"She said it was her contribution to the party."

"Maybe she thought of it as a peace offering?" Susan suggested. "You know, maybe she was trying to make up for some of the grief she's been causing you?"

"Susan, give me a break," Rebecca replied. "She wanted to ruin my party—just like she's been trying to ruin my marriage. And I'm not going to let her!" Rebecca stopped talking and looked around the kitchen. "Now what did I come in here for?" she asked, looking at the trays of canapes ready for serving on the counter before her.

"Serving tongs," Barbara answered. "Remember? Your guests can't pick up the Swedish meatballs."

"Of course." She looked at Susan curiously. "Why are you here?"

"A glass of water. I was going to take a Tylenol. I have a headache and the downstairs bathroom is occupied."

"Oh. Well, glasses are to the right of the sink," Rebecca said, as tongs in hand, she left the room. "Try some of Evan's eggnog. It'll kill the pain as well as anything."

Susan, who had been considering the possibility that too much of that particular concoction had caused the pain, found a glass and took her pill. Then she, too, returned to the party, where she was immediately accosted by her husband.

"What are we going to do about this?" he asked anxiously.

Susan stared at him a moment before answering. Not that she wasn't happy to see he cared about Kelly, but it wasn't like Jed to get so upset about neighborhood problems; usually he stayed just a bit removed from his hometown. Susan had come to think of it as the commuter's dilemma—they lived in town and at the same time they were separated from it.

"I'll give her a call tomorrow and we can talk. I don't really know what else I can do," she answered.

"Give her a call? What are you talking about? What if she marries him?" Jed asked.

"I don't think Rebecca is going to let that happen," Susan answered, looking around the room.

"Rebecca? What does Rebecca have to do with this?" Jed asked, waving to acknowledge the greeting of Derek Stevenson.

"Wait a minute. Who are we talking about?" Susan asked.

"My mother. Who else?"

"Your mother? What's wrong with your mother?" Susan took a caviar-covered cracker from a proffered tray and popped it in her mouth.

"How can you ask? It's that man she brought to the party with her—Dr. Bobby Barr. Oh, no! Here they come. Try to be nice to him," Jed requested anxiously as they were approached by his mother, who was accompanied by a short, bald man around fifty-five years old.

Susan, with no intention of being anything but nice, smiled happily at the couple.

"Susan, I haven't had a chance to tell you how much I love that dress. What a wonderful shade of green. And how slim you look in it," Claire said.

"Thanks. I'm glad you like it. Kathleen picked it out for me."

Everyone smiled at one another and there was one of those awkward silences.

"Isn't the food lovely?" Susan said, hoping to attract the attention of one of the young men handing around the appetizers. She was especially interested in the small crab puffs and said so.

"You're not eating that stuff, are you, my dear?" Dr. Barr seemed horrified. "Crabs are bottom eaters. Never, ever, consume bottom eaters! You might as well be eating raw sewage!"

Susan stared at the light crisp of pastry and crab in her hand and thought for a moment. How much did she owe a guest of her husband's mother? But greed beat any good intentions she may have considered and she gobbled up the food. Then, hoping to atone for her sins, she chose a wine spritzer over more eggnog.

"I cannot let you do that," insisted Dr. Barr, taking the goblet right out of her hand. "Sulfites, you know."

"But I'm not allergic to sulfites," Susan protested, watching him pour the wine on a defenseless poinsettia.

"How can something that so many people are allergic to be good for you? Think, my dear, think," Dr. Barr said in an attempt to explain his actions.

"I think—" Jed began.

But Susan wasn't going to let this go any further.

"I see the Stevensons over by the Christmas tree," she said. "Let's go see them, Jed. We have to talk to them about the New Year's Day party at the club, remember?"

He didn't, mainly because there wasn't a New Year's Day party at the Hancock Field Club, but he followed his wife toward the other couple. And, more importantly, away from his mother and the man she rather adolescently was calling her date.

"Did you hear about Kelly?" Elizabeth asked immediately. Susan wondered how many times this greeting had been exchanged during the evening so far.

"Yes. Have you talked to her today?" Susan asked immediately.

"My wife," Derek explained to Jed, "is very, very worried about Kelly Knowlson. We all are, of course."

"Kelly and Derek went to prep school together, you know," Elizabeth elaborated. "We're really dreadfully worried about her."

Susan wondered if some archaic concept of "old school ties" was the only reason for Derek's expressed concern.

"But have you talked to her today? Do you have any idea why she came over here with the salad?"

"I spoke with her this morning. She seemed fine. A little sad. Of course, that's only natural. Some of her best friends are here tonight. In many ways this is the same party that she and Evan used to give every year. A half-dozen couples enjoying a very elegant evening. I think it's fair to expect that she'd be sad about it."

"But bringing food . . ." Susan tried to find the right words. "It's a little odd, don't you think?"

"A little." Derek conceded.

"But Rebecca threw it at her," Elizabeth responded. "That shows a certain lack of class, don't you think?"

"We're not here to criticize our hosts," her husband reminded her.

"Of course not." His wife fell into line at once. "But, if you don't mind, I think I'll sneak off and call Kelly. If anyone sees me, I can say that I'm calling home. That would be all right, wouldn't it?"

"An excellent idea," her husband agreed, taking her empty glass and setting it down on a nearby table.

"I heard an interesting story about the new V.P. of personnel at your company," Jed commented to Derek.

Susan knew it was her cue to circulate; it was time to find her host. When she had arrived at Evan's house, he had been busy explaining his new and very complicated stereo system to Jeffrey St. John. Maybe he was free now. After a quick search, she found him standing beside a hard-disk computer with Jeffrey still at his side. Evan had run his hands through his thinning hair too many times for neatness and was waving around his horn-rimmed glasses to make a point. Susan thought, not for the first time, that whatever he had that made women devote their lives to him, it had nothing to do with his looks. Although usually impeccably groomed, he was a grown-up nerd. He smiled at her appearance.

"Susan, help me escape from this man. Let's talk about something other than machinery. Tell me, did you get out to Quogue last August? We wanted to see you, but we were so busy with my boring business colleagues the first two weeks and then, of course, there was that trip to the fjords in Finland. You must go there—you would love it; it reminded me terribly of New Zealand, only much more civilized. Some of the best food in the world; just your type of place." Although shorter than Susan, Evan Knowlson put his arm around her shoulder while talking and led her toward a large couch covered with a Navaho wool rug.

"Doesn't everything look wonderful?" he asked her as they sat down. "Didn't Rebecca do a wonderful job?"

"Perfect," Susan agreed, feeling slightly uncomfortable and wondering if it was the itchy wool poking through her light silk dress or the questioning.

"She planned everything perfectly," Evan agreed. "And it was quite a job—we've only been back from Vermont for two weeks."

"I hadn't seen this place since the housewarming you gave last June. You've done a lot with it." She looked around the large, sweeping combination living room and dining room.

"Everyone is surprised that it's so different than the house Kelly and I built."

"Yes, but how many people have the chance to do two different things so perfectly?" was Susan's tactful answer. She had actually been thinking not about how different the houses were, but how similar. Both places were designed more for entertaining than family living.

"You're a woman who's grown over the years . . . You must understand that a person needs change," Evan continued. "Kelly refused to change. Oh, I don't blame her. She knew what her needs were and stayed with them. I accept that as real wisdom, but I need something different. All this," he amplified, waving a well-manicured hand around the room, from the antique Indian saddle blankets hung over the two-story-high railing on the second floor to the heavy iron abstract sculpture displayed over the large, free-form stone fireplace. His eyes fell on a framed photograph of Rebecca's two teenage sons, and he stopped speaking for a moment.

"That reminds me of something I wanted to ask you, Susan, dear. I've been so busy at work that I haven't had a chance to give you a call. But now Rebecca and I are taking a good long break. We're actually closing the office until after the New Year. But I do have to think about some family things. I wonder if you could help me.'' He sounded a little hesitant. ''I'm looking for someone to write recommendations for the kids for jobs next summer—they're hoping to wait on tables out in the Hamptons or something. And I wondered if you and Jed would help us out.''

Why not? ''Sure. I don't usually speak for Jed, but I can't think of any reason he'd object. It would be nice if they could work out there. Then you all could spend the summer together on the Island.''

''Yes. Just like a normal family,'' Evan agreed somewhat vaguely. ''I mean, like a real father and mother, not like a stepfather,'' he elaborated. ''It's not always easy being a stepfather.''

''I can imagine.''

''Sometimes I think I'm not a very good parent,'' he continued, looking sadly at his guests.

''I'm sure you're—''

''Well, look who's here. Your husband and my wife.'' Evan changed his tone as he interrupted her. ''And who is this lovely lady they have with them?''

The two men exchanged Christmas greetings before Jed introduced his mother. Susan wondered vaguely where Dr. Barr had vanished to. Well, since he wasn't around, she'd get another glass of wine—or two. She smiled and hurried over to the bar set up near the two-story balsam that filled the end of the room opposite the fireplace.

The bartender took her order, pouring white wine from a bottle with the label of an expensive French vintner. This was something else that hadn't changed: Only the best was ever served to guests at Evan's house, no matter who its mistress might be.

''Susan, I've been looking for you.'' It was Kathleen, and standing beside her was a very attractive woman in her early fifties who could only be her mother. "Susan, I want you to meet—"

"Your mother," Susan finished for her and took the woman's hand. "I'm very, very pleased to meet you. I've been looking forward to your visit. How was the trip up from Philadelphia?"

"Not bad. I had been worried about snow on the roads, but they were clear. The only problem was that horrible bit of the Jersey Turnpike around New York City. I'm always afraid I'll make the wrong turn and end up on the George Washington Bridge." She took Susan's hand and squeezed it warmly. "Call me Dolores; everyone does. I've been looking forward to meeting you and your children. You have two of them, don't you?"

"Yes." Susan was surprised by this transition. "Chrissy is fifteen now and Chad is twelve."

"Most people who choose to live in the suburbs have children, don't they?" Kathleen's mother continued.

"Yes, I suppose so," Susan agreed, wondering what she was getting into.

"I've always thought Kathleen would be a wonderful mother. Don't you think so?"

Susan took her time sipping her wine. But she could sit down and finish the entire bottle and she wouldn't think of an answer to that question—not one that would satisfy everyone. "She's very good with children."

"Well, then . . ." Kathleen's mother appeared to find that a sterling endorsement. "And I'm sure Jerry—"

"Mother, not now. We'll talk later. But not now," Kathleen hissed.

"Maybe I'm wrong. Maybe you can't even imagine how a mother feels. How much she wants to be a grandmother."

"Exactly. You're exactly right, ma'am."

Susan and Kathleen twirled around. It was the bartender, the man who wouldn't wash off the front steps, speaking.

"My son and his wife have been married for six years and still no children." He put his head closer to Kathleen's mother and handed her a glass of red wine. "They say they're too busy. Do you believe that? Too busy. Where would he be if his mother and I had been too busy?" He turned his attention to Kathleen. "And what would you like?"

"Double Scotch. No ice."

NINE

HAPPILY, SUSAN WAS ALMOST IMMEDIATELY PROVIDED WITH an excuse to leave this particular discussion behind.

"Susan, there's a telephone call for you. It sounded like your daughter. There was some loud music playing in the background and I couldn't hear very well," Rebecca said, joining the group near the bar.

"Thanks. It's probably Chad. He seems incapable of turning down his music unless someone orders him to do so." Susan hurried off to the wall phone in the kitchen, thinking of accidents, dismemberment, fires . . . She picked up the receiver.

"What? I can't hear what you're saying. What's wrong?"

Susan heard herself start to scream. One of the caterers gave a started glance in her direction, and she lowered her voice. "Chad, turn down that music right now!"

"You don't have to yell, Mom. I can hear you." But he turned down the volume, and Susan felt her grip on the phone relax.

"Why are you calling, Chad?"

"The hospital called."

"What?"

"It's okay. They said not to worry, that everything was okay."

"Who's okay? Where's Chrissy?" Susan asked, confusion replacing panic.

"Right here. I was trying to tell you. The hospital called and said there had been an accident."

"Chad! Who was hurt?"

"Mrs. Knowlson."

"Rebecca? That's not possible, I just saw her . . ." The explanation occurred to her as Chad spoke.

"Kelly Knowlson. She was in an automobile accident. The man on the phone called it minor. She's in the emergency room at the hospital and they want you to come, pick her up, and take her home."

"Of course," Susan relaxed. "When did you get the call?"

"Just a few minutes ago. The man said that you didn't have to rush. I think I got the whole message, Mom."

"I'm sure you did, honey. Thanks a lot. Now go to bed soon, okay?"

"Sure. Does this mean you and Daddy are going to be home later?"

"Don't plan on it, Chad," she answered. "Thanks for calling. 'Bye, honey."

Susan hung up as her husband entered the room. "Oh, Jed. There's been an auto accident and Kelly Knowlson is in the emergency room. They called and asked if I could give her a ride home.''

"The hospital called here?"

"No, Chad got the call at home and relayed the message. I wonder what Chrissy is doing?"

"Probably too involved in a TV movie to pay attention. Don't worry about her. What about Kelly?"

"I guess I'd better go to the hospital and pick her up."

"Do you want me to come along?" he offered.

"No, and I don't think we should say anything about this. There's too much talk about Kelly at this party already. I'll just tell Rebecca that there's a small problem at home and that I have to leave for a while. I should make it back here in less than an hour."

"Unless Kelly needs you to be with her," Jed suggested.

"True." She hesitated.

"If there's a problem and you're needed there, I can get a ride home with Jerry. You'd better run. No one likes to spend extra time in a hospital."

"You're right. Oh, Jed . . ." She stopped on her way to the door. "What about your mother?"

"I think Mother is just fine. Dr. Barr has detached himself from her side and she's chatting with Elizabeth Stevenson."

"I'll get my coat," Susan said, not wanting to get into a family discussion now.

"No, I'll get it. You go explain to Rebecca and I'll meet you at the front door. It's lucky we were a little late, otherwise the car might be parked in."

They had been late and, for once, it hadn't been her fault, Susan remembered. Jed's mother had changed her outfit half a dozen times before their departure, modeling all the beautiful silks and leathers that she had picked up in her travels. Susan couldn't help thinking of all the shopping the woman had done and how she had ended up with a vegetable juicer.

On the other hand, there was something satisfying about seeing Jed irritated at his mother instead of his wife.

She was thinking about it during the short drive to the emergency room. And thinking, too, of Kelly having an accident during her ex-husband's party. If it really had been an accident. But there was no reason to anticipate more trouble than she had right now, she lectured herself, turning off the road and into the emergency room parking area. She was as familiar with the area as any mother whose son had played on Little League, on soccer teams, and on the swimming and diving team at the club would be.

But Chad wasn't involved in winter sports, and she was surprised to discover the reception area decorated for the holidays. A large gold paper banner on the far wall ordered everyone in the room to HAVE A HAPPY HOLIDAY. Cards were taped to a string draped around two computer terminals and up over a tall file cabinet. A tabletop Christmas tree with multicolored blinking lights obscured the view of the nurse at the desk.

"I'm here to see Kelly Knowlson," Susan told the woman, who was looking at her somewhat suspiciously.

"Are you a patient?" the woman replied.

"No. I got— That is, my son got a call that Mrs. Knowlson was here and needed a ride home," Susan explained inadequately.

"Mrs. Knowlson works here?"

"No, she was in an accident."

"Oh, she's a patient here." The nurse seemed pleased at her discovery.

"Yes. Don't you have a record of her admittance?" Susan asked, wondering if she had gotten the information wrong.

"Are you a relative?"

"No, but . . ." The entrance of a large, burly man wearing a pea green surgeon's gown solved the problem.

"Susan, what are you doing here? Is someone hurt?"

"Dan, I'm fine, but I'm so glad to see you!" Susan accepted his hug and returned the kiss of her next-door neighbor. "What are you doing here?"

He chuckled. "This is a hospital. I'm a gynecologist. I belong here, remember?"

"Dan, have you seen Kelly?"

"Kelly Knowlson? No."

"I got a call— That is, Chad got a call that she had been in an automobile accident and was here, but now I can't find her," Susan explained.

"I've been in surgery so I haven't seen her, but certainly that's easy enough to find out," Dan Hallard replied, reaching toward the woman behind the desk. "Nurse?"

"These are Mrs. Knowlson's admission papers as well as the report on status. That new young resident with the long hair is looking at her now." The nurse answered the unasked question and placed a manilla folder in his hand.

He looked through it quickly, then handed it back. "No problem. According to this, her car slid off the road. X-rays look fine, but she is feeling some pain in her neck, so the resident will probably put a brace on it. He's just being cautious. Let's go find her."

Susan followed him through double swinging doors and into a large area partitioned into half a dozen small rooms. Kelly was sitting on an examining table in the cubicle nearest the door, a large pink plastic circle around her neck.

"Susan, thank goodness you got my message. I don't think I could have stood another minute of this place," Kelly cried, and burst into tears.

Dan took both her hands in his and murmured comforting words. Susan, whose second child had been delivered by this man, remembered when his "calm down, you're going to be just fine" had sounded like an impossibility followed by the biggest lie she had ever heard. But Kelly was childless and it seemed to work for her. She sniffed a few times, blew her nose into the handkerchief offered, and even attempted a smile.

"Can I go home now? I need to be at home."

Susan looked to the doctor for instructions.

"Of course, you may. But remember that you have an appointment with the hospital orthopedist tomorrow—I was reading your chart, and it's down there. It's nothing to worry about; he'll just check the fit of your brace. He's a good man. You'll have to take a taxi or find someone to drive you around for the next few days, though."

"I'll be fine. I have a lot of friends," Kelly assured him. "Even friends who leave parties to help me." She looked at Susan. "I really appreciate this, Sue."

"Don't even think about it. I'm just glad you're not hurt," Susan said, as Dan helped Kelly down off the table. "Here's your purse. Did you have anything else?"

"No, I don't think so," Kelly answered. "Just that and my coat. Everything else was left in the car, and the policeman who brought me here said it would be towed to the Gulf station on the other side of town."

"They have the contract for all emergency towing in town," Dan explained. "Anything left in the car will be safe there."

Susan had helped Kelly put on her coat. "I don't know how to check you out of here," Susan said.

"Don't worry," Dan said. "I'll take care of it. You two just head on home. Kelly will get an extraordinarily high bill in the mail in a few weeks, but her insurance company will cover it."

Kelly smiled. "Thanks, Dan. It'll be good to get home."

Susan thought that perhaps Kelly was going to begin to cry again and urged her out of the hospital and into Susan's Maserati, adjusting the headrest to make the injured woman more comfortable. They waved to Dan Hallard and drove off.

"How did it happen?" Susan asked. "Or don't you want to talk about it?"

"I don't mind. It's just that I'm not sure I know the answer. I was driving down by the old mill— You know where that is?" As Susan nodded yes, she continued. "Well, I was just driving along and the car skidded off the road. I guess I must have hit a patch of ice or something."

"There's a stream along the road there, right?"

"Yes, and my car slid right into it. But there isn't much of a drop between the pavement and the water, and the car didn't even topple over or anything. The policeman who brought me to the hospital said I was lucky that it didn't happen four miles earlier. The water is about twenty feet below the road there and the drop is pretty steep. The car might have rolled in a place like that."

"Yes. I guess you were lucky," Susan agreed, thinking that if Kelly had in fact been trying to kill herself, she would probably have chosen a more suitable, more dangerous place to do it. Especially when it sounded like one was readily available.

"You know, Susan, I was very upset about Evan's party tonight. I was crying. That's probably why I didn't see the ice."

Susan wondered if Kelly was going to mention the salad— or if she should, since it was, by now, common knowledge among their friends and neighbors. "I heard that you were at Evan's new house earlier today," she began.

"I just wanted to be part of the party in some way," Kelly said, fumbling in her jacket pocket for a handkerchief and coming up with a pair of pigskin gloves.

"This must be very difficult to you. It's your first holiday season in town since the divorce," Susan commiserated. "Maybe you'd be happier with your mother?"

"No. Absolutely not. I'm needed here." Kelly stopped sniffing and seemed to gather herself together emotionally.

"I thought all this out very carefully. You know how much the holidays mean to me, and Hancock is my home. It's time to get on with my life."

"Maybe you'll meet another man," Susan suggested, thinking that a new love had cured the unhappiness of others in this situation.

"Not me. I'm not that type of woman," Kelly said as Susan entered her driveway and followed it around to the back of the house. "Evan is the man I loved—the man I'll always love. I'm just going to continue my life and wait for him to come back to me."

"But he's married to Rebecca," Susan said, shutting off the ignition and turning to look at her passenger.

"He was married to me first, and that was his only real marriage. This thing with Rebecca can't be permanent."

Susan didn't know what to say about that. "Don't move," she said. "Let me come around to your side of the car and help you get out. You don't want to strain your neck."

Kelly did as suggested, and Susan helped her hobble up heavily salted back steps and into the house. "I'm going to stay here until you're in bed," Susan announced, turning on the lights in the kitchen and helping Kelly remove her coat. "You may have some trouble putting on your nightgown. Do you want to shower?" Susan took off her own coat and threw it on an antique kitchen stool.

"The cloakroom," Kelly reminded her, looking at the casualness of the arrangement with distaste.

"I'll hang up yours, but mine might as well lie here. I can't stay very long. How about something to drink? Or maybe," she suggested, thinking of possible medication, "just some warm milk?"

"I'll make cocoa," Kelly said. "Then I think I'll get ready for bed. It's been a long day."

"I can make it."

"I want to," Kelly insisted.

Susan had always been impressed with Kelly's determination—and knew the futility of fighting it. "Fine. I'll go hang up your coat." She passed through the hall and into the cloakroom, hanging the coat next to the mink jacket that Rebecca had spoken of earlier in the evening. It looked as if she had been telling the truth about their encounter. A tiny leaf of lettuce hung off the fur's stand-up collar.

The house was chilly, and she hurried back to the kitchen. Kelly was sitting at one end of the long trestle table. The place to her right was set with a mug, spoon, and napkin identical to those before her. A steaming pot and matching tray of cookies sat on the table and the air was fragrant with chocolate.

"Come sit down. I thought we could both use a little snack," Kelly said, nodding to the place next to her and picking up the pitcher. As she poured the hot liquid into Susan's mug, two marshmallows bobbed to the surface. "I always like the marshmallows best, don't you?"

Susan lied and agreed, wondering if her children's tastes were more mature than Kelly's. But she sipped her drink and even found herself nibbling at a cherry-decorated wreath cookie. Kelly did the same.

"Did you have any dinner tonight? Would you like me to make you an omelet or something?" Susan offered.

"No, I'm more tired than I thought I would be, though. I think I'll just leave everything on the table and go upstairs."

"I'll go with you," Susan said. "You might be a little shaky and there are a lot of steps."

Kelly finished her cocoa and seemed to consider the effort. "Okay. We can go up the back way. It will be easier."

"The back?" Susan was surprised when Kelly went over to what she had always supposed was the door to a utility closet and opened it, revealing a small winding staircase.

Kelly turned and smiled at her. "Most people don't know about this. Evan insisted on it when we were designing the house. He said it was foolish to sleep on the second floor of a house with only one stairway, that too many people burned to death in accidents. But I think he just liked the idea of a secret entrance to our bedroom.'' She smiled a little sadly.

Susan wondered if this was a peek into some sort of sexual ritual and decided that she was too tired to be interested. She followed Kelly up the stairs. She didn't need help, as there were curving railings attached to the walls on either side.

They left the stairway through another door; this time it led directly into the bedroom that Kelly and Evan had shared.

''I think I can get washed by myself,'' Kelly announced, heading toward the adjoining bathroom. ''I'll call you if I need any help with this brace.''

''Fine.'' Susan sat down in one of the two Lawson chairs set before the fireplace. She waited until Kelly had closed the door behind her to take more than a surreptitious glance around the room. But, when she could concentrate on it, she was surprised at what she saw.

Not that the room wasn't as well thought out and luxurious as the rest of the house. If anything, it was more so with its four-poster bed hung with embroideries done more than a hundred years ago, its hand-loomed carpet, and stenciled walls. The fireplace she sat in front of was faced by another chair and a love seat covered with needlepoint pillows, all signed with the initials of their maker: K. K. Two doors led to walk-in closets. Two recessed windows displayed tiny brass electric candles hung in wreaths. None of this surprised her.

But the fireplace still glowed with the embers of a fire lit a few hours before. And, on either side of the bed, lights were set on a low wattage to illuminate four plump pillows that had been relieved of the spread. Each side of the bed had been turned back invitingly. If Susan hadn't known better, she would have thought that Kelly was anticipating a romantic evening.

Not that she had dressed for it. The door to the bathroom

opened, and Kelly emerged wearing light blue tailored pajamas with white piping around the collar and cuffs. Susan had once bought Jed an almost identical pair when he went to the hospital for some minor surgery. She must have been staring, because Kelly seemed to feel the need to explain.

"The doctor said that I could take off the brace at night."

"Oh, of course. Let me help you get into bed."

"I can do it, but would you go downstairs and find my purse? They gave me some painkillers and I'd like to take one."

"Did you leave them in the kitchen?"

"Yes."

Susan hurried down the stairs. The front stairs this time. She found the purse easily, sitting on the kitchen counter right inside the back door, and was on her way through the hall and back to the stairs when a light in the living room caught her eye. Might as well turn it off now. She tucked the tiny plastic cylinder in the pocket of her skirt as she entered the room.

"Oh, I . . ." She didn't know what to say. "Evan?"

Evan Knowlson was sitting in one of the plaid chairs in front of the fireplace. A small lamp disguised as a candle was lit on the table by the chair; its light beamed down on a cup of creamy liquid beside a plate of tiny cookies shaped and decorated to look like wreaths. He held a book in one of his hands; the gold letters on the leather binding identified it as a copy of *The Night Before Christmas*. It took Susan a few moments to realize that he must be dead; no one could live with a hole the size of the one he had in his right temple.

"Susan? Why is it taking you so long? Are you okay?" Kelly appeared behind her.

Susan heard her gasp, but then there was almost a full minute of silence before the other woman spoke.

"I told you he would come back, didn't I?"

TEN

A LARGE STAIN HAD SPREAD ACROSS EVAN'S COLLAR AND down the front of his perfectly starched shirt. He would have hated to be found looking like this, Susan thought.

"Evan always read that book on Christmas Eve. He gave it to me right after we were married. It's a first edition."

Susan reached out and grasped a corner of the wall beside her, taking a deep breath.

"He's dead, Kelly. He's dead," she repeated.

"I know. It looks like someone killed him, doesn't it?"

"We have to get help," Susan insisted.

"You do it. I'll stay here." Kelly walked slowly toward the body.

"I think you'd better come with me." Susan grabbed her arm. To her surprise, Kelly offered no resistance and allowed herself to be guided to the kitchen phone. But the line was dead.

"I don't understand," Susan said, shaking the receiver. "There's no storm, no winds."

"We're not supposed to call anyone."

Susan looked at Kelly before the impact of her comment struck. The killer had cut the phone line. "We're getting out of here." Mindful of Kelly's fragile state, and unwilling to move around the house more than necessary, she threw her own coat over Kelly's shoulders, grabbed her purse, and pushed Kelly before her out the back door. The cold air shot through her silk dress, but this was no time to worry about comfort. The car was parked at the bottom of the steps, and she shoved Kelly into the passenger seat, slammed the door, and ran around to the driver's side, her keys already in hand. The car started instantly, and they were out of the driveway in seconds.

"Where are we going?" Kelly asked as Susan steered the car out to the street.

"To Evan and Rebecca's house. There will be people there to help us." She pushed down on the accelerator. The two Knowlson houses might share a common property line, but the road from one to the other led around a very large block.

"We're not going to be able to park close. It isn't just Evan's party; there was also a big party going on next door," Susan said, pulling the car over to the side of the road.

Kelly didn't answer, but she got out of the car by herself and followed Susan down the sidewalk, toward the commotion. They were stopped from getting any closer to the house by a uniformed policeman hired for the evening as security for one of the parties.

"A little cold to be out without a coat, isn't it?" he asked Susan.

"I'm so glad to see you, Officer. Something terrible has happened." She heard Kelly start to cry. "Could you please come up to the Knowlson house with us? Please!"

He looked carefully at the two distressed women and followed without a word.

Susan didn't know what she had expected to find inside, but not this. The party was still going on, just as when she had left. If anything, it was even more convivial, more jovial. Jed was playing the piano in one corner of the room and proving that drinking excessive amounts of eggnog didn't turn a group of middle-aged suburbanites into the Vienna Boys Choir. Dr. Barr had just backed into the Christmas tree, and a uniformed girl was rushing over, dustpan in hand, to sweep up a shattered ornament. Both her mother-in-law and Kathleen's mother were examining the back of his suit jacket for damage. It appeared that a good time was being had by all. Except, of course, the host.

She waved to Jed, hoping to get his attention. What she got was the attention of everyone else in the large room. Susan had forgotten that Kelly was wearing pajamas.

"Susan. What are you doing? Are you mad?"

Susan's arm was almost pulled out of its socket as Barbara St. John grabbed her and spun her around. "We've got to get Kelly out of here before Rebecca sees her. She's in the kitchen now, but she's bound to be back soon," she continued, latching on to Kelly. "And look at Kelly. She isn't dressed. She looks terrible. What possessed you to bring her here?" She kept asking questions while pulling Kelly toward the large powder room near the door.

"Barbara, stop this. I have to talk to Kathleen. Evan's dead!" Susan turned and headed back into the room.

"Evan's dead?" Barbara repeated in a shocked voice, dropping Kelly's arm. "How could he be dead?" She looked around the room as though expecting to find him sprawled on the floor.

"Who's dead? And who brought *her* here?" Rebecca appeared in the open doorway, there was no mistaking the anger in her voice.

"Rebecca, there's been an accident . . ." Susan began, knowing that she was lying, but wanting to prepare her for the shock.

"I know. Kelly was in some sort of stupid car crash. Evan

overheard you on the phone and told me about it. But I don't understand why you brought her here. Surely there are more appropriate places. Or was this no accident? Is she just trying to get Evan's attention by playing another of her stupid little tricks?''

"Rebecca . . ." Susan began again.

"Susan, let me take Kelly home," Jed offered, appearing at her side.

"Jed–" Susan resisted the urge to rush into his arms and hide "—something terrible has happened."

"Let's go back into the hall," he answered. "You come, too, Kelly. I think—" he looked over his wife's shoulder at Rebecca "—I think something terrible is about to happen."

"You don't understand. Evan is dead."

"Evan—?"

"What did you say?" Rebecca interrupted Jed.

"How could you say such a thing?" Barbara asked.

"Wait one second. Repeat what you said, Susan." This last from Kathleen Gordon who had joined them.

"I said that Evan is dead." As she spoke, she heard Kelly begin to weep again behind her.

"Is this some sort of horrible joke?" Rebecca asked. "Or have you gone mad, Susan?"

"Now wait. We've got to figure this out. It may ruin your party, Rebecca, but right now there are more important problems here," Kathleen stated, taking control of the situation. "Where is Evan?"

"At Kelly's house."

"In the bedroom."

Susan and Rebecca answered simultaneously.

"He can't be in both places. Why do you think he's in the bedroom?" Kathleen asked Rebecca.

"Because that's where he went about half an hour ago to make some calls. There was a problem with one of the projects he's working on."

"So he'd be on the extension up there?" Kathleen asked. "But I was on the phone myself just a few—"

"No. There are two lines into the house. One is unlisted; we use that for business purposes."

"Right," Jed agreed, taking action. "Why don't I just go and check on him?"

"I'll come with you," the police officer, who had been silently sizing up the situation, insisted. The two men walked off quickly.

"We'll wait here until you get back," Susan said.

"No, we'll wait in the media room," Rebecca corrected. "Barb, will you just tell everyone that something has come up—don't make a big deal about it—and that Susan, Kathleen, and I are needed elsewhere for a few minutes?"

"Of course."

"No need to mention Kelly," Rebecca added.

"Certainly not," said her ever loyal friend.

"I think you all know where we're going—except Kelly," she added rather nastily.

"Evan always wanted a room just for his equipment on the ground floor," Kelly said. "I think I can figure out where he would have put it. I lived with him for—"

Susan literally put herself between the present Mrs. Knowlson and the past Mrs. Knowlson, and hurried both of them into the "media room."

"Good heavens," she said, momentarily distracted from the problem at hand by the place. "I don't think I've ever seen such a large television. Ever." Or want to, she added to herself.

"This room wasn't finished until last week. Everything is the most recent model. The TV is computer controlled—or maybe just the tape machine is." Rebecca ended less confidently than she had begun. "Evan had the best of everything put in here. Everything," she repeated for emphasis.

Kelly was looking around the room in wonder. "This isn't

at all like my place.'' She sat down on a plump red leather couch. ''I can't really believe all that's happening.''

Susan looked at her closely. Was she getting paler or did the dramatic recessed lighting make her appear so? ''Kelly? Are you feeling all right? You don't have your neck brace and you didn't take a painkiller before leaving the house. Maybe I should call a doctor.''

''My mother is a nurse,'' Kathleen announced. ''Do you want me to call her?''

''I'm okay,'' Kelly insisted. ''Just let me close my eyes for a few minutes.''

Susan sat down next to Kelly, and Kathleen joined them, sitting on the arm of the couch near Susan. Rebecca sat down at a desk and, her back to them, turned on the personal computer placed there. Except for some muted ticking as she typed something at the keyboard, the room was silent. Susan wondered if some sort of soundproofing had been placed in the walls when the house was built. She sighed. Kelly was still sitting with her eyes closed; Susan wondered if everything that had happened had been to much for her and if asking Kathleen's mother to look at her would be a good idea. Kathleen had discovered a chipped nail that she was running over her front teeth to smooth down as she stared off into space. Rebecca gave up typing and reached to turn off the screen as Jed returned to the room.

Susan looked up despite herself.

''Well, he's not there—and I didn't see any sign of a note or anything explaining why he left the house,'' Jed said.

''But we don't know that he left the house. Only that he's not in the bedroom,'' Rebecca insisted, beginning to sound a little panicked.

''He's not here. I checked everything out pretty thoroughly, Rebecca. You know—'' he hesitated and looked at his wife ''—with what Susan and Kelly are saying . . . and that policeman *is* talking to the policemen who showed up earlier about filing a report . . . well, maybe something *has* happened to Evan. Not that he's necessarily dead,'' he added as Rebecca stood up quickly. ''After all, how close did you get to him, Susan?''

''He was six, maybe seven feet away, but, believe me, he wasn't alive.''

''That explains it,'' Rebecca said, sounding relieved. ''You just thought he was dead. Evan's had a hard week, there are problems at work, and the party and—and everything. He probably just fell asleep.''

Susan didn't think that problems at work—or even whatever it was that Rebecca didn't want to mention—could have taken Evan over to his ex-wife's house and shot a hole in his head, but she shut up. They would be seeing for themselves soon enough. Then she realized she might be missing something, too. ''What did you say about the police showing up?''

''They came to the door with a stupid story. Someone called the dispatcher and said that there had been a murder here. Just some sort of kid prank—'' Rebecca began, and then looked around the room slowly. ''You don't think there's any truth in this, do you?'' she whispered, her eyes wide open.

Susan opened her mouth, but the door that Jed had carefully closed behind him swung open, and her mother-in-law entered the room.

''Jeddy! I want to go home—and I want to go home now!'' she said, imperiously demanding his attention.

Susan, sitting between one bereaved ex-wife and one about to find out that she was bereaved wife, had enough of her wits about her to be surprised that Jed's mother had a mug of eggnog in one hand and large chunk of pork pâté in the other, and was alternating sipping and munching. Had Dr. Barr and his diet died, too?

ELEVEN

"WE'VE GOTTEN OUR REPORT WRITTEN, MA'AM. IF YOU OR your husband would just sign it, we can be on our way."

"Of course. I—I don't know where my husband has gone to . . ." Rebecca laughed a little self-consciously at the policeman who had appeared in the doorway immediately after Jed and his mother's exit.

Susan couldn't wait any longer. "I think, Officer, that I have something to tell you and then—" she paused, thinking of the gaping hole in Evan Knowlson's head and how the blood had shimmered in the light of the candle "—and then, I have something to show you. There's been a murder."

"Murder? Say, are you the person who called claiming that someone had been killed here?" he asked, folding the paper he held in half and slipping it into his pocket. "Because if you are, I need to talk to you before turning in any report."

"No, I didn't call, but I do know something about the murder. That is, I know where to find the body," she added modestly.

"I can't stand this anymore! Nothing is making any sense!" The announcement came from Kelly as she stood up and fled from the room. Susan made a move as if to follow, but the policeman stopped her.

"You said something about a body," he reminded her firmly.

"Oh, yes." Susan looked around and found help in Kathleen.

"I'll make sure Kelly's all right," Kathleen offered, getting up.

"Don't let her go back to her house. Evan's there and—"

"My husband is at *Kelly's* house?"

Susan heard the outrage in Rebecca's voice, but did nothing. What could she say? *Don't worry about it. He's dead.*

"Your husband is not my concern right now, ma'am. There's been a report of a killing and, whether it's a hoax or not, I have to investigate. So I think we'd better get to the bottom of that immediately. Now where did you say this body is?" he asked Susan.

"At Kelly Knowlson's house."

"Hey, wait a minute. I thought we were at the Knowlsons' house. Are you telling me that we went to the wrong house?"

"I don't know. There are two Knowlson houses in town." Susan decided an explanation could wait. "All I know is that we'd better go to Kelly's house. I guess Rebecca should come, too." She'd added this last a little reluctantly.

"I certainly will," Rebecca agreed indignantly. "This is really the last straw. What did Kelly do now? Kill someone and then call Evan for help?"

The policeman looked at her, opened his mouth, and then closed it again. "Can you show us the quickest way to this place?" he asked Susan.

"We'll have to go in my car—"

"Why not take the short cut through the storage shed? Everyone else does!" Rebecca said.

"The what?"

"That damn storage shed. Come on, I'll show you." Rebecca sighed and got up from the computer terminal.

They returned to a very quiet living room. Nothing like police presence to kill a party, Susan thought, remembering one particular St. Patrick's Day celebration in her sophomore year of college. Rebecca didn't even make an attempt to change the mood of her guests; she led them through the kitchen and out the back door.

"There's a path beaten in the snow. Not that this isn't going to ruin these shoes anyway."

"This is no time to worry about that." Susan urged them on. She saw no sign of either Kelly or Kathleen and was beginning to worry. The policeman was listening to Rebecca's explanation of the shared shed.

"It's on our property now, but originally it belonged to the owner behind us."

"And who was that?" he asked, waving his flashlight toward the structure at the rear of the acre of backyard.

"At the time it was Evan, my husband. He lived there with his first wife." Rebecca tugged nervously at the large silver bangles she wore. "They built that house years ago, when they first moved to Hancock, and they added the shed for extra storage when they discovered that the basement stairs were too steep for easy access. Actually the first structure had been put up by the builders to keep their tools in while they built the house, so when Evan discovered that they needed a shed, he just altered the one that was already there. Unfortunately the builders had been a little casual about choosing a site. A lot of the building was on this property."

"This house doesn't look that old," the policeman commented, glancing behind him.

"It's brand new. Evan tore down the house that was here and rebuilt. You see, the man that owned the property in those days waited until Evan and Kelly had finished the shed and then sued for possession. It turned out that it actually had been built almost entirely on his property and the court turned it over to him. Then, about two years later, when the man died and his wife wanted to move to the Midwest somewhere to be with her son, Evan bought the property.''

"Sort of to get back his own?" The policeman sounded bemused.

"Something like that," Rebecca agreed.

"And he built this house recently . . . and you and he live here right behind his first wife?"

"It is quite valuable land in a very desirable part of town. There was really no reason we shouldn't build on it, was there?" Rebecca sounded defensive. "Well, here we are," she added, pulling open the door to the building they'd been discussing. Called a shed, it was actually a substantial structure about fifteen feet square, faced in cedar that matched the siding of the house that loomed up behind them. "Kelly probably passed through here. She even left the lights on."

Except that whoever had come through the shed would have had to walk right through the bodies of Rebecca's two sons.

"Mom!"

"Thomas! Travis!"

Susan thought it was like that question on TV: Parents, do you know where your children are?

In this case, what they were doing was getting high on an eclectic collection of wine coolers, gin, and eggnog. Susan felt her stomach lurch. She also understood the nervous looks on the faces of the boys. Travis and Thomas were in high school and older than Chad and Chrissy, but they were still too young to drink. And they both appeared to have had a lot to drink. Travis brushed his too-long hair out of his eyes and looked up from the redwood lawn chair where he was sprawled. Thomas was avoiding their eyes and staring at the floor, nervously running his hands around a glass full of clear liquid.

"Do you boys want to explain just what you think you're doing here? When I asked you to help out at the party, I didn't expect you to drink up all the booze."

"We . . ." Travis began, and then stopped. After all, what could he say?

"How long has this been going on?" his mother persisted. "How long have you been here instead of inside helping?"

"Quite a while," Thomas answered, looking up quickly. "We've been here for a while, haven't we, Travis?"

Travis just looked at the adults and nodded his head.

The policeman cleared his throat before speaking. "I think we were on our way to a body, ma'am. Maybe when we come back this way everything will be cleared up."

"I'm sure it will be, Officer," Rebecca agreed, and walked in a large circle around her sons.

Sure enough, the back wall of the shed had another door. They passed through to the outside. Susan was surprised with what they found.

"It looks like more than a few people know about this route," the policeman said, echoing her thoughts.

The snow was trampled down here, too. In fact, it almost looked as though someone had given a large party in Kelly's backyard. Footprints covered most of the area, except for the large lump indicating the location of the swimming pool.

"This is very strange," Susan said. "Maybe we shouldn't walk across the lawn."

"Don't be ridiculous. It's time to clear up this story. And I certainly don't plan on leaving Kelly and Evan alone in that house longer than necessary."

"I don't think you have to worry about them. We don't even know where Kelly is," Susan protested, following Rebecca in a path straight toward the house.

"I can tell you where she is. Look! She even left her back door open." Rebecca pointed as she spoke.

"That certainly is odd in this cold weather," the policeman commented. He hurried his steps slightly, and the women increased their speed to keep up.

"There's a patch of ice on the back steps," Susan warned the other two.

"If there is, Kelly made it herself," Rebecca replied.

"Why on earth would anyone do that?" the policeman asked. "Someone could get killed slipping on the top of tall steps like these."

"Because Kelly Knowlson is crazy, that's why," Rebecca replied, pushing the door open further and entering the kitchen.

Kelly was sitting at the table, her head resting in both hands so that they couldn't see her face. Susan pushed around her companions and rushed over to her.

"Kelly, you didn't go back in there? You didn't go in alone?" she asked quickly.

Kelly looked up, an expression of fear on her face. "I think Rebecca's right, Susan. I think I am crazy."

"Kelly, you're not crazy. You've just had a horrible, horrible experience, that's all." Susan brushed Kelly's hair back off her forehead and looked Rebecca square in the eye. It was time to tell the truth. "Rebecca, Evan is sitting in a chair in the living room with a bullet hole through his head."

"Don't be stupid, Susan. We're giving a party. He can't be dead. He's the host."

Kathleen appeared, breathless from running, at the back door. "I looked all over, but I couldn't find her— Oh, Kelly, there you are."

Susan decided that it was time for a display of the evidence. Now that Kathleen was here, she wouldn't have to leave Kelly alone. "If you'll stay with Kelly, I think the rest of us should go into the living room."

"No, Susan; don't go in there!"

"Kelly, this man is a policeman. He has to see this."

"But there's nothing to see!" Kelly protested.

Susan wondered if perhaps she had been hasty in supporting Kelly's sanity. But she was getting tired of this. "If you'll just follow me," she said to the policeman. He followed willingly, Rebecca at his heels. They walked quickly through the hall and into the still dimly lit living room, stopping at about the same place where Susan and Kelly had stood less than an hour ago. Susan didn't even know that Kelly had followed them until she spoke.

"See, Susan? I told you there was nothing to see."

TWELVE

LIKE THE OTHER GUESTS AT LAST NIGHT'S PARTY, SUSAN and Jed were still discussing Evan's vanishing act at breakfast the next morning.

"And there was nothing there."

"That's what you said last night, but surely—"

"Jed, you were too tired to understand anything I was saying last night. I'm telling you that Evan's body wasn't there, not that the room was empty. In fact, it was really pretty creepy.'' Susan leaned across the kitchen table and poured coffee into a red mug printed with a Christmas tree.

"Thanks. Why creepy?"

"Well . . ." She paused to take a sip from her own mug. "Were you listening when I told you about how Evan was sitting in the living room?"

"With a drink and a book open on his lap, wasn't it?"

"Yes. And a plate of Christmas cookies on the table by his side. It was as though someone was trying to make him comfortable.''

"As comfortable as a person can be with a large hole in the side of his head.''

"Right. Except for the wound, it was like the body was a dummy in some sort of domestic display.''

"And later, when the policeman was with you? Were the cookies and everything else still there?"

"No, not quite.''

"Not quite. Susan, did you get a really good look around?"

"Yes. Let me explain.'' She took a deep breath and remembered the scene in detail. "The room was perfectly clean, no sign of blood or that there had been a body in it recently—or ever for that matter. The light by the chair that Evan had been sitting in was turned off and some candles were lit—a good half dozen or so on the mantel . . . You know how Kelly has all those brass candlesticks on one end, and there were two on the table behind the plaid couch closest to the fireplace. In front of the couch, votive candles were burning on the coffee table that Evan made from an antique child's sled. There was a plate of cookies nearby—a different plate than the one that had been near Evan. This was one of the cut-glass plates that Kelly's mother gave her for a wedding present. You know Kelly; she's shown them to me a dozen times at least. The one next to Evan had been white china. And there was also a tray on the table, with a steaming teapot and a cup—oh, and a plate of lemon slices with a clove in the middle of each one. Kelly likes to display them like that.'' Susan stopped and stared at her husband.

''You mean it looked like something that Kelly would set up?''

''I mean it looked like something that a person who cares about how things look would set it up. Kelly isn't the only person I know who puts cloves in lemon slices. I've even seen it done in magazines.''

''You don't have to defend her to me.''

''I know.'' She sighed. ''It's just that I've been thinking how much it looked like something Kelly would do.''

''But there was absolutely no sign of Evan?''

''None. And I looked. It wasn't just that the plate was different; the cookies were different too. The glass of eggnog had vanished. *The Night Before Christmas* book was gone. And the chair that Evan had been sitting in has down stuffing and it wasn't just empty, it had been fluffed up. You know how down gets when it's had any weight pressed on it.''

''Especially a dead weight,'' Jed said.

Susan looked at him suspiciously. ''You wouldn't think it was funny if you had been there.''

''You're right, and I'm sorry. Go on.''

''There isn't anything else to say. The room looked as if someone had prepared it for Kelly to come in and have a snack before going off to bed. Rebecca took one look around, announced that she had to get back to her party, and stormed out. Kelly started to cry again and said that she didn't understand anything anymore and that her neck was hurting her, so Kathleen suggested that her mother check it out . . . Did you know Kathleen's mother is a nurse?''

''Yes, she and I had a nice long chat at the party. But go on.''

''And then the policeman gave me a look suggesting that

I was crazy, and asked me a lot of questions, and wrote down some of my answers—and then Jerry Gordon came over and offered me a ride home. And I took it.''

''What did Dolores say about Kelly?''

''Dolores?''

''That's Kathleen's mother's name.''

''Oh, I haven't had much of a chance to talk to her. Actually I don't really know what happened to Kelly. Jerry said everything was being taken care of, and I left it at that.'' She reached out for the wall phone. ''I should call Kathleen and find out.''

''Wait an hour or so, why don't you? They may still be in bed over there.''

Susan put down her hand. ''You're right. I'm sure Kathleen wouldn't have left Kelly alone unless everything was okay. I wonder how your mother is doing this morning?'' she said, changing the subject.

''Good question. I heard her wandering around in the middle of the night.''

''She seemed awfully mad last night.''

''Yes. I'm not sure why. She announced that she didn't want to talk about it and stomped up to bed as soon as we got home.'' Jed resisted the temptation to add that it had reminded him of something his wife would do. ''Whatever happened, it sure threw her off her diet. She was eating everything in sight at the end of the party.''

''I hope she cheers up. I'd hate for her to have a rotten visit. After all, it *is* Christmas. Kathleen and I are taking both her mother and yours out to lunch today. Maybe in her present mood, she'll eat something.''

''Good idea.'' Jed walked over to the toaster and popped in two halves of an English muffin. ''But you know what I've been wondering about?''

''No. What?''

''I've been wondering if Evan is still missing.''

"Of course he is. He's dead."

"Is it possible that he was just made up to look wounded?" Jed asked as his breakfast popped up. "Some theatrical makeup can look pretty real, you know."

"I know a dead body when I see one," Susan insisted, and removed the smaller muffin half from the plate he brought to the table. "So, since Evan is dead, is the person who moved him from Kelly's house the same person who killed him?" She bit into the bread, and butter dripped down her chin. "And why hide a dead body?"

"I can think of half a dozen reasons easily."

"Name three," his wife challenged him, getting up to toast another muffin.

"To give the murderer time to cover his tracks. To keep the police from beginning a murder investigation. To allow the body time to decompose before an autopsy is carried out. To keep the will from being probated—"

"Okay, okay. No need to show me up. Do you want half a muffin?"

"I wanted a whole muffin, but you seem to have consumed the other half of mine."

"There are three hundred calories in each half of a buttered English muffin." Jed's mother stood in the doorway in a bright pink terry cloth robe. "I'll have mine with strawberry jam as well."

"Good." Susan leapt from her seat. "I made strawberry jam this year. I even went out to a farm and picked my own strawberries."

"Only cost twice what it would have in the stores, too," Jed teased, going into the refrigerator for the jam jar. He put it on the table, within reach of both women. "Maybe you should call Rebecca and make sure that Evan is okay," he suggested to his wife.

"You don't believe me," she protested. "Okay, fine."

She stood up and walked over to the phone. "I'll call. Then you'll believe me."

The phone rang as she reached for it. "Hello? Kathleen. Yes, everyone is fine here. I was just going to call Rebecca . . . You did? He is? Isn't anyone going to call the police? Okay. Well, how does noon sound? Great. See you then."

Susan turned to her husband immediately upon hanging up. "Are you driving in? You're going to miss your train, if you don't hurry."

"Where are the kids?" his mother asked, putting artificial sweetener in her coffee and piling jam on another muffin.

"They both have to be at school early on Mondays—Chrissy has chorus, and Chad is in the school dance band. They were out of here almost an hour ago."

"And I'm on my way now." Jed leaned over and kissed his wife. "If a large package from Burberry's arrives today, just put it in the hall closet. And don't open it!"

"Have a nice lunch," he said to his mother, and was gone.

"Lunch?" She looked at Susan curiously.

"I thought we would have lunch with Kathleen and her mother today."

"I hope you haven't made a lot of plans," was Claire's stony reply.

"Well, nothing special." Susan put Jed's dishes in the dishwasher. "Just reservations at the new Swiss restaurant in town. I've never been there, but everyone says it's wonderful. And, then, if you're feeling like it, I thought maybe we could do some Christmas shopping. My list is nowhere near complete— Hey, I thought you'd left." Jed had pushed back into the room.

"I forgot to remind you—I'm going to be at the graphics department's Christmas party tonight. I have to go. So I'll be home late. I think I'll take the car."

"Fine. I'm glad you haven't left. Do you want me to look for a gift for Gloria? Or have you found something?"

"I can look at lunch . . ."

Susan recognized the hesitancy in his voice. "No, your mother and I were just talking about going shopping. I'll do it today."

"And if you find something for Glen or Arthur . . ." Jed began on his way out the door.

"I'll find something," she promised and then, as the front door slammed, turned to her mother-in-law.

"Presents for his secretary and some of his colleagues," she explained. "I can use your help. I don't see enough of these people to know what to get them. It's a problem every year."

"I'd really rather not go to lunch with Dolores."

"What . . . ? Who's . . . ? Oh, Kathleen's mother. Why not?"

"I would just rather not." She got up and started from the room, her back straight.

Susan was wondering just what she had done to offend the woman, when Jed's mother turned back around.

"I suppose I owe you an explanation. I have had a severe disappointment."

"What's happened? Is there something I can do?"

"I caught Bob—Dr. Barr—and Dolores flirting last night. I don't think I can trust a woman like that. And, of course, I would prefer not to socialize with her. You understand."

"Yes," Susan lied. Was she talking to an adolescent or a grown woman? "I understand. I'll call Kathleen and cancel. Do you still want to go shopping?"

"Of course. I certainly wouldn't want to change any of your plans."

Susan, glancing up to see if Claire was being sarcastic, was surprised to see tears in her eyes.

"Oh, my goodness. I didn't know you cared so much—" she began, when the phone rang again. "Hello? Oh, yes. Just let me see if she's free to take your call." She pressed the receiver against her chest and whispered, "It's Dr. Barr. He's asked to speak to you. I could tell him you're busy . . ."

But the phone was suddenly wrenched from her hands.

"Hello? Bob?"

Wow. Susan saw, for the first time, which parent had contributed Jed's great smile to his genetic mix.

"Of course, I'd love to. I promised my little granddaughter that I would take her shopping after school, so it can't be too early. I don't want to disappoint the child. Of course, seven would be perfect. I'll see you then." She hung up and turned to Susan.

"That was Bob Barr," she explained unnecessarily. "He's asked me to dinner. I told him yes. I knew you wouldn't mind. Well, I'd better take a shower and get dressed. It's going to be a full day, isn't it? Lunch with Kathleen and her mother, and then shopping with you, and then with Chrissy. And then, of course, dinner with Bob." She sighed happily. "This is such a busy time of year."

THIRTEEN

"SO WHAT DO I GET HIS SECRETARY THIS YEAR?" SUSAN asked Kathleen, stopping in the middle of the aisle of the crowded department store.

"Gloves?"

"And a cashmere scarf last year."

"Perfume? Scented soap?"

"The first year she worked for him."

"A wallet? Leather purse organizer?"

"The year before last."

"A gift certificate?"

"Jed thinks they're impersonal."

"Jed's not doing the shopping; you are."

"I noticed." Susan sighed. "Let's try another store. Maybe Saks . . ."

"Susan, we've been to Macy's, Lane Bryant, and Lord and Taylor. What makes you think you'll find the perfect present at Saks Fifth Avenue?" Kathleen leaned back against a glass counter and lifted the weight off her left foot as she spoke.

"You're right." Susan smiled as though an idea had just struck her. "We'll go to Bloomingdale's."

"You are the most optimistic Christmas shopper in the world," Kathleen commented.

"What choice do I have? Jed seems to be incapable of thinking about Christmas until the second week of December—and then he's too busy going to parties at work and at home to do his own shopping." Susan looked down at the jewelry in the counter. "I have a great idea: bookends!"

"Bookends?" Kathleen peered at the rhinestone-encrusted bracelets and strings of cultured pearls. She looked at up Susan. "Bookends?" she repeated.

"Brass bookends. It's the perfect thing for one of the men in Jed's department. Now who would carry them?"

"We were going to go into the city Wednesday. Do you want to look for them there?"

"If I have to, but let's try Bloomingdale's first. And that decorators' store down by the river. I'd love to get this shopping finished. Besides, there are some things I want to find for Chad. He's beginning to get interested in clothes."

"You don't mean that we're going to see him wearing shirts without New York Mets or skulls printed across the chest?"

"Hard to believe, isn't it?"

"Sure is, especially since I bought him a bat signed by some members of the team for Christmas."

"Kathleen, you didn't! He'll love it!"

"I hope so." She slipped her foot back into her shoe. "Bloomingdale's?"

"Bloomingdale's. And a cup of coffee."

"Only if it's accompanied by a great big creamy French pastry. I'm starving! Never again do I eat lunch with two dieters. Susan, what are we going to do about our mothers?"

"Your mother, my mother-in-law," came the correction.

"Fine. So what are we going to do about them?"

The two women started down the aisle of the store. "I don't think we're going to have to do anything. I think they're going to diet themselves to death."

They both laughed.

"Seriously, Susan. What about this Dr. Barr?"

"I'm not sure. Do you think he's a quack?"

"I don't know. What sort of doctor is he?"

"Good question. I guess I just assumed that he was an internist. What sort of doctor monitors diets?"

"What sort of doctor names diet food after himself?" Kathleen asked sarcastically. "I think we should find out more about him."

"Hmm . . . Last night was something, wasn't it?" Susan asked. "Your mother was telling me at lunch that Kelly went back to the hospital this morning."

"Yes, but that doesn't mean anything. She had to have an orthopedist look at her; there wasn't one on duty last night. I guess she'll return to her house after that."

"Probably," Susan agreed.

"I wonder what Rebecca is doing."

"I called there this morning—you know, to thank her for the party last night—and the answering machine was on." She glanced in the window of a small stationery store they were passing. "Hey, what about pens? Do you mind stopping in here?"

"Not at all," Kathleen said, following her through the door into the wood-paneled interior.

"Susan! Kathleen! I was just thinking about you. Tell me what happened last night. I've been worried sick about Kelly." Elizabeth Stevenson hurried down the main aisle toward them, her arms full of packages. "I called and I called and, when no one answered at the house, I drove over early this morning. No one was home. The bed wasn't even slept in."

"You—" Susan started.

"The house was left unlocked last night?" Kathleen interrupted quickly.

"No. I have a key. Kelly had to have someone to water her plants and check out the house when she was gone last year, and I volunteered. I still had the key on my key ring."

"And the key that turns off the burglar alarm?" Kathleen persisted.

"I have that, too. Not that I had to use it. The system was turned off. I guess Kelly's gotten a little careless about security since Evan left."

Both Susan and Kathleen knew this to be untrue, but neither mentioned the fact to Elizabeth. "Kelly is at the hospital being checked out by an orthopedist. It's routine; nothing to worry about. She spent the night at Kathleen's house."

"My mom is a nurse," Kathleen explained.

"Thank goodness. I can't tell you how worried I've been." Her concerns apparently at an end, Elizabeth turned to a more interesting subject. "Was that some party last night? What do you think happened? I think Rebecca and Evan had a fight, and he's left her. But Barbara believes the story that there was some sort of crisis at his business and he had to drive to the city."

"I—" Susan began.

"I was in the bathroom when Rebecca explained his leaving. What did she say exactly?" Kathleen asked quickly.

"Well, that's the problem. She just said that it was necessary for him to leave and asked that everyone excuse him."

"Then—" Susan began again.

But Kathleen seemed determined to make a career of interrupting her. "When did she say this?"

"Well, I don't know exactly. It was after the policeman came, and then Kelly barged in in her underwear . . ."

"Pajamas," Susan corrected.

"Okay, pajamas. And then everyone disappeared for about fifteen minutes and, when Rebecca came back, she announced that Evan had to leave and that he was sorry, but, of course, he wanted everyone to stay and have a good time. But, by that time, Jerry and your mother were talking about leaving. We were sitting with the St. Johns, wondering what to do. And you came in and got your mother just then, Kath. So I said that we had to get home to the sitter and Jeffrey St. John said something about being tired.'' She shrugged. ''We were both lying. We all ran into one another at the inn ten minutes later.''

''And ended the evening guessing why Evan had disappeared,'' Kathleen said.

''What else? After we got home, Derek made this big deal about not talking about other people's affairs, but even *he* was fascinated. How many other parties have you ever been to where the host disappeared in the middle of the evening without a word?''

''For that matter, how many parties have you been to where the police appeared?'' Susan asked.

''I'll admit that hasn't happened since college,'' Elizabeth said. ''In fact, that's what I thought when I saw them.''

''What?'' Kathleen asked the question.

''I thought that either Thomas or Travis had gotten into some sort of trouble again.''

''Again?'' Kathleen asked.

But, before Elizabeth could reply, they were interrupted by a saleswoman offering assistance.

''Would you show me some fountain pens?'' Susan responded to her question.

''Of course. If you'll just follow me?'' They went toward the back of the store, leaving Kathleen and Elizabeth to talk without interruption.

''Have the boys had trouble with the police?'' Kathleen asked.

''Oh, you don't know?''

Kathleen would have thought she was being put off if Elizabeth hadn't leaned toward her. "Well, they tried to keep it quiet, of course. Who can blame them? But I understand that both boys have been brought home by the police. And you know what that means."

"No, I don't." In Kathleen's years as a police officer, being brought home by the police could indicate something as innocuous as a minor spill off a bicycle or something more serious.

"It means that they've been in trouble."

"What kind of trouble?" Kathleen persisted, wondering if Elizabeth actually had any facts.

"Oh, who knows? I heard something about a big drinking party over in Darien. And, of course, there are always drugs around. I've never understood it myself. These children have been brought up with all the advantages; they have everything any child could want. Nice homes. A good social life at the club. The right schools. I can't understand how they get in trouble. I had to fight for every single thing I have, and these kids are just given everything. It makes me furious sometimes."

"But Rebecca's kids . . ." Kathleen tried to return to the subject that interested her.

"Maybe it's different with them. They weren't brought up in Hancock, you know. I don't even know where Rebecca and her first husband lived before she came here. Maybe they didn't have all the advantages after all." The idea seemed to restore order to her world and she cheered up. "I shouldn't be standing here gossiping. I have tons of shopping to do. I still haven't found the right thing to give the Duchess."

"The Duchess?"

"Derek's mother. That's what the family calls her. She's very particular. Her gift is always a problem."

"I always have trouble shopping for my mother," Kathleen said sympathetically.

"Oh, that's no problem. I can buy my mother almost anything. But the Duchess is another story.'' She looked around the store. ''I better get going; I don't even remember what I came in here for.''

''Good talking to you. I'd better go along, too. I can see Susan waving to me.''

They hurried off in opposite directions.

''Which do you like? The black or the maroon?'' Susan greeted Kathleen, holding two pens out for comparison.

''When in doubt, choose black is the rule, isn't it? Besides, I like the black better.'' Kathleen looked at the price tags. ''Wow. Isn't that a lot of money for something so easy to lose?''

''Jed can't give cheap gifts to the men who work for him, can he?''

''Don't ask me. I'm still new at all this, remember.''

''Jerry must have given presents last year.''

''I think he bought a case of champagne and passed it out December twenty-fourth.''

''Expensive champagne?''

''Very.''

''And a label that everyone knows is expensive?''

Kathleen laughed. ''Maybe you're right.''

''So you'll take a pen, ma'am?'' the saleswoman asked.

''Two of them. And can you gift wrap them nicely?'' Susan requested, handing over her American Express card.

''Of course!''

''As soon as this is done, how about that coffee? I need to sit down—and the caffeine won't be unwelcome, either.''

''There's a coffee shop just around the corner,'' the saleswoman announced while Susan was signing her charge slip.

''Sounds great. I wonder if we could go there and then stop back here for the pens?''

''Excellent idea. Our gift wrapping department is very busy at this time of year. I'll have the packages wrapped and waiting for you at the customer service desk, shall I?''

"Fine," Susan agreed. "Let's hurry. I'm starving."

They rushed around the corner to the place that had been suggested and found it surprisingly crowded for the middle of the afternoon.

"Oh, yes," the waitress said after seating them. "A lot of ladies get hungry after a few hours of shopping. We always do a good business this time of year. Now what can I get you?"

"A cup of coffee and a slice of that lemon meringue pie we passed on the way in," Susan replied.

"I'd like coffee, too. And a hot fudge sundae."

"I'll be back in a second, ladies." She hurried off, almost bumping into Chrissy and her grandmother, who were on their way to a booth on the other side of the room.

"Chrissy!" Susan waved to her daughter. "Imagine running into you here. You must have just gotten out of school a few minutes ago."

"Half an hour," her daughter corrected her, after first greeting Kathleen. "Grandmother and I were just going to have a small snack before we start shopping."

"Do you want to join us?"

"That's a nice offer, Susan. But we're going to discuss some presents that you don't need to hear about," her mother-in-law replied, with a smile. "Oh, look, Chrissy. They're going to give away our table. We'd better get going."

"Right. 'Bye, Mom. Mrs. Gordon."

"What a nice combination," Kathleen said, watching them leave. "I like to see the different generations getting along so well."

"I think your mother would be happy to get along with any future generations you care to produce. At least, that was the impression I got last night."

"My brother and his wife have six children. If my mother

wants to be with grandchildren all she has to do is drive to Bryn Mawr and see them.''

Susan was too good a friend to pursue the subject, nor did she get a chance to. Chrissy, having ordered, rushed back to their table.

''Mom, I forgot to tell you. I was with Seth at lunch today and he had just had gym with Thomas and Travis. They have that really awful teacher that I had last year. Remember? Well, anyway, they were together and Thomas—or Travis—told Seth that Mr. Knowlson didn't come home last night. And that their mom hadn't heard from him when they left for school, either. They said that she's frantic. I thought you might want to know.'' Chrissy rushed off.

''That's interesting,'' Susan commented.

''Why?'' Kathleen asked. ''You didn't expect a dead body to walk in Rebecca's front door, did you?''

''No. But I would love to know if Rebecca is upset because her husband has vanished or because he's dead.''

''Or because he's both,'' Kathleen suggested.

FOURTEEN

"I SUPPOSE YOU'D JUST TIE A BOW TO ONE OF THE TOP branches and leave it at that," Chad commented, wandering into the room sucking a candy cane.

"What are you talking about, Chad?" Susan looked up from where she was sitting on the floor of her bedroom, surrounded by rolls of colored paper, ribbons, gift tags, and all the paraphernalia of wrapping presents.

"That's the only way you could wrap a partridge in a pear tree. It's the song on the radio," he explained. "Of course, you could tie a bow around the bird's neck. But it might get caught on something and then the bird would hang himself."

"Chad!" his mother protested. "What an awful thought." She looked around and lifted up some papers near her feet. "Have you seen my scissors anywhere?"

"Didn't you have them in your hand just now?"

"Probably. But it doesn't mean much. I can lose scissors faster than anything. I'll look for them. I'd better stand up; my back is killing me. Would you take that pile of presents off the bed and arrange them under the Christmas tree?"

"You mean these are to stay here?" he asked, leaping up.

"Yes. Don't drop them, Chad!"

He was too busy reading the tags to answer. Susan smiled at him and, stretching, walked over to the window. Snow had been falling lightly an hour ago when Jed's mother had left on her date, but it seemed to have stopped. Susan was relieved. Jed had a long drive home from the city, and she always worried about him in bad weather, especially this time of year when there were so many Christmas parties, so much drinking. She leaned farther to the right to see the beam of the streetlight on the corner. Maybe there were still a few flakes coming down . . . Was that what she thought it was?

"Cha—" She started to yell her son's name and then, deciding that what she was about to do could be dangerous, decided to do it alone. "Chad! I'm going out for a walk. Tell Chrissy. I'll be back in a few minutes," she called as she ran down the hall and grabbed her coat from the chair where she'd left it earlier in the evening. Flinging open the front door, she dashed toward the scene under the streetlight, slipping on the fresh snow, but managing to stay upright. She didn't know what she was going to do when she got to them. She didn't have a gun; no one would listen if she yelled something like, murderer, murderer. She felt a sharp pain in her ankle, but was determined to continue onward toward her prey when, to her surprise, they turned, not *away* from her, but *toward* her, calling her name.

"Mrs. Henshaw, are you okay?"

"Has something happened?"

They had dropped him—it—and were running toward her! Susan was astounded.

"I saw you two under the light. I saw you carrying something," she began, and then didn't know how to go on. If they were coming to help her, then it couldn't be the body of their stepfather that they had been carrying, now could it?

Travis and Thomas looked at each other. It was Travis who spoke. "We were just moving—"

"You know, Travis, maybe Mrs. Henshaw can help us," his brother interrupted him.

"How?"

"Would you keep something in your garage for us until Christmas Eve?"

"Till Christmas Eve? You want me to help you hide a Christmas gift?" Susan asked. She'd been wrong. Why would they want to hide Evan's body until Christmas?

"Yes. Do you mind?" Thomas asked. "It's pretty big, though."

"Well, as long as the two of you can get whatever it is into the garage," Susan agreed.

"Fine. It's right back there. We'll bring it over now, if that's okay with you?"

"Sure. I'll just go open the garage door. The button is kind of hard to find." She walked back to her house feeling slightly foolish. It was Christmastime. Everyone was hiding presents.

Within a few minutes, she was in the garage, Travis and Thomas following behind closely, the giant thing slung between them.

"What is it?" Susan asked, motioning for them to put it down. "It looks like . . ." She didn't want to say what she thought it looked like. "It looks heavy," she ended.

"It should be. It's a punching bag; we had it made specially. Weighs over a hundred pounds. It's for Evan. He's building a gym in the back of the garage, you know."

"No, I didn't," Susan said.

"Yeah, and we were having a lot of trouble figuring out a place to hide this. It was in the shed. No one but us ever went there in the winter." Susan noticed that Travis had the grace to look embarrassed at this admission. "But with the police running around and all, it's no longer a safe place. And we really want to surprise Evan.''

"Has he— Has Evan gotten back yet?" Susan asked, knowing, of course, the answer. Did this mean that the twins didn't know about the murder?

"Not yet. Mom's expecting him tonight," Thomas answered. "At least that's what she told us at breakfast this morning."

"Do you think we can just leave it leaning against the wall, or should we put some sort of cover over it?" Travis asked, standing back and gazing at the three large black garbage bags that had been taped together to hold the punching bag.

"Just leave it like that," Susan answered. "It's not as though Evan is going to walk into the garage and ask what that big thing in the corner is." Actually, she reminded herself, there was no way that Evan was ever going to find out about this . . . period. She looked at the gigantic rectangle, now stored neatly against the wall, and shivered.

"You must be cold, Mrs. Henshaw," Thomas said.

"Yes. And we'd better get going or we'll be late for dinner," his brother said. "We open our presents on Christmas Eve, so we'll pick this up sometime earlier that day, if it's all right with you."

"Fine." Susan walked them out of the garage and then returned to her house. How strange it was that they had been wandering about the neighborhood looking for a place to hide a Christmas gift. The phone was ringing as she entered the hall.

"I've got it," Chrissy yelled from upstairs. "It's for me."

Well, it usually was. Susan went into the living room. She was shivering; the last few minutes had upset her more than she realized. But there was a large pile of presents under the tree. Chad was sitting on the couch staring at a big flat one with a smile on his face. "That's a new drum pad for my synthesizer, isn't it?"

"No answers, Chad."

"Just one hint!"

"No hints."

He sighed. "Where are you going?"

"Back upstairs. I still have a lot of wrapping to do. And you don't have to bother to come up and hang around. None of *this* pile is for you!"

She hurried back up to her bedroom. On the way through the hall, she noticed the phone's receiver was lying next to it. She replaced it and called to her daughter. "Chrissy, you left the phone off the hook."

There was no response, and she hurried back to the task at hand. She was busily wrapping a large bottle of Jerry Gordon's favorite aftershave (the scissors having been discovered hiding under a roll of paper printed with penguins sporting red bows around their chubby necks) when Chrissy appeared at the door.

"Hi. Why are you wrapping presents in your bedroom? You never do them in here."

"Because your grandmother is staying in the guest room where I usually work," Susan replied, trying not to be impatient.

Chrissy walked in and sat down on the bed. "I like this pink marbleized paper," she commented, fingering it. "What did Mrs. Gordon want? She sounded upset."

"Kathleen? When did you talk to her?" Susan asked. "Here, put your finger in the middle of this ribbon. I can't seem to get it tied neatly," she said before her daughter could answer.

"She was on the phone," Chrissy explained, putting down her finger as asked. "She said she was in a hurry."

"You didn't tell me she called," Susan protested.

"Yes, I did. You must not have heard me. If we had a built-in intercom system like Sandy's parents, this—"

"Chrissy, it was your responsibility to let me know that

the call was for me. And especially if Kathleen had a problem." Susan cut short her lecture and reached for the phone extension near her bed.

Chrissy muttered something about people who were too cheap to buy the proper equipment and flounced off to her room.

Susan dialed quickly, but was disappointed when Jerry answered, and doubly so when he announced that Kathleen had just left.

"Did she say anything about why she'd called me?" Susan asked after explaining what Chrissy had done.

"I didn't talk to her. I was starting into the driveway, when she almost backed her car into mine. She rolled down the window and said that she had left a note on the table and drove off. Faster than the speed limit, I might add."

"And the note?"

"Said that she had to leave and that she'd call; it didn't even say where she was going. In fact, I was going to call you just now. I hoped you'd know."

"I would, if Chrissy had told me Kathleen was on the phone. I don't know what's happened to that girl. She seems to have her head in the clouds half the time."

"She's just growing up," Jerry said, laughing. "Don't worry about her. Let me know if you hear from my wife, will you? I'm a little concerned."

"Of course, but I wouldn't worry. Kathleen knows how to take care of herself. Where is her mother tonight?"

"Visiting an old friend who lives in Darien. Say, maybe I'll call there. Maybe she knows what's going on."

"Good idea. And I'll call you right away if I hear anything."

"Great," Jerry said.

Susan hung up and, resisting an urge to scream at her daughter, returned to her packages.

Every year Susan spent a remarkable amount of money on

printed paper, assorted bags, ribbons and bows, stickers, and gift tags. It was a Christmas gift to herself; she loved wrapping presents. She pulled a large wooden rack designed to hold fifty cassette tapes from under the bed, sat it down in front of her, and stared at it critically. Thank goodness it didn't need a box; she'd never find one that fit. Maybe gold and blue, she decided, reaching for a roll of paper.

So now two people were missing, she thought, applying tape to the seams she had made and then looking around for some wide silver ribbon. Ah, there it was!

Evan and Kathleen were both missing, she continued her thought while forming an expert bow with the glittering band. Could it be a coincidence? It seemed unlikely. So what could Kathleen be doing? And where was Evan's body? Or did Kathleen know where Evan's body was and was that the reason she had vanished?

She was still worrying about the double problem when Chad reentered the room.

"Hey, you're putting my name on that tag," he cried, bouncing as he sat down on the end of the bed. "You told me you weren't wrapping anything for me!"

"Christmas fib," Susan admitted, handing the box to him. "You can add this to the pile under the tree."

"I'd rather look through that pile of boxes," he said, eyeing a half-dozen red boxes waiting to be wrapped.

"Sure. Just don't mess anything up."

"That means there's nothing there for me," Chad said, losing interest—almost. "Unless you just said that because you don't want me to look," he cried, changing his mind.

"Do whatever you want," his mother said, laughing. "I'll take this downstairs. And then I think I'll make a few phone calls."

"Chrissy is on the phone," Chad told her, making up his mind and delving into the pile of unwrapped gifts.

"Well, she's just going to have to get off it for a while. I need to track down Kathleen, and I can talk while I make cheese balls for the party. They can go in the freezer for a few days.'' But she was talking to herself; Chad's interest lay in the pile of packages. Susan considered party preparations as she headed downstairs. She usually spent most of the week before this, their annual Christmas party, cooking and baking. But this year she was beginning to wonder if her guests were going to starve unless she got busy and ordered a large amount of deli food for Friday night.

Or maybe Dr. Barr would spend the rest of the week converting all her guests to his diet plan. Then she could just microwave a few thousand of the little plastic bags that had been littering her kitchen since her mother-in-law's arrival, she thought, looking at the mess her kitchen had become.

''Hi!''

Susan spun around. ''Kathleen! Jerry and I were just on the phone, wondering where you were. What are you doing here?''

''I came over to talk to you. Are you busy? I called and talked to Chrissy, but someone cut me off.''

''That was my fault. Sorry.''

''No problem. So, anyway, since my mother is gone for the evening, I thought I'd come for a chat. Okay?''

''Great. Jed's at a party, so I'd love the company. But do you mind if I cook while we talk?''

''Of course not. You're behind schedule for preparations for your party?''

''That's putting it mildly. Claire's early arrival was the one thing I didn't need.'' Susan pulled cheese from the refrigerator and threw a piece of it into her food processor as she spoke.

''It doesn't look as if she's exactly underfoot all the time,'' Kathleen said, going over to Susan and pulling plastic wrap from some of the chunks of cheese.

"That's true. Dr. Barr keeps her pretty busy. They're out together right now, in fact."

"Dr. Barr is one of the reasons I'm here," Kathleen said, handing Susan the last piece of cheese.

Susan turned off the machine and looked at Kathleen. "What about him?"

"I think he may be doing what used to be called toying with your mother-in-law's affections."

"Kathleen! Not you, too. Jed sounds like a jealous teenager whenever he mentions the man."

"The opposite of my mother. She spent an hour or so with him and she keeps raving about what a fascinating person he is. And you saw the way she was acting today at lunch."

"No worse than Claire. When they weren't comparing words of wisdom from Dr. Barr, they were trying to outdiet each other. Could they have anorexia at their age?"

"Who knows? My mother has spent her entire life telling me to clean my plate, now she just picks at her food—and I made my special lasagna for her!"

"Your mother's already thin. She probably doesn't eat very much anyway."

"My mother eats like a horse. Always has. But the point isn't the food, the point is that I think Dr. Barr is working to control these women."

"Control?"

"Maybe that's too strong a word." Kathleen paused.

"And maybe not. Tell me what you're thinking."

"I'm not thinking so much as guessing. It's a gut feeling that I have, but it seems to me that our Dr. Barr is interfering an awful lot in the lives of the women who like him. And it makes me nervous when people change their lives because someone else thinks they should."

"Interesting point." Susan walked over to a cabinet hung on the wall over her stove and took out a few small spice bottles. "I was wondering about all this myself." She added some sage leaves and dried basil to the cheese. "In fact, I was going to ask you exactly what happened with your mother and Claire last night, but I didn't know how to put it."

"What do you mean?"

"Well, your mother obviously got the idea that Dr. Barr was interested in her . . ." Susan stopped, embarrassed.

"And you wondered if Dr. Barr did anything to encourage the idea or whether she's the type of woman who thinks things like that about all men," Kathleen finished for her.

"To be honest, yes."

"Well, I'm not sure I know the answer. I would have said that my mother was always very sensible, but what I've seen in the last twenty-four hours doesn't fit in with that. Her story is that Dr. Barr got bored with your mother-in-law at the party and approached her. He complimented her on the dress she was wearing and they talked for an hour or so. She was obviously very impressed by him. Maybe he has some sort of strange power over older women—or maybe my mother has become more vulnerable."

"I think it's Dr. Barr. Claire seems to have abandoned her common sense, too. Do you think we should do something about this?"

"I don't know what we can do. But I think Bob Barr should be watched pretty carefully."

"Good idea— Would you get that?" Susan asked when the phone began to ring. Her hands were covered with bits of herbs and cheese.

"Hello? Yes, it's Kathleen. Of course, I'll come at once." She hung up.

"It was for you?" Susan asked, scraping the cheese mixture out of the bowl and onto a piece of aluminum foil.

"It was Kelly. She asked that I come over there. The police are questioning her. And they've suggested that she find a lawyer."

FIFTEEN

"But did they arrest her?" Jed asked, hanging up his coat in the hall closet.

"I have no idea; they were questioning her. Kathleen said she would call, but I haven't heard from her yet. They were looking for a lawyer. Do you think that means that they're going to take Kelly to jail?"

"I don't know, but they're smart to get a professional in there right away."

Susan sighed and picked up a discreet grey-and-purple paisley cashmere scarf from the floor. "You dropped this . . . and you're right," she said, handing it to him. "Kathleen asked me to call and tell Jerry where she was going, but . . . Maybe that's her now." She hurried over to the phone in the hall.

"Susan. I must say I thought Chrissy would answer. Jeffrey St. John says the phone company should have a direct line put in between your house and theirs."

"Elizabeth. Hi." Susan recognized the caller.

"Did you hear about Kelly?"

113

"About the police questioning her? Yes." Susan immediately became more interested. "Who did you hear it from?"

"Kelly herself. Well, not quite. She didn't talk to me. She talked to Derek. I was in the shower. So I don't have the whole story," she added regretfully. "You know how men are about getting the details: impossible. But I know that she is afraid of being arrested. She called here to see if we knew the name of a good criminal lawyer."

"Did Derek know one?" Susan asked.

"Oh, yes. Remember his old partner who was charged with securities fraud? Derek gave Kelly the name of the man who got him off. Derek says his partner was guilty as sin, so the guy must be a good lawyer."

It made a certain amount of sense.

"Did Derek ask if there's anything else anyone can do?"

"Probably not. He got the impression that Kelly wasn't alone."

"Kathleen is there."

"She's not Kelly's closest or oldest friend," Elizabeth protested.

"But she's had some professional experience with murder," Susan reminded her. Leave it to Elizabeth to get her feelings hurt in the middle of a murder investigation.

"Well, you've had experience with murder, if that's all she wants. I wonder if that good-looking detective who came to town with Kathleen a few years ago is back. I wonder if that has something to do with her involvement."

"I'm sure Kathleen only wants to help. She's married now, remember. Besides there isn't— I heard that no one had found Evan's body," she corrected herself. "So how can there be an investigation of murder? I'd better get off the phone, though. Kathleen may be trying to get through if she needs something . . . Of course, I'll call the second I hear." She hung up.

"Find out anything?" Jed asked from the living room, where he was pouring himself a drink.

"You are going to get me one, aren't you?"

"Sure. Who are you calling?"

"Rebecca. I wonder if the police are at her house, too. It's a little odd that they would concentrate on the ex-wife instead of the present wife in a murder investigation."

"They don't know it's murder—unless they've found the body," Jed answered, handing her a drink.

"True, unless— Rebecca, it's Susan. How are you doing?"

The answer took long enough for Susan to consume a fair amount of her drink. Jed lost interest in his wife's constant "uh-huhs" and returned to the living room. He was pouring himself more Scotch when she joined him.

"Want another?" he offered, waving the bottle to show what he was talking about.

"No. I'm confused enough as it is."

"So what did Rebecca say about all this? Were the police there, too?"

"They were over this afternoon." Susan sat down on the sofa. "Rebecca wasn't too anxious to talk about that. She said that the police don't understand how Evan could have a business problem and just take off and disappear. Rebecca insists that there's nothing strange about it—that they are just following up on that odd call last night."

"But that's a change for Rebecca, isn't it?"

"I guess so. She isn't talking about Kelly abducting him anymore. And she claims that Evan's business frequently calls him out of town in the middle of the evening. She insists that he'll call or fax when he gets a chance."

"Is that all she said?"

"It was really a weird conversation." She elaborated in response to her husband's raised eyebrows. "She seemed almost disinterested. All she really wanted to talk about was what she and the twins were getting Evan for Christmas. Don't you think that's odd?''

"Yes, but she knows you're friends with Kelly as well as with her; maybe she was intentionally avoiding talking about Evan's disappearance.''

"Maybe.'' Susan was doubtful. "Of course, she could be mad at me for insisting that Evan is dead.''

"That's a good point,'' Jed agreed.

"Although—'' Susan paused "—it's a little strange that she didn't mention it.''

A dull thud against the front door ended their speculation. Susan hurried into the hall to see what had caused the noise and discovered something blocking the storm door. "Jed? Would you help me?'' she called out, watching a large van drive off down the street and into the darkness.

"What is it, hon?'' Drink in hand, Jed joined her.

"There's something leaning against this,'' Susan explained inadequately, pushing against the door.

Her husband put his drink down on a nearby table. "Move over and let me help. Can you see what it is?'' He peered out through the glass at the top of the door. "It looks like boxes.''

Susan sighed. "It's probably a delivery from one of the stores in town. They try to keep the packages dry under the overhang, and I guess this man just got a little carried away— or there are more packages than usual.''

"I think I'd better go out the garage door and move these away from the outside. Pushing like this might just break something.''

"Good idea . . . Oh, look. There's a car coming into the drive. Jed, it's your mother and Dr. Barr. They can move the boxes for us.''

"Good. I'm glad to see that they're home early.'' Jed picked up his drink again and leaned back against the wall to wait for their guests.

"They may not be coming back to stay," Susan said, peering out. "Your mother left her purse in the car."

"She probably just forgot. They're old. They'll be wanting to get to bed early."

Susan looked at her husband out of the corner of her eye, but she couldn't detect any sign that he knew what he'd just said.

They watched the doctor shove his shoulder against the pile of packages, slowly moving them off to the side, away from the door.

"You don't think those boxes are too heavy for Dr. Barr, do you?"

"He claims to be in such good health," Jed said, shrugging his shoulders.

Susan decided she was going to have a long talk with her husband—and soon. But not when his mother was entering the door, a wide smile on her face. "They had you trapped? It was a good thing Bob and I came home when we did."

"Yes. You decided to make it an early evening, I see," Jed said, moving the large pile of packages through the doorway and into the hall, one at a time, as he spoke.

"Oh, we're not back for good. I just came home to change my clothes. Bob's taking me sledding."

"What . . . ?"

"On the hill at the club!" Susan's exclamation interrupted her husband.

"Yes, we were driving by and saw the lights, and Claire mentioned what fun she had sledding as a child, so I said, why not?"

"I'm afraid we're going to look a little foolish . . ."

"Not you, my dear," her escort protested gallantly. "I may, of course, but the exercise will do me good."

"If you're sure," Claire replied. "I'll just run upstairs and put on some slacks. It will only take me a minute or two. Maybe you'd like a drink?" She directed that suggestion not at Dr. Barr, but at Jed. It had been years since she'd been forced to remind him of his manners!

"Yes. Of course." Jed took the hint. "Maybe a Scotch?" he asked, waving his still full glass as an illustration.

"Or some carrot juice?" Susan added quickly. After all, they didn't want to offend his professional sensibilities, and she did have two large containers of the stuff crowding the top shelf of her refrigerator.

"Nothing. We had ample refreshments at the restaurant. Overeating kills more Americans than most people know. Not to mention overdrinking." This last was said with a pointed look at the glass in Jed's hand.

"Jed . . ." Susan started. Since she didn't know how she was going to continue, her son's noisy appearance at the top of the stairs was a relief.

Chad was chuckling rather loudly to himself, a stereo headset connected to a Walkman in his shirt pocket.

"Chad, if we can hear the music down here, it's too loud," his father shouted up at the child.

"Many children do permanent damage to their hearing with those contraptions," Dr. Barr informed the Henshaws.

"We know that there is a danger. That's why my husband was telling him to turn it down," Susan said.

"I'm ready, Bob," Jed's mother announced from the top of the stairs. "Chrissy loaned me this sweater; isn't it cute?" She paused for a moment in her descent for everyone to admire the oversized, hot pink, mohair turtleneck. "I'm going to wear her neon yellow down vest, too. She says all the kids love the combination. Well, we'd better be going."

Dr. Barr pulled the collar up on his coat and reached for the doorknob. "Maybe we'll break the diet just this once and go out for hot chocolate after sledding, my dear." He turned to Jed and Susan. "Don't wait up for us. I'll see that Claire is taken care of. And"—he smiled at Jed—"I'll move any packages that we find blocking your front door. It could be dangerous for anyone to do it unless they're in pretty good shape.''

''Too bad you weren't around when the twins were dragging that big bag into the garage,'' Jed responded angrily. ''They're young, but they're probably not in shape according to your standards, either!''

''Jed.'' Susan placed a hand on his arm, hoping to calm him down.

Happily Dr. Barr didn't say anything else, appearing startled into silence at Jed's angry response to his offer. ''Come with me, Claire,'' he urged, and they hurried out of the house as Kathleen entered it.

Susan didn't know what else Jed might have said if Kathleen's arrival hadn't provided him with an excuse to say nothing.

''So what's happening?'' Susan asked Kathleen as Jed took her coat.

''The police are very interested in an insurance policy that Kelly has on Evan's life.''

''They've arrested her?'' Jed asked. The three of them returned to the living room and sat down in the comfortable chairs near the glimmering Christmas tree.

''No, they haven't actually arrested her. I don't think they're going to, either. They are asking her to assist in the investigation of Evan's disappearance,'' Kathleen explained. ''And, yes, they're considering the insurance very carefully. A two-million-dollar profit is quite a motive for a murder— if there's been a murder.''

''I know—''

''That Evan's been shot. But since the body is missing, the police certainly would have a hard time charging anyone with his murder.''

''Fine. So where does the insurance policy come into it?''

''It was part of Kelly's divorce settlement.''

"A two-million-dollar life insurance policy on her ex-husband?"

"With the premiums paid by the ex-husband," Kathleen elaborated.

"That's some divorce settlement," Susan said.

"But it makes sense. Not only is Evan committed to paying alimony for as long as he lives and Kelly doesn't remarry—"

"And she doesn't appear very anxious to do that," Susan commented.

"True. And, in case he dies, he's insured for two million dollars, and Kelly is set up for the rest of her life."

"Wow. That's social security. He must have wanted that divorce pretty badly. I had heard that the alimony payments were more than generous, and to be making large insurance payments on top of it all . . ."

"I don't know if it's unusual these days or not. You said that Kelly and he did a lot of entertaining for his business. Maybe the court decided that he owed a lot of his financial success to her and that this was one way of paying her for that contribution."

"Do you have any idea what the police think of Kelly?" Jed asked.

"Behind her back, they're calling her a fruitcake," Kathleen answered. "And I don't think it's a tribute to the season. I'm not sure I blame them. After listening to the story about finding him—and how happy she was to see him in his favorite chair . . ."

"Oh, God. She might as well put on a sweatshirt with the words I'M GUILTY printed across the front of it," Jed said, getting up and moving aside the curtains for a better look out the window.

"I'm afraid so," Kathleen agreed.

"It's a mistake to think that Kelly could harm Evan. She loved him too much," Susan insisted.

"You may be right, but the police don't know her. And, when they find that body, they're going to start looking for a murderer right away— What is that noise?" Kathleen interrupted herself.

"Chad's radio," Jed answered, leaving the window. "I'll go. Maybe you ladies can solve this crime between the two of you. You've done it before."

Susan watched him leave. "Do you think we can?" she asked Kathleen, not taking her eyes off the doorway her husband had gone through.

"We don't even seem able to find the body," came the rueful reply.

"I thought I'd seen it earlier this evening," Susan said, and then explained what had happened with Thomas and Travis. "I felt pretty foolish when it turned out to be a punching bag."

"I suppose it could have looked like a body. I'd be embarrassed, too . . . But you did check inside the bag, didn't you? You wouldn't want a body hanging around your garage."

"Check inside?"

"Inside the leather bag. You did look, didn't you?" Kathleen insisted.

"I . . . ?" Susan thought about the thing standing in the corner of her garage, now covered with a plaid wool blanket that she and Jed had picnicked on and snuggled under years ago when they were first dating. "It really did look like a body," she repeated.

SIXTEEN

SUSAN AND JED WERE LYING IN BED, STEALING SOME TIME together while the rest of the family slept.

". . . and you found out that it really is a punching bag," Jed was whispering.

"Of course. I don't know how I could have thought it was something else—twice."

"Nothing wrong with checking. I'd hate to think we have a dead body leaning against the wall of the garage. It wouldn't be very Christmassy."

"True."

"And think of what my mother would say about your housekeeping," Jed kidded his wife.

"Think of what Dr. Barr would say," was Susan's reply.

"Oh, God!" Jed slipped further under the down comforter. "What are we going to do about that man?"

Susan lifted up the thick covering so he could benefit from hearing every word she spoke. "We are going to do nothing about Dr. Barr. He is your mother's friend. She's an adult. She can choose her own friends."

Jed sat up quickly. "If he were just a friend I wouldn't worry. But he's running her life."

"Jed, don't be silly. She's happy. She looks good. Damn it, she's thinner than I am." Susan, out of bed by this time, tugged a bulky sweater over her head.

"That just proves it," her husband insisted. "She was always dieting when my father was alive and she never lost any weight."

Susan knew there was an answer to that, and that her husband wouldn't want to hear it. "Whatever. But I don't think she'll appreciate interference in her life, Jed. Besides," she continued before he could make his next point, "this is just a holiday romance. Dr. Barr will return to his work after Christmas, and your mother will go home. They'll probably never see each other again."

Jed stood up. "Maybe you're right," he said, seeming to think it over. "It's not as if they were next-door neighbors," he concluded on his way to the bathroom.

"Where is Dr. Barr's home?" Susan called after him.

"Somewhere around Boston, Mom said. But he runs his business from New York City, for some reason."

"So why is he spending Christmas in Hancock?" Susan persisted.

"His family kicked him out because they were sick of him criticizing the way they were eating."

"What?"

"Just joking." Jed stuck his head out the door. Shaving cream covered his cheeks. "I've been wondering about that myself."

"Did you ask your mother?"

"Yes. She said he had a business meeting here."

"Here or in the city?"

"In the city, I guess. And that he had never seen New York City at Christmastime."

"Where has he been all his life? Boston isn't that far."

"That's exactly what I thought," Jed agreed. "And he's not staying in the city. He's staying at the inn. You know, I think he's really just in town to see my mother, and all this stuff about a business meeting is just an excuse."

"Maybe . . ."

"And that's why we have to put a stop to it," Jed insisted, heading back to the bathroom.

"And exactly how are you going to do that?" Susan muttered.

He didn't answer.

Well, she just hoped he wasn't going to make a fool of himself over this thing. She was going to leave well enough alone. Claire was being entertained and was happy. And Susan had to get going and make breakfast. She hurried downstairs.

"Good morning!" The voice greeted her as she entered her kitchen.

"Claire!" Susan was startled. "I—I didn't think you'd be up so early."

"I wouldn't say that older people need less time in bed, Susan, but they certainly need less sleep."

"Would you like some coffee?" she offered, too surprised to remember that coffee was one of Dr. Barr's favorite no-no's.

"Of course not. I made myself some nice herbal tea. Did you know that there was a phone call for you about fifteen minutes ago? You and Jed didn't seem to hear the ring, so I picked it up."

Susan, remembering what she had been doing with this woman's son fifteen minutes ago, turned away in case she was blushing. "Thanks. Who was it?"

"She said her name is Elizabeth Stevenson. Isn't that the woman I met the other night who kept using the word *gracious* and waving her hands around in a rather affected manner?"

"Uh . . . yes. Did she say what she was calling about?" Susan picked up a large mug of strong black coffee and took a sip. It was bitter and burned her throat—wonderful.

"Something about a murder, if you can believe that. Probably one of those murder parties that everyone is going to these days—although it doesn't seem very Christmassy. We had a murder party on the boat that I took around the Mediterranean. It was fun. Dr. Barr guessed the murderer early, but he didn't want to ruin everyone else's fun, so he kept the solution to himself. He's so thoughtful."

"Yes. He sounds like it," Susan muttered, dialing the phone. "Hello? Elizabeth? I heard that you called. And it sounded—"

"Hi, Mom. Hi, Grandma. What's for breakfast?" Chad appeared in the doorway, followed by his sister.

"They were only questioning her last night— What?" Susan removed boxes of cereal from the cupboard as she spoke. Her children took juice and milk from the refrigerator and filled the bowls she handed them. With a quick check to see that her guest had everything she needed (in this case, very lumpy and strangely gray granola concocted from a recipe of Dr. Barr's), she turned to look out the window and concentrate on the person whose call she had returned.

". . . naturally we thought this was all silly. I mean to suspect Kelly of kidnapping was one thing. You hear about people kidnapping children from their divorced husbands and wives all the time, but murder is something else. Derek thinks that the police will be calling it murder sometime soon, and we really can't be involved in that, can we? I don't know what Derek thinks we should do; we were too busy to talk much this morning. He has an absolutely huge deal that he absolutely has to complete before Christmas. By the way, did I tell you that he's giving me a full-length sable cape? It's supposed to be a surprise, but I found out about it a few weeks ago. I can't wait until Christmas. And I know I'll get a lot of use out of it. We have to go to so many formal functions these days . . . But I was talking about Kelly, wasn't I?''

"Yes."

"Okay, don't let me get distracted again, Susan. The reason I called before was to ask you what we should do if she is arrested for murder. She could be arrested, and tried, and convicted."

"Well, with a good lawyer . . ."

"You haven't told anyone that we helped find one, have you?"

"No, but—"

"Please don't. If we had known how serious this all was, we wouldn't have gotten involved."

Susan finished her coffee before answering. "But she needed a lawyer and—"

"Susan, we didn't expect a murder case."

"That just means that she needs a good lawyer more than ever."

"It won't do us any good if anyone knows we're involved in this. We have our standing in the community. And Derek's business. He can't have it known that he's helping a murderer."

"No one knows that!" Susan protested.

"Okay, a possible murderer, if you want to quibble. It's the same thing as far as the business and our reputation in the community are concerned. Derek has lived here all his life, Susan. He's been president of the club for two terms, he was a city councilman for five years. In fact, he's the person who pushed so hard for the new Christmas decorations in the downtown area . . . they were even mentioned in the *Times*, you know. That's important for a town like Hancock. It will bring people in to buy houses and raise real estate prices. We'll all benefit."

"So what does that have to do with Kelly?" Susan asked,

remembering that Elizabeth had said she didn't want to change the subject.

"We think she should be asked to resign from the club."

"What?"

"It's an official way of eliminating her from our social circle. Of course, I'll remain her best friend in private. This is really just a business arrangement. I know it sounds cruel, but Derek says we have to protect ourselves and what we've worked for."

"I don't understand what—" Susan began, and then she did. "Can I call you back in a while? I have to get the kids and Jed out of the house and—"

"Of course, I'll be home all morning. I have about a million things to do."

"Okay. I'll call later." Susan hung up, unable to deal with the problems of being the newly elected membership chairman at the club and feeding her family breakfast at the same time.

"Who was that?" Jed asked, passing by with a cup of coffee in his hand.

"Elizabeth Stevenson." Susan glanced at her children as she spoke. "Do you have clean clothes for gym, Chad?"

"Nah. why bother? Vacation starts in less than a week. Gotta go. Charlie's mom is driving us to school." Her male heir ran out of the room, smashing his backpack against the much-dented woodwork, and slamming the door behind him.

"Chad!" His father protested ineffectively.

"You were just like that at his age," his mother said, beaming at him.

"Now we know who to blame," Susan muttered to herself, pouring out another cup of coffee and trying to remember if she had washed her son's gym clothes since he'd taken them to school the first week of September.

"I'll be home late tonight," Jed announced, kissing his

wife good-bye. "The department Christmas party is after work. 'Bye, Mom."

"You don't mind him going to office parties without you?"

Susan ground her teeth for the first time that day. "Of course not," she lied.

"My parents have a very sane marriage," Chrissy surprised her by announcing. "They don't have to sit in each other's pockets to be happy. They are independent human beings, with separate lives and separate needs. We learned all about it in family life class this year. 'Bye. I'll be late, too."

"Aren't you intending to find out where she is going to be after school?"

"Chrissy knows where she can go and where she can't go," Susan answered. "And she'll call if anything comes up." Another phone call got her off the hot seat. Actually she *would've* liked knowing where Chrissy was intending to be, but hadn't had time to ask.

"Hello? Oh, Barbara. Good to hear from you. I was planning to call later today. Do you know anything about Kelly?"

"That's just what I was calling you about. We must be simpatico," trilled the voice at the other end of the line.

"Then you know something."

"Just that Derek Stevenson found her a high-powered criminal lawyer—and you know what that means."

"No. What?"

"Well, she wouldn't need one unless she was guilty, would she? Anyway, Rebecca is really worried. That's why I called you."

"I don't understand," Susan said, thinking that Elizabeth wasn't going to be terribly happy to hear that her part in getting legal protection for Kelly was being exaggerated.

"Rebecca and I are thinking about psychiatric help."

"Well, I have bad days, too, but getting involved in therapy . . ."

"For Kelly. We've been wondering about having her committed."

"What?"

"Susan, surely you don't think she's been behaving normally since Evan left her?"

"Well . . ."

"And Rebecca is scared. Kelly is telling all sorts of horrible stories—and someone might believe them, no matter how fantastic they are. We think that having Kelly put away is the only good idea here. It's for her own good, you know."

"I don't know what to think, Barb. But I don't know why you've come to me. Surely, even if something like that is called for . . ."

"Because you're friends with Kelly. Maybe you can talk her into seeing someone. I just talked to Elizabeth; she says that Kelly and she are no longer friends and that she doesn't want to be a part of this, but we thought that you . . ."

Susan had had enough. "Barb, you're being ridiculous. If Kelly needs therapy, she can find her own therapist. Besides that, only a family member could have her committed to an institution. This is none of our business." Susan paused for a moment. "I have to go. My mother-in-law—"

"Oh, I forgot you had company. You're probably having to fix pancakes for her breakfast and things like that. I'll call back in a while. Okay?"

"Fine," Susan agreed, putting off the problem until she had time to think about it. She hung up and turned to explain to Jed's mother why she had used her as an excuse. To her surprise, she found that she was alone in the kitchen.

"People certainly do disappear these days," she muttered to herself, and turned back to the phone. She took a deep breath, made her decision, and dialed Kathleen.

When her friend answered, she asked the question without any preliminaries. "How would you like to investigate a murder with me again?"

SEVENTEEN

"You really love Christmas Carols, don't you?" Kathleen asked, raising her voice to be heard over the small CD player impregnating the room with imitations of Olde English cheer.

"Turn it down if you want," Susan said, rolling out cream cheese pastry and cutting small circles to fill with ham and mustard before baking. "I was just trying to keep the spirit of the season—which isn't all that easy with a murderer loose."

"And you are convinced that it isn't Kelly?"

"Definitely."

"And that, once the police find the body, they will assume it is Kelly and won't look any further," Kathleen continued, picking up a small piece of dough and popping it into her mouth on her way back from the radio. "I think you underestimate your police department."

"I can't sit around and do nothing when she's in trouble. And she's making it worse for herself all the time."

"I can't argue about that. But I don't necessarily think that—if Evan *is* dead—Kelly isn't the one that killed him."

Susan paused, looking up from her work. "Kathleen, I saw Evan, and he was shot through the head. I know Kelly, and she could not have killed that man. She loved him obsessively. Maybe her feelings weren't rational, but she didn't kill him. Now are you going to help me find out who did?"

Kathleen looked around Susan's kitchen where they were discussing this problem while Susan cooked. A huge round of Stilton sat on the counter surrounded by bags and bags of dark green spinach. Artichokes marinated in a gigantic ceramic bowl. Hundreds of tiny cream puffs had just been taken from the oven and were cooling on racks balanced on every available space. A light dusting of flour, evidence of an improperly sealed container, covered everything including Susan's hair. Kathleen considered her life, and that she was bored running a security company in the suburbs, and that her mother was going to drive her crazy, and that it was only a few days until Christmas and she hadn't decided what to buy the most wonderful husband in the world. Sure, why not investigate a murder where no one could even find the body?

"I think we should start by talking with Rebecca."

Susan grinned. "Just let me finish these. I can make them all up and put them in the refrigerator downstairs and bake them tonight. I don't know how I'm going to get finished before Friday."

"Maybe you're doing too much. Roast goose, plum pudding, eggnog . . ."

"Spinach tarts, salmon-and-caviar spread, chicken-pistachio pâté, chicken liver pâté, etc., etc." She paused and waved her arms around the room. "Not a sign of goose or plum pudding. This isn't for Christmas Day."

"Are you having goose for Christmas Day?" Kathleen asked, thinking about the turkey sitting in her freezer.

"Yes. And plum pudding. Why don't you and Jerry come

eat with us? And your mother, of course. We'd love to have you.''

''And we would love to come. So what can I do to speed up this process? Because I think you're right. When can we find Rebecca?''

''Help me stuff these crescents and we'll go right over to her house.''

''I could call and let her know that we're coming,'' Kathleen suggested. ''She's probably pretty busy. Or maybe not. Maybe she stopped doing all the Christmastime things that we all do when Evan disappeared.''

''Or maybe she's going ahead and doing them to make everyone think that everything is normal for her—that she's not guilty of murder,'' Susan said, fingers flying as she worked on the appetizers.

''The wife is always suspect,'' Kathleen muttered to herself, grabbing the pad of paper that hung on the wall near the phone. ''Where's a pen?''

''That drawer.'' Susan pointed. ''I thought you were going to help me with these.''

''In a minute.'' Kathleen had found a pencil and was writing furiously. In a few minutes she looked up. ''Nine suspects. There were nine people who could have killed Evan that night. If you leave out the caterers.''

''And we probably can—they do half the functions in town; they wouldn't be that popular if they killed their employers.''

Kathleen looked startled.

''I was just kidding,'' Susan explained. ''But we probably can eliminate them as long as there's no personal connection between one of them and Evan.''

''We should check into that, though.'' Kathleen added a note to the paper.

''So who are the nine?''

''Rebecca, Kelly, Thomas and Travis, Barbara and Jeffrey

St. John, Elizabeth and Derek Stevenson, and Dr. Barr.''
Kathleen read the list she had made aloud.

"Dr. Barr? Did he have a connection with Evan?''

"Not that I know of, but when you think about it, we really
don't know very much about Dr. Bobby Barr.''

"That's what Jed was saying this morning,'' Susan mused.

"There's a book though—a physicians' directory or something similar—that we can start by looking him up in. The
library probably has a copy of it.''

"And how do we know that the other eight are the only
other suspects?'' Susan asked.

"Because no one else could get in and out of the security
system in that house. I know. I helped design it. It's run
through the computer in that media room of Evan's. It was
turned off when guests were expected and turned back on
when everyone had arrived. After that it recorded everyone
coming and going. And I don't think anyone did. But, of
course, we can check that out.''

"The computer system?'' Susan mused. "Rebecca was
sitting at the console later in the evening. Could she have
been turning it off?''

"Or on. Or checking the records of comings and goings.
We'll have to look into that.'' Another note.

"Are you putting in a lot of security systems like that?
Computerized and everything?'' Susan asked, beginning to
put the pastry in plastic bags.

"Nope. His was the first. And last, I suspect. It's very
expensive and requires a lot of discipline on the part of the
owner—making sure it's turned on and off at the right times
and things like that. It's much easier to just wire up a place
and then hire a security company to check things out whenever the wire is tripped.''

"So why did Evan go to all that trouble and expense? Did
he have a lot more to lose than most people?''

"I don't know. The house is new, of course, and very

expensive to build, but I don't know that he was protecting anything in particular in it. But that's true of a lot of security jobs I do. Unless the person who hires me wants to protect something in particular—like I once wired every painting in a house and, even more unusual, I once put a very expensive system into a garage and ignored the house, those people collected antique Porsches—I just put in a whole house system without knowing what needs protecting in particular."

"He didn't say anything about why he was doing it?"

"No. To tell the truth, I think he's—was—a technology junkie. What I put in was the most advanced system of its kind. I think he appreciated that for its own sake."

"He moved from the perfect country Cape to the perfect architectural modern with ease. I think what mattered was not what it was, but that it was perfect. It makes sense that he would want the most up-to-date system. The same way he insisted on real beeswax candles when he lived with Kelly."

"But you know what I keep wondering," Kathleen said, gathering up her paper and pen and putting them both in her purse.

"What?"

"If Rebecca was as anxious to work and create the perfect life-style as everyone says that Kelly did for all those years."

"Good question. Can you think of any excuse to appear at Rebecca's front door and start asking questions?" Susan took off her apron and pulled an elastic band from her hair. Her ponytail fell loose. "Just let me comb this out and get my coat."

"Fine. I'll go say hello to Jed's mother."

"Claire . . . I forgot. I can't just leave her alone all day!"

"You appear to think I have no inner resources, Susan." Claire Henshaw appeared in the doorway. She was dressed in a Chanel-style suit and very high heels. "Good morning, Kathleen. I was just going to tell my daughter-in-law that I wouldn't be home for dinner tonight. Bob is taking me into

New York City for the day. We'll be stopping at an inn he knows near here for dinner this evening. How is your mother, Kathleen?''

"Just fine, thank you. She's visiting some cousins that live in Rhode Island today. In fact, I'm glad I ran into you. My mother is going to cook our traditional family dinner Christmas Eve. I was hoping you and Dr. Barr would come. Susan's already been invited, of course.''

"What a good idea. I'll have to check with Bobby, but I think you can depend on us being there. If Jed and Susan don't have any other plans.''

"No, and it sounds wonderful.'' Susan waved her hand for quiet. "What is that noise?''

"Just the limo that Bobby hired scraping its trunk at the bottom of your driveway. I'll get going. Don't wait up for me.''

"Have a good time,'' Susan called out to Claire's back as she hurried out the door. "Everything's in the refrigerator. Let's get out of here, too.''

"Fine. Why don't I drive so you can comb your hair in the car?''

"Okay.''

They hurried out the front door just as there was a repeat of the limo's scraping bottom. Kathleen chuckled and hurried on, but Susan stopped in the middle of an unnoticed wave to Jed's mother.

"Kath . . . ?''

"Like it? It's an early Christmas present from Jerry.''

"I love it. It's fabulous.''

"Once, back when I first met Jerry, I told him that this had been my dream car ever since I was a kid. And he remembered.'' She sighed happily and opened the door of a restored white Jaguar XKE. "Isn't it beautiful? The upholstery was just redone.''

"Hmm.'' Susan got in and sank down into the soft leather

seat. "Smells like one of those expensive leather shops in Florence.

"Why the early present?" she asked as Kathleen started the engine.

"There was some sort of mix-up in the delivery schedule and I took the phone call from the delivery company. Jerry said, since I knew about it, I might as well drive it."

"What are you getting Jerry?"

"Don't ask. I still have no idea. Absolutely none." Kathleen shifted quickly and ground the gears. "Damn. I wake up in the middle of the night trying to think of the perfect gift, but so far, nothing."

"Well, there are a few days left. You'll think of something."

"I hope so— Hey! Wasn't that Thomas and Travis going in the opposite direction? In that black Jeep?"

"It certainly looked like them. I wonder why they're not in school."

"They go to Hancock High?" Kathleen asked.

"Yes. They're seniors, I think."

"Where is their father?" Kathleen asked, turning the corner onto Rebecca's street.

"Ev— Oh, you mean their real father. I'm not sure. In fact, I don't know very much about Rebecca before she married Evan."

"She caused the divorce?"

"Who knows what causes a divorce?" Susan answered with a question. "All I know is that she was Evan's secretary before the divorce . . . and his wife almost immediately afterward."

"Does she still work in his office?"

"Yes, but she let everyone know that Evan has a new secretary. She's now his partner in the business."

"What precisely is his business?"

"I was afraid you were going to ask me that," Susan said. "Listen, drive around the block and I'll tell you what little I know."

EIGHTEEN

"I DON'T KNOW ALL THAT MUCH—ALTHOUGH, OF COURSE, I've heard some rumors and some gossip. You know how it is."

Kathleen did. A quick comment in the checkout line at the grocery store, someone whispering about a neighbor's behavior at a party the weekend before during a lull in the PTA meeting, a joke or two in the locker room at the club before the weekly handball game. There was usually a bit of truth around somewhere. "So tell me."

"Well, the first time I heard about Rebecca was three years ago. Around Christmas, in fact. I ran into Kelly at Bergdorf's, she was looking for a present for Evan's secretary."

"And that was Rebecca."

"Yes. I don't think she had been working for him very long at that point because Kelly said she didn't know her very well; we talked about how hard it was to buy a gift for someone you don't know—that type of thing."

Kathleen, driving carefully around an icy corner, nodded her head. She had heard a similar conversation recently.

"But she also said that it had to be a really nice gift—that Evan really liked this new secretary and wanted to keep her. The whole thing is a little ironic, thinking about it now."

"You got the feeling that the relationship was more than professional even then?" Kathleen asked.

"No, nothing like that."

"Why not? An affair with your secretary is pretty cliche."

"For a lot of reasons. In the first place, Kelly and Evan seemed so together. They looked like the ideal suburban couple: working together on their house until it was perfect, giving parties, playing on mixed-doubles teams in both tennis and paddleball, doing local charity work . . ."

"Like what?"

"Let me think. Kelly ran two of the auctions that the volunteer group at the library held when they were raising money for the computer system, and she worked hard with one of the groups from their church to organize a shelter for the homeless somewhere near Stamford. She also was very involved in the replanting of the parks the year that the hurricane hit and the stream overflowed downtown. And I think she—"

"You're telling me that Kelly did a lot of volunteer work, not Evan."

"Well, Evan always went to the benefits and everything . . ." Susan paused, then laughed. "I guess you're right. It's the wives that do that type of thing in Hancock. We have the time, I guess."

"So Kelly was the family volunteer."

"Yes. But Evan was very busy at his work. He owns his own business, you know."

"I thought he was a stockbroker."

"No, he's a venture capitalist."

"You're into something I don't know very much about,"
Kathleen admitted.

"Neither do I. But I'm not finished telling you about Rebecca."

"I'll drive through the park."

"Fine. Let me think. The first time I met her was the
spring after that."

"After you heard about her in the city?"

"Yes. It was at a party, and Evan asked me about getting
Thomas and Travis jobs for the summer." She remembered
the last conversation she'd had with Evan and wondered if he
thought she ran an employment service. Kathleen must have
been thinking the same thing.

"Why you?"

"I had been on the committee down at the club that picked
kids to help out with the pool and the grounds the year before
that. You know the summer hiring that we do. Well, I didn't
have anything to do with it that year, but I told him who
did."

"And so Thomas and Travis worked at the Hancock Field
Club that summer."

"No, I don't even know if they applied, but I'm sure they
didn't get jobs there; I would remember seeing them around.
I didn't meet them until Evan announced his engagement to
Rebecca and that was later, of course. I wouldn't even remember that it was Thomas and Travis he'd been talking
about except that he'd explained that they were the sons of
his secretary, and she was divorced, and he wanted to do
something for her. I remember meeting Kelly in New York
a few days later and asking her about it."

"What did she say?"

"I *think* she said something about the two boys being a
problem, but that may be something I heard later. She didn't
seem surprised that Evan was looking for jobs for the boys—
at least I don't remember anything like that. So, if the rela-

tionship had become personal, she probably didn't suspect it at that point.''

''And that was it until after the divorce.''

''No, not at all. Rebecca moved to Hancock a few months after that.''

''She did? I didn't know anything about that.''

''Yes, she rented that little cottage over near Baxter's Castle.''

''I don't think—''

''You wouldn't. It's an estate right on the edge of town. It was built before the turn of the century by a man who made his money in mustache wax, of all things, and it's gigantic. Something like forty rooms. A real white elephant. The house had been empty for years. There was a rumor that a school was going to buy it, but the residents over there got up in arms and stopped that from happening. Recently there's been some talk of turning it into expensive condominiums—something like that might go through. I know that it's been empty and uncared for for a dozen years or so and there are a lot of people who don't like seeing a building like that deteriorate— especially if they live nearby.''

''But Rebecca and her boys lived on the property for a while?''

''Yes. There's a coach house built right next to the main gate and they lived there. That building has always been occupied—at least as long as I've known anything about it. In fact, there's a young couple living there now. They just joined the club a few months ago. They'll probably be at the club Christmas party.''

''You've met them?''

''Just in passing. I'm on the membership committee, but I missed the meeting where they were considered. Chad had cracked a bone in his leg playing soccer that day, and I was still in the emergency room.''

''You're going to the party, though?''

"Yes. We can look them up, if you want."

"Great. Go on."

"There isn't too much more. I met Rebecca once or twice at Kelly's house. The first time was at a barbecue in their backyard. It was a memorable night. The caterer set up a long fire and was cooking a dozen or so suckling piglets over it when the contraption that was holding the pork broke and everything fell into the flames."

"Oh, no."

"Yes. And what's interesting is that Rebecca got right in there and helped salvage the party. Huge orders of cold cuts and salads were sent from two delis and Rebecca took Kelly's station wagon and picked up emergency supplies."

"I don't understand what you're getting at."

"Just that she acted more like a host than a guest. Most of us just kidded around and had another beer, but Rebecca helped solve the problem."

"You think she had gotten close to Evan by then?"

"Not necessarily. But she wasn't just another guest. Maybe that doesn't say anything. In fact, maybe it just means that she was the only person who was an employee and could be called on to solve a problem."

"And Travis and Thomas?"

"They went to boarding school somewhere in Vermont and they weren't around in the summer, either. Off at camp probably. I don't remember where they were, actually. I didn't meet them until they were living with Evan and Rebecca after their marriage. In fact, and this is strange when you think about it, they didn't even come to the wedding."

"That *is* interesting. What do you know about her first marriage? Or the kids' real father?"

"Nothing. Absolutely nothing. To be honest, I hadn't re-alized it until you started asking me these questions. There was such a furor in town over Evan leaving Kelly that I didn't really think very much about Rebecca or her background.

Actually an ex-husband probably accounts for how little we see of Thomas and Travis. They've probably been spending time with their father.''

"But you don't know that for a fact. You've never heard them talk about going to visit their father."

"No. Strange, isn't it?"

"Yes."

"Or maybe not," Susan contradicted herself. "Have you ever noticed that we don't really ask all that much about how anyone new got to Hancock and what they did before?"

"I guess I understand what you're saying," Kathleen said after taking a moment to consider the question. "Most people know that I was a cop before marrying Jerry and moving here, but that may be because working on a case brought me to Hancock originally. There really haven't been all that many questions about my past before coming here, come to think of it. To be honest, I've appreciated it. I also doubt if it would have been like that if I hadn't married into Hancock, so to speak."

"Good point," Susan said, staring out the window at a plastic Santa about to topple off the roof of a large Tudor house onto a bright red BMW sitting in the drive.

"So how did Rebecca come to be known as Evan's wife-to-be? I remember hearing that he and Kelly were getting a divorce, but that's all."

"It all happened while you and Jerry were in Florence last spring," Susan said. "A lot of people knew that there was going to be a divorce, and Evan had moved out of the house, and Kelly had gone home to her mother; then all of a sudden, there was demolition on the property behind the Knowlsons' house."

"You mean tearing down the house that was there before?"

"Yes. I don't know what everyone else thought, but I assumed that he and Kelly had sold off the land. Who would ever have thought that Evan planned to live behind his ex-wife?"

"No one. It still strikes me as bizarre. But when did he announce his impending marriage? I remember people talking about it when we returned from our vacation, but I don't know how it came about."

"He gave a party for her. It wasn't a large party. It was in the hotel suite he had moved into—in the city. Jed and I were invited, and the Stevensons, and the St. Johns, and one or two other couples. And Rebecca was there. I don't know how he worked it with everyone else, but he told me as I came in the door. I was late. There had been an accident on the Merritt and I was the last to arrive; Jed had gone straight from work. Anyway, I walked in the door and Evan hurried over to me, handed me a glass of champagne, and suggested I congratulate him on his forthcoming marriage to Rebecca."

"So you did."

"What else could I do? Actually I think I stood still with my mouth hanging open for a minute or two before I remembered my manners. And then Rebecca came over and said hello to me—and I asked them where they would be living after their marriage. That's when Evan explained that he was building the new house right behind Kelly. Although he just referred to it as the property he owned in town, not the location."

"It must have been an interesting party."

"That's one way of putting it. I don't know about everyone else, but I was so startled that I didn't relax until the drive home. As you can imagine, Jed and I didn't talk about anything else."

"And the divorce went through quickly, didn't it?"

"I guess so, looking back. But it's always easier when there aren't any children."

"And property?" Kathleen asked

"Well, there have been a lot of rumors that Evan paid through the nose for that divorce, but I have no idea of the truth of them. Kelly always says that he provided for her well, but, then again, she never says anything against Evan."

"We ought to see if Kelly will be a little more specific with us; she'll have to be with her lawyer. Time to go see Rebecca?"

"Definitely." Susan sat back and looked out the window. "There really are a lot of interesting decorations this year. Look at the huge wreaths they hung on all their windows." She pointed to the large modern house they were passing. "And have you seen the models of three deer that are in front of the home around the corner? I don't know if they're visible during the day. It's the house right next to Evan— Kathleen! Look! He's not dead! He's standing there next to Rebecca right in the middle of their lawn!"

NINETEEN

"Susan, it's . . ." Kathleen parked the car at the top of the driveway and looked back toward the middle of the lawn.

"Oh, no!" Susan was halfway out the door before she recognized them. "I don't believe it. They're cutouts of some kind. Photographs."

"I guess they're supposed to be decorations." Kathleen got out, and together they walked over to examine the life-size photographic cutouts of Evan and Rebecca standing in the middle of the front lawn.

"We had them made last fall. Evan thought they would make an interesting greeting for the holidays." Rebecca appeared in her open doorway. She joined the women who were now examining the figures. "They're a little bit larger than life. Evan thought that was important, as they were to be seen from such a distance. What do you think?"

Susan looked up at Evan Knowlson, towering over her head. "They're covered with some sort of plastic coating, aren't they?"

"Completely waterproof," Rebecca assured her, studying the image of herself. "I think I should have worn more eyeliner. From the street, it looks like I'm squinting."

"They're so unusual. How did you ever get the idea?" Kathleen asked.

"Evan thought of it. He wanted something different for this house and for our first Christmas together. Look, why don't we go inside? Even with this coat, I'm cold. I just made coffee, if you want some."

"I'd love it."

"Me, too," Susan agreed. "Rebecca," she started as they made their way to the house, "were these here for your party?"

"Yes, but the lighting wasn't working so no one saw them, I'm afraid. The electrician got all that fixed and they're lit up at night now. They seem to be making quite an impression; I've had a lot of people call about them."

Susan, whose heart was still slamming against the walls of her chest, wondered if anyone else could possibly be as shocked at seeing Evan in the middle of his yard, seemingly alive and smiling, when her last image of him had been dominated by the hole in his head. Anyone who had seen Evan dead would feel the same way. Maybe . . .

"Who called?" she asked. After all, the murderer would be more surprised than she had been.

"Almost all the neighbors. I think some of them were a little startled the first night the illumination was working. Why don't we have our coffee in the kitchen?" she suggested.

"Fine. Who else?" Susan asked, dropping her coat across the banister of the large open stairway in the living room.

"Who else? A lot of people. Why are you asking?"

Rebecca sounded irritated, so Susan dropped the subject. "Just interested. Maybe you'll be copied all over town, and next year we'll see the Stevensons in front of their house, and Jerry and Kathleen in front of theirs—"

"There certainly are a lot of interesting decorations in town," Kathleen interrupted. "Jerry and I just hung a wreath on the front door. I feel as if we're not quite keeping up the town's image." She hoped that Susan hadn't put Rebecca off by her talk about the figures on the lawn.

Rebecca retrieved handmade ceramic mugs from the cherry cupboard above her sink, took the Melitta coffee maker off the stove, placed it on a heavy mat woven from exotic weeds, and poured, filling the three mugs. "I'll just get the cream and sugar."

As both women protested their need for such embellishments, Rebecca sat down on a chair and sipped the steaming brew. "You came here to talk about Evan's disappearance, didn't you?"

"Yes. We were worried and wanted to see if we could help out in any way," Susan said.

"Well, I don't know what you can do, Susan. But I'm glad to see Kathleen. I've been thinking there was something unusual about his disappearance and I was considering calling her."

Susan, distracted by the discovery that there were tiny goldfish embossed inside her mug, didn't answer, and Kathleen stepped into the breach.

"How can I help you?"

"I was hoping that I could hire you to find Evan."

"Hire . . ." Kathleen resisted looking at Susan to see how she was taking this surprise.

"What a good idea," Susan said immediately, giving up trying to figure out the mind of someone who would buy mugs decorated in such a strange manner. "Kathleen had a lot of experience looking for lost people when she was on the police force."

"I . . ."

"In fact, she was thinking about offering you her services."

"Oh? I wondered why you were here," Rebecca said as Kathleen glared at Susan. "Does that mean you'll take my case?" She got up to put the coffeepot back on the stove. "I don't know how you arrange these things—contracts, payments. Do you get a daily fee for your work plus expenses, or . . . ?"

"We don't have to worry about that now," Kathleen assured her. "I'd be happy to help you find—with your problem. You don't have to hire me officially."

"No, I want everything to be on a professional basis. Knowlson Enterprises will pay you to find Evan. Just draw up the contracts and I'll sign them. I can give you a check now or . . ."

"Later will be fine," Kathleen said. She turned to her friend. "Maybe Susan had better leave now . . ."

"There's no reason for that. She's been involved in Evan's disappearance from the beginning. She may as well stay involved."

"But—"

"Really, Kathleen, it's okay. Susan can stay."

Since everything was working out as she wanted, Susan decided to shut up and drink her coffee.

"Well then, I'm afraid I have to start by asking you a lot of questions."

"Go ahead. Unless you want something to eat. There's food left over from the party—and we got a large package of cakes from someplace in Oregon in the mail yesterday. A gift, of course, from one of the people we do business with. We could open one of them."

"Nothing, thank you." Kathleen echoed Susan's refusal. "Do you mind if I start?" she asked, taking a notebook from the large leather purse she carried.

"No, let's get going."

"How did you and Evan meet?"

Rebecca looked a little startled, but evidently decided that it might be appropriate for Kathleen to ask some background questions, so she answered.

"I was hired a couple of years ago as a summer replacement when one of his secretaries took an extended honeymoon vacation."

"And then he hired you permanently?"

"She got pregnant and didn't come back so I stayed. I had trained as a bookkeeper as well as a secretary, so I was a real asset. And, I suppose, Evan and I were already becoming interested in each other."

"You knew he was married?" Kathleen asked.

"I didn't steal him from Kelly." Rebecca's voice had hardened. "I know she's worked very hard for the image of the wronged woman, but it isn't true. Evan had lost interest in Kelly long before I met him. She was too domestic—only interested in having the perfect house in the perfect town. Evan was bored with her."

Susan looked around at the kitchen of another perfect

house, in the same perfect town, and wondered if there was another reason for the dissolution of the marriage. Could Evan *really* have disliked Kelly for her domesticity? Kelly appeared to think he reveled in it. But she didn't say anything.

"Kelly wasn't even interested in Evan's business. Evan created the company, and its success is due entirely to him. It's very important to him. And it became very important to me. I think that you can just be a typist and a bookkeeper, or you can be a real help to your boss. I became something like his personal assistant—keeping the office running while he was out of town making deals, even starting to do some of the research in our smaller projects."

"I understand Evan is a venture capitalist," Kathleen said, remembering to use the present tense.

"Yes, and a very successful one."

"That means that he invests in smaller businesses . . ."

"Businesses or parts of businesses that are just beginning," Rebecca corrected her. "He's very successful," she repeated. "Mainly because he's very good at picking out people who are going to succeed. See, he concentrates on the person, not the idea. Evan says that there are some people who can make anything work, some people who can make a good idea work, and some people who will screw up any deal—no matter how good it is." She shrugged. "So he only invests in the right people. And he always makes sure that his investment in that person is guaranteed."

"Makes sense," Kathleen commented, wondering if it could be that simple.

"Evan is the smartest man I've ever known."

"What a nice way to feel about your husband," Susan said, thinking how lucky Evan had been—married twice and worshiped by both wives. Had he *really* been something special? Or did his ability to pick the right people extend into his personal life?

"I have to ask a personal question here . . ." Kathleen began.

"I know. Don't worry about my feelings. The most important thing is finding Evan."

"Good. Then will you tell me how you and Evan got together?" Kathleen asked.

"Well, we were working very closely over a proposal from a group interested in doing travel programming for cable television. It was Evan's first investment in the cable industry and he wanted a lot of background material. My first husband was in television news, so I knew something about the field."

"That's Thomas and Travis's father?"

"Yes. But our marriage ended almost ten years ago, and we didn't stay in contact—"

"You didn't have joint custody? Or regular visitation periods set up in your divorce settlement?" Kathleen interrupted, hoping that Rebecca would tolerate these questions.

"Oh, the law said he was to maintain regular contact with the kids but, unless the judge was planning on picking the man up and dumping him on our doorstep, it was never going to happen. That man was too much of a child himself to be interested in raising children."

"You speak of him in the past tense," Susan noted.

"He's dead. Fell out of a helicopter over LaGuardia Airport doing a story on the dangers of flying since deregulation. He hadn't even kept up the payments on his life insurance. We got nothing. If I hadn't married Evan, I don't know how we would have made it."

"Evan and you told each other about yourselves while you were working on this programming proposal?"

"Yes, just a few months after we began working together. Then, while on a trip to Detroit to check into some work being done there, we fell in love."

Sounded like the same old sleazy story to Susan, but the

people involved always thought of it as something else. And maybe, for them at least, it was.

"When did he decide to leave Kelly?" Kathleen asked.

"Right away. We were in love, and he said he would get a divorce as quickly as possible."

"He thought Kelly would agree to that?" Susan asked.

Rebecca paused. "Evan must have known that Kelly wouldn't let him go easily. That woman is a possessive monster. But Evan always told me that she would agree in the end, and she did." Rebecca smiled. Possibly satisfied that her perfect husband had been right again.

"Do you know anything about the divorce settlement?" Kathleen asked. "I heard some gossip about a large insurance policy."

"Then you heard right. Kelly is being supported in the style to which she became accustomed during her marriage to Evan—her lawyer saw to that all right—and Evan and she had a very nice life together. Not only that but, as a guarantee that this life-style will continue whether or not Evan is alive, he is forced to make massive quarterly payments on a two-million-dollar life insurance policy. With Kelly as beneficiary. It's extortion, that's what it is!"

But it also meant that Kelly benefitted more from his death than anyone else.

"You stayed involved in his business after your marriage, didn't you?" Kathleen asked.

"Yes. In fact, Evan trusted me so much that he made me a partner. Something he would never have done with Kelly. She had no head for business." Rebecca smirked.

"Am I right that a lot of people would like him to invest in their businesses and he has to pick and choose?"

"Yes. He's small, but very well known."

"Is it possible that he's made some enemies along the way? Most people who have power over the lives of others do," she added, perhaps to soften the question.

"Probably. But you're not going to be able to connect this crime with anyone but Kelly, no matter how hard you try," Rebecca insisted.

"I have to check into everything—just in case it turns out that Kelly is telling the truth . . ."

"And that he's dead," Rebecca ended. "If he is, she murdered him."

TWENTY

SUSAN WAS BEGINNING TO WONDER IF THERE WAS SOME sort of immutable rule that she couldn't leave the house unless she went shopping, that she couldn't return without her arms full of packages.

"You promised me!"

"I don't remember promising anything, Chrissy." Susan put down the heavy brown paper bag sporting printed greetings of the season from a national grocery store chain.

"You did. Last weekend at breakfast. You said you would drive me out to the mall so I could shop for Seth's Christmas present."

"That was before your grandmother arrived early, Chrissy.

Besides, you went shopping with your grandmother yesterday . . .''

"That was for my presents to you and Dad," her daughter explained, a smile on her face, guessing that she was close to winning this battle.

"There are a few more bags of groceries in the car. Bring them in and give me a chance to unpack and we can leave. Unless—'' Susan raised her voice''—unless your grandmother has something she wants to do.''

"Grandma is out with Dr. Barr—and she wasn't planning to be home for dinner. Don't you remember?'' her daughter called over her shoulder on the way to the garage.

Susan stared at the box of imported pasta in her hand. "Maybe we could stop at the library," she said, remembering the book Kathleen had told her about earlier. "Where's your brother?'' she called.

"He had chorus practice. The school concert is tomorrow night. You didn't forget that, too, did you?''

She had, but she certainly wasn't going to admit it. "Of course not. We'll have to remind your grandmother. She won't want to miss it.'' Susan smiled to herself. How could a grandmother refuse to go see her grandson's junior high Christmas concert? She remembered last year when the trumpet section had been so off-key that most of the audience (parents of the young musicians included) had spent the evening stifling wails of laughter, and friends spent the next day comparing who had the sorest diaphragm muscles. She smiled again as the phone rang.

"It's probably for me, Chrissy. Kathleen was going to phone," she called to her daughter, picking up the receiver. After talking to Rebecca, they had parted; Susan to buy groceries, and Kathleen to see if she could find and talk to Kelly, as Rebecca had insisted she do immediately. But Susan suspected that Kathleen's conscience was bothering her; she had led Rebecca to think that she was looking for Evan professionally. Susan hoped that not charging Rebecca for these false services would make Kathleen feel more comfortable.

When she picked up the receiver, Susan was anxious for information about Kelly. But the caller was Seth St. John.

"Chrissy!"

"I'm right here, Mom. You didn't have to yell." Her daughter appeared behind her, three bags precariously balanced in her arms.

"Chrissy! You're going to drop—" But the girl had everything placed on the counter and was reaching out for the receiver before she finished.

"It's okay, Mom. Hi, Seth. Hang on while I take this upstairs, okay?" She handed the receiver back to her mother. "Hang this up when—"

"I know, Chrissy." Susan took the phone with one hand and, returning to domestic concerns, started to pull groceries out of the bag with the other. How was she going to have everything ready for the party? She looked around her kitchen. She had stored so many staples along one long counter that it looked like a shelf at the grocery store. The liquor store had delivered her order; half a dozen cases of wine were stashed under the kitchen table and an equal amount of hard liquor sat on top. She sighed and glanced out the bay window at the bird feeder in the backyard. It was almost empty, and they were running out of seed. Jed had said something this morning about not having any clean shirts so she'd better stop at the cleaners on the way to the mall.

"Are you ready?" Chrissy asked from the doorway, pulling on a parka.

Susan looked at the phone still in her hand. "I didn't hear you tell me to hang up."

"Don't worry about it. We didn't talk. Seth decided he had to go when he heard that I was on my way out to buy his Christmas gift. We are on our way, aren't we?" she prodded.

"Yes, we are. This minute, before anyone calls." She would get back to Kathleen later.

"Great!" Chrissy smiled happily and picked up her purse from the counter. "I've decided what to get Seth," she said.

"Wonderful. What?"

"A wall rack for his tapes. He has over seventy of them and, sometimes when he's on the phone, I hear his mother yelling at him to put them away. What do you think? Not personal enough?"

"I think it's a wonderful idea. If you want it to be more personal, maybe you could put in a tape of your song."

"Our song! How 1950s. We don't have a song, Mother. For heaven's sake. What sort of dumb people do you think we are?"

Susan assumed it was a rhetorical question and changed the subject. "So what store do you want to hit first?"

Chrissy got into the car and considered the question. "Sam Goody. They'll have what I need."

She was right and, an hour later, they were on their way home again, the backseat of the car filled with bags from the record store. "What a good idea you had, Chrissy. Chad will love the carrying case I bought him, and your father is going to be thrilled with the Beatles CDs. What luck finding the wrapping paper with Jed and Chad printed on it. And I love the ribbon with glitter sprinkled over it."

Chrissy seemed preoccupied. "Yeah. Mom . . ." she started, and then stopped.

"What, honey?"

"What do you think happened to Mr. Knowlson?"

"What do I— Oh, there's the cleaners. I almost forgot about your father's shirts. I promised him I'd pick them up." She turned into the parking lot, nearly hitting a large gold Mercedes; the driver was backing out without bothering to check his rear. "What the . . . ?"

"Mother! It's Mrs. St. John. Be careful!" Her daughter

was apparently more worried about embarrassment than the consequences of eighty thousand dollars' worth of foreign cars becoming a hundred dollars' worth of scrap metal.

At the last minute, Barbara St. John checked in her rear-view mirror and put on the brakes. She looked as embarrassed as Chrissy claimed to be feeling, and she pressed the button that rolled down the window near her seat and stuck her head out. "Sorry about that. I was just thinking about what I have left to do before Christmas."

"Don't worry about it. Everyone has a hard time concentrating these days. You know, I think what makes Christmas so difficult is that all the normal chores and errands don't stop before the holidays: there's still laundry, and cleaning, and car pools, *and* the routines that fill our time the rest of the year."

"I know what you mean," Barbara answered, looking over her shoulder at the car honking behind her. "Do I know the woman driving that car?"

"I think she wants us to move," Susan said. "We're blocking the entrance here," she pointed out as the car honked again.

"Some people! No Christmas spirit!" Barbara St. John took the time to glare at the other driver before accelerating into the street.

Susan pulled into a nearby parking space, ignoring the sounds of the still-angry driver. "Is Seth a good driver?" she asked quietly.

"His mother didn't teach him, if that's what you're wondering," Chrissy answered, and then laughed. "Mr. St. John says his wife takes out all her hostilities on the road. Seth says that she didn't learn to drive until a few years ago, and she had to take so many Valium to pass the driver's test that she almost passed out while they were taking her picture for the license. He showed it to me; she looks dead." Chrissy paused. "Mom . . ." she began again.

"Let me pick up your father's shirts and then we'll talk," Susan said, noticing the change of tone in her daughter's voice.

But after going into the cleaners, greeting half a dozen friends, paying for and picking up a dozen starched shirts and one silk blouse that she had forgotten about, she returned to the car—and a daughter who had apparently changed her mind.

"Nothing. It wasn't important," was all Chrissy would say when Susan started the conversation.

Susan was afraid she had lost another fleeting chance at making contact with her adolescent daughter. "You were asking about Evan Knowlson," she prompted.

Chrissy had developed an apparently intense interest in the dozens of evergreens lining the sidewalk of Hancock's small shopping area.

"Chrissy? Is something wrong?"

"No."

"Kathleen is going to investigate Evan Knowlson's disappearance," Susan announced, deciding to introduce the topic herself.

"Oh?"

"If your friends know anything about it, they could talk to her. She would keep it confidential, I know." Susan kept her eyes on the road, but she heard her daughter take a deep breath and then let it out.

"I heard you and Dad talking," Chrissy stated. "You think that Evan's dead."

"I saw him sitting in Kelly's living room. He had been shot," Susan said as calmly as possible. "But his b— He disappeared after that. I don't know what to think," she lied.

Chrissy took another deep breath as her mother stopped the car for a red light. "Mrs. Knowlson—the second wife— I don't know what her name is . . ."

"Rebecca."

"What does she say about her husband's disappearance?"

"She doesn't seem to believe that he's dead, but she's worried. That's why she hired Kathleen." The light changed, and Susan started the car. She was choosing her words carefully, trying to keep Chrissy talking. She was afraid that asking a direct question could bring their discussion to an end.

"I don't know Thomas and Travis. They're seniors, you know."

"I heard that."

"Seth knows them a little, though. Thomas and Travis are on the varsity wrestling team and Seth is on J. V. But they all work out together."

"Oh?" Susan had to bite her tongue to keep from asking what Seth thought about the twins.

"The twins think that Mr. Knowlson is dead, too."

"They said something at practice?" Susan had to respond.

Chrissy didn't answer, and they were almost home. Susan searched for a way to prolong the drive. It was obvious to her that this was worrying the girl. "I need to go to the library and look up something in the reference department. Would you mind if we stopped over there?"

"No. I need some books to read during vacation anyway."

Susan turned a corner and they drove through a large, rolling park toward the town library. Susan pulled into the paved lot provided for patrons and turned off the car.

"Mom, Seth says that he overheard Thomas and Travis in the locker room after school and they were talking about 'Mr. Knowlson's body.' "

"Did he hear any more of the conversation than that?" Susan gave up subtlety as her daughter appeared ready to confide in her.

"I asked him and he says no, he just heard the phrase 'Evan's body'—'moving Evan's body,' in fact. He says that they were whispering, and when he walked around to the other side of his bank of lockers they shut up.''

''Oh.''

''Do you think I ought to call Kathleen and tell her?''

''It might be a good idea. I could do it, if you want me to.''

''Oh, would you?'' Chrissy seemed relieved. ''But you won't tell anyone else about this? And Kathleen won't, either, will she?''

''Not unless she has to . . .'' Susan began.

''Mom, you can't tell anyone. Not even Kathleen—unless you know that it isn't going to get around. Seth would kill me.''

''I don't understand.'' Susan looked at he daughter straight in the eye.

''Because I promised Seth I wouldn't say anything about it,'' Chrissy said. ''You see, he told me about it while I was at my locker at the end of the school day yesterday, and I didn't think anything more about it, but last night he mentioned it to his mother . . . and she got really mad.''

''Mad?''

''Yes, Seth said that she yelled at him to mind his own business and not to repeat anything that has to do with Mr. Knowlson to anybody. And Seth didn't want to talk about it when he called this afternoon.''

''So you want to be sure this doesn't get back to Barbara,'' Susan said.

''Yes.''

''I think we can be sure that Kathleen will be discreet. You were right to tell me, though,'' she added, placing her hand on her daughter's arm. ''This is a very serious thing, you know.''

But her daughter was peering out the window at the group of high school students standing on the steps of the old red sandstone building.

TWENTY-ONE

Susan called Kathleen immediately after returning home. Once again, she found herself juggling the phone while cooking.

"It might just be Barbara. She's like that, you know."

"Like what?"

Susan put her hand over the receiver. "Have some more. Everyone else has already eaten."

"What?"

"Oh, sorry, Kathleen." She returned her attention to the caller. "I'm feeding Chad a late dinner. He had to stay after school to rehearse for the holiday concert tomorrow night. Hold on a second." Susan put the receiver to her shoulder. "Would you like to eat in the study? You can watch TV."

"Yeah!" Chad popped up from the table enthusiastically.

"Do you need help getting the food there?"

"No, I'm fine!"

Susan turned her back on her son and returned to her conversation. She didn't want to be looking if the large bowl of beef stew hit the floor.

"I can talk now." She heard the kitchen door swing shut behind her son. "What were you saying?"

"Nothing. You were talking about Barbara St. John."

"And why she is so anxious for Seth to be quiet about what the twins were saying about Evan's body. Well, I know it sounds significant, but it might just be Barbara. What people think of her is very important."

"More so than the rest of us?" Kathleen asked.

"In a more superficial way . . . I hope. She's very worried about class. You know, whether she does the correct upper-middle-class thing."

"You're not being bitchy enough."

"What?"

"Susan, you're being so nice and polite, and that doesn't help me. Just tell me what you think."

"I think that she thinks she married beneath her. I know she's always worried about her husband doing the right thing. Jeffrey comes from Wisconsin or Minnesota, and she's always talking about how she had to teach him to dress and what to eat. She even talked about selecting 'power clothes' for him to wear."

"You're kidding?"

"No. She says that she checks him out before he leaves the house each morning—otherwise he doesn't look right."

"Ouch."

"Yeah, it's pretty emasculating. Actually more than a little—because she also complains about him to her friends—even to me, and it's not as though we're all that close. I feel sorry for him . . . sometimes."

"Sometimes?"

"Sometimes I think that it's his own fault that she's running his life. She not only picks out his clothing, she tells him how to be a father, how much exercise to get, when to go on a diet. She treats him more like he's her son than her husband. I've even heard her complain about what she thinks he's doing wrong with his business.''

"So maybe he wants a mother instead of a wife."

"Exactly. She's the same about Seth. Always making sure he does just the right thing."

"So you think that maybe she doesn't want Seth to say anything about Evan just because it's tacky to gossip or something?"

"It's possible. And, remember, she's one of Rebecca's best friends."

"That's interesting," Kathleen commented.

"It is, now that I think about it. After all, it's not like having an ex-secretary for a friend is exactly status."

"Maybe Evan is status enough."

"Maybe, but, you know, even though most people tried not to take sides after the divorce, many of us ended up closer to Rebecca or Kelly."

"I suppose that's inevitable," Kathleen commented. "And Barbara came out of it more Rebecca's friend than Kelly's."

"Definitely. Say, did you talk to Kelly?"

"Yes. She's coming over to your house after dinner this evening. In fact, she should be there any minute now."

"What?"

"I left a message on your answering machine. Didn't you get it?"

"No. Probably one of the kids played it back and then didn't bother to tell me."

"Well, when I told Kelly that I wanted to talk to her, she agreed immediately, but asked that we meet someplace besides her house. She says she thinks it's good for her to get out these days. I knew you would be busy cooking, but I did want you to hear this. We can just sit and talk while you work. You don't mind, do you? I'll be over soon."

"Fine. I was going to make dips for the party tonight. You're going to get to spend more time in my kitchen."

"Just don't let me eat anything. I can't believe how much weight I've gained in the last two weeks."

"Don't mention weight. Claire has been driving me crazy— Oh, there's the doorbell. It's probably Kelly. Hurry over. I don't know what we'll talk about until you get here." She hung up without waiting for a reply as Kelly entered the kitchen.

"Hi! You're looking so much better. That was Kathleen on the phone. She's on her way over." Susan hoped she was telling the truth about that last thing. Kelly, in fact, didn't look better. She looked terrible. Except for the dark circles under her eyes, her skin was pallid, and even her lips were almost white. She wore jeans, a wrinkled linen shirt, and a pullover that must have belonged to Evan in his college days. It was the first time Susan had ever seen Kelly without discreet eye makeup and freshly washed hair. "Have a seat. Would you like some tea?"

"No." Kelly sat down on a stool pulled up to the counter. "Or maybe I will have a cup. If it wouldn't be any trouble."

"Of course not." Susan reached for the kettle and put it on the stove. "I have to get ready for the party, so we're going to—to visit in here, if you don't mind." She prattled on while she made a pot of tea and got out mugs, sugar, and cream. Kelly didn't say anything. She just sat on the stool and stared at the bunch of mistletoe that was sitting on the end of the counter.

"I bought that this afternoon—at one of those stands in the middle of the mall. I was going to hang it for the party, but I can't decide on a place. Any ideas?"

When Kelly didn't answer, Susan added, "You always have such good ideas about decorating."

"Evan had all the ideas. I just carried out his wishes."

"Kelly, that can't be true . . ." Susan began, and was rewarded with the first spark of animation her guest had shown.

"But it is. Evan was the creative part of our partnership— even he used to say so. He decided how everything was supposed to look, and told me what to do, and then I did it. Do you know that, in all the years we were married, Evan made every decision. And you can't imagine what a wonderful relief it all was."

"A *relief*?" To Susan, it sounded like slavery.

"Yes. I didn't have to worry and plan. Evan did it all. I can't tell you how difficult it's been since he died. I really don't know what to do next."

"Maybe you'll enjoy making your own decisions," Susan suggested gently, spooning tea into the china pot.

"Oh, no," Kelly protested. "I know already that I'm going to hate it."

Susan didn't know what else to say.

"Those are poison, you know."

"What?" Susan looked around the room, wondering what Kelly could be talking about.

"The berries on mistletoe. They're very poisonous."

"I've read that," Susan said. "But I don't think anyone is going to reach up to the ceiling and take a nibble. Not unless I don't get the rest of my cooking done. Maybe mistletoe doesn't belong in the kitchen, though, come to think of it." As she picked it up off the counter some of the waxy white berries fell from the bunch and rolled on to the floor.

"I'll get them," Kelly offered. She slipped off her stool and knelt on the quarry tiles. "Some of them have gotten down in the mortar," she murmured.

Susan put the greenery into a large plastic bag. "Just throw those in the garbage compactor. I'm going to put this into the garage. It's cooler out there, maybe it will stay fresher. It would be nice if there were some berries left on it for the party." She hurried off, and returned to the room in time to pour the now-boiling water over the tea leaves.

"You'd be surprised how many common Christmas decorations are poisonous," Kelly was saying as Kathleen entered the room.

"Chad opened the door for me," she explained, pulling off her coat and sitting down at the kitchen table. "If that's hot tea, I'd love a cup. My mother has been cooking huge meals and my stomach is in shock."

"I'll pour," Kelly offered. "You better get on with your cooking, Susan."

"Thanks."

"You must want to ask me questions about Evan," Kelly stated calmly, pouring tea into a mug and passing it to Kathleen.

Susan thought about Kelly's tendency to come directly to the point. Did it show an admirable forthrightness or was it merely the result of a lack of imagination? It was something she hadn't considered before.

"You know things that no one else knows," Kathleen answered, watching as Kelly slopped tea on the tablecloth.

"That's true." Kelly answered slowly, reaching out for the sponge that Susan handed her.

"We don't mean to pry into your life," Susan added. "You and I are the only ones who saw Evan in your living room. We're the only ones who know he's dead."

"Except for the person who killed him and the person who moved him," Kelly said.

"That's a good point." Kathleen sipped her tea. "I wonder if there were two people or one."

Susan thought about this for a moment. It might be the most interesting question asked thus far.

"Would it upset you to tell us about the day of Evan's murder?" Kathleen asked gently.

"No. I can do that," Kelly answered. "But Susan was with me and she saw what I saw."

"I'd rather hear the story from you," Kathleen asked. "Why don't you start with the salad?"

"With making it?" Susan thought Kelly sounded oddly upset by the thought.

"With when you decided to make it," Kathleen persisted.

Susan wondered if it was panic that flashed across Kelly's face before she answered. But whatever it was, its effect appeared to be momentary.

"I wanted to contribute something for the party."

"Was it just a spur of the moment thought, or had you been planning—"

"It just came to me the morning of the party," Kelly interrupted Kathleen to answer. "I wanted to do something for Evan—to make something for him, that is. I'm not explaining very well, am I?"

"That's okay. Just tell me how you thought of it."

"I don't know," Kelly answered. "I just thought of it."

"So you made the salad in the morning . . ." Kathleen prompted, thinking she had better get the story going.

"No, I never leave a salad sitting around; it should be fresh. I washed all the ingredients in the morning and put them in the refrigerator to crisp. Then I put together the salad in the afternoon and put the salad dressing on it right before I left the house." She stopped and seemed to be thinking hard.

"I heard that it looked wonderful," Susan said, hoping to jog her into continuing.

"I make a nice salad." Kelly accepted the compliment and it seemed to encourage her to continue. "I put it in the car and took it over to Evan's other house about an hour before the party was supposed to start."

"Was that around seven o'clock?" Kathleen asked.

"Around seven-thirty. In Hancock, when you invite people for eight, they really don't start arriving until eight-thirty."

"And what happened when you got to the house?"

"I rang the doorbell, and Rebecca answered. She was still

wearing her robe and there were curlers in her hair. She— she seemed surprised to see me.''

''What did you say to her?''

''I was very polite, just like I was supposed to be. I said Merry Christmas and that I had brought the salad as a contribution to her party.''

''Was there a top on the bowl or could she see what was inside?'' Kathleen asked.

''It had cellophane covering the top. She could see what was inside by just looking down.'' Kelly seemed to be remembering. ''Anyway, Rebecca said something like 'How could you do this to me?' She didn't even say hello or anything! She took the salad from me, and I was wondering if she was going to invite me in when she threw it at me—bowl and all. Luckily it was one of my collection of antique wooden salad bowls or it might have shattered and cut somebody. But it did leave a large bruise on my shin!''

Susan thought that Kelly was still surprised by Rebecca's action. ''Did she say anything then?''

''Yes. She said to get away from her house and leave her alone. I never expected her to greet me like that. Never.''

''And then you . . . ?'' Kathleen's voice was gentle.

''I was so upset. I wiped the salad off my boots as well as I could—most of it landed there—and then I walked back to my car, and got in, and started to drive. I've never done that before. But I didn't know what to do. I didn't have to be at home, and I couldn't stand the thought of just sitting around the house and waiting for the party to end, so I drove around.''

''For how long?''

''An hour or so, I guess.''

''Kelly, was it an accident that your car slipped off the road?''

''Of course. Kathleen, you thought I was trying to kill myself!''

"We—" Susan began.

"Everyone thinks that I was trying to kill myself," Kelly continued, her voice rising. "How could my friends think such a thing?"

"No one thinks it," Susan lied. "Kathleen just has to check out all the possibilities. It's her job."

Kelly appeared to accept the explanation and continued. "I really don't know what time the accident happened. I looked at my watch as I turned on to Mill Road and it was eight-forty. There was a clock on the wall across from my bed in the emergency room and I noticed that it was almost ten o'clock when they called you, Susan. I suppose you and I got to my house around eleven?"

"Probably."

"You didn't do anything but drive around before your car slid off the road?" Kathleen persisted. "You didn't stop anyplace or talk to anyone?"

"No. I had filled the car with gas earlier in the day. I just drove around. It was interesting actually—looking at all the different Christmas decorations. And one of the radio stations was playing Christmas carols. It wasn't as bad as I thought it was going to be."

"You were under a lot of strain—what with Evan and Rebecca giving the party and all," Susan suggested. She was confused by the tone of Kelly's answers. There was something so matter-of-fact about her, almost like it didn't matter.

"Yes. I was very nervous."

"When you and Susan entered your house, you didn't go into the living room right away, did you?" Kathleen asked.

"No. We entered through the back door and went up to my bedroom using the stairs from the kitchen."

"They were pretty much a secret, weren't they?"

"The stairs? Well, most people didn't know about them, but they weren't exactly a secret," Kelly said, and Susan again wondered about some sort of sexual ritual.

"How long were you in the house before you went to the living room?"

"About—"

"I want Kelly to answer," Kathleen said, stopping Susan.

"Probably half an hour at the most," Kelly guessed. She looked at Susan for confirmation of her answer, but Kathleen didn't give anyone time to say anything.

"And you didn't see or hear anything out of the ordinary until you entered the living room?"

"Nothing. Nothing at all."

"How long do you think it was between the time you left the house and when you returned?"

"You mean when we went over to Evan's other house?"

"Yes."

"Well, awhile," Kelly answered slowly. "Maybe half an hour or forty-five minutes."

"Did you go all the way around the block to get back to your house?"

"Oh, no. I cut through the shed, of course."

"The twins weren't there then?" Susan asked.

"No, no one was there," Kelly answered.

"The twins?" Kathleen asked.

"Yes, they were using the shed as a place to get away from adult supervision and do some drinking," Susan explained, remembering that Kathleen didn't know about it.

"Really?"

"Yes, when Rebecca and I—and the policeman, of course—cut through, they were sitting there drinking up a storm: eggnog, wine coolers, gin."

"That's interesting," Kathleen commented.

"I thought it was nauseating myself," Susan said.

"Huh?"

"The liquor," Susan explained, wondering why Kathleen wasn't paying attention.

"That's not what I'm talking about," Kathleen explained.

"I'm just wondering why the twins weren't there when I followed Kelly through the shed just a few minutes earlier."

"Maybe we ought to have a chat with Travis and Thomas," Susan said quietly. "There are a lot of paths leading to them," she added, thinking of what her daughter had told her earlier.

"Tomorrow afternoon," Kathleen said. "We'll just have to come back from the city a little early."

"The city?" Kelly asked.

"Susan and I are taking her mother-in-law and my mother in to New York for the day," Kathleen explained.

"Evan and I used to visit the Christmas tree at the Metropolitan Museum each year." Kelly began to tear up.

"New York City," Susan mused. She'd forgotten all about it.

TWENTY-TWO

NEW YORK CITY CAN BE AN ENCHANTING PLACE IN DECEMber. The stores are beautiful, the streets are full of happy shoppers, the very air seems cleaner, purer. Unfortunately Claire and Dolores didn't see it that way.

"You mean we have to park all the way down here?"

"It doesn't look very safe."

"When Bob and I were here, we went to this nice garage—
it was very clean and everything—and this very attractive
young man took the car and parked it for us. Couldn't we go
there?"

"We're already in this garage, Claire," Susan answered.
"And this is a very safe area of the city. I come here all the
time."

"Susan used to live in the city," Kathleen started to explain to her mother.

"In this tiny little apartment with only one window. And
the stairs that they had to climb to get up there . . . it was
horrible. Very strange cooking smells came from the other
apartments," Claire elaborated. "I can't tell you how glad I
was when they moved to Connecticut. So much healthier for
the children. Dr. Barr agrees."

Susan ground her teeth. They had left Hancock late because neither mother could decide what to wear. There had
been a broken-down truck in the middle of the already heavy
holiday traffic. They had been very lucky to find a garage
with space available this close to Rockefeller Center. And
still complaints from the backseat. Ho. Ho. Ho.

"So where should we go first?" Kathleen asked, and, to
Susan, her voice seemed a little strained.

"I thought we were going to see the Christmas tree at the
skating rink," Claire answered.

"I don't know about the rest of you, but I could use a cup
of coffee," Dolores stated.

"I'll go along with that," her daughter agreed.

"Why don't we go to one of those restaurants near the
rink?" Claire suggested. "I can remember coming into the
city and taking Jed there for hot chocolate when he was just
a little boy—younger than Chad. They're nice places; they
probably have herb tea."

"Great idea. Just let me give the car keys to this man," Susan said.

"Does he really look trustworthy, dear?" Claire peered out the window at the uniformed garage attendant; above his grease-stained, gray coverall uniform his long hair was spiked in four different directions, and each point of the compass had its own assigned color.

"I'm sure he is," Kathleen assured her.

"It's only a Maserati," Susan said casually. Her hand was shaking as she gave the young man her keys and took her receipt. "We're only a few blocks from the tree," she said. "Why don't we walk?"

"Of course," Dolores agreed. "I can almost smell that coffee."

"I should have worn different shoes," Claire said. "I didn't think about walking."

Susan bit her lips and said nothing. Fortunately the streets were dry and the tree was so beautiful that everyone forgot everything else while contemplating it. Almost everything else.

"Where did you say that restaurant is?" Dolores asked Claire, who was leaning against a railing and slipping her shoe off her heel.

"Right down there. I don't remember how to get there . . . Oh, look. They must have added an elevator . . ."

Forty-five minutes later they were on their way up that elevator. "I think they added more than this elevator. I cannot believe that they have the nerve to charge two dollars for a cup of coffee." Claire was echoing her previous statement.

"And Danish pastry for three-fifty. Disgraceful. It wasn't even homemade."

Susan and Kathleen, of one accord, moved a few steps back from the older women.

"It's going to be a long day," Kathleen commented.

"Very. I wonder if we could suggest that Claire stop in Saks or someplace and buy a pair of comfortable shoes. I don't know how she thought we were going to get around the city without walking."

"Dr. Barr had a limo that took them from place to place and waited for them all day yesterday. She told us about it when you were in the ladies' room," Kathleen explained.

"You and your mother are certainly being good sports listening to all this talk about Dr. Barr," Susan said.

"It's better than listening to talk about how Jerry and I should start a family," Kathleen said.

"She really is pretty insistent about the subject," Susan agreed.

"She's driving me crazy," Kathleen admitted. "That, and the fact that I still haven't thought of anything to give Jerry for Christmas."

"Well, here we are on Fifth Avenue. If we can't find anything here, there's something wrong with us."

"Trump Tower! I've always wanted to see it in person," Dolores cried, looking down the street.

"I've heard it's very tacky. At least that's what Bob said," Claire Henshaw said disagreeably.

"It's definitely something that everyone should see once," Susan assured Kathleen's mother. "I think that should be our first stop. All right?"

"I suppose so, if we can go to F.A.O. Schwarz after that. I want to find a stuffed animal for the little girl who lives next door to me. Then maybe Tiffany's. I wonder how it's decorated for Christmas. And . . ."

Susan and Kathleen resigned themselves to following along.

Two hours later, they were still following; this time, however, Claire and Dolores were comparing the prices and selections of the various menus hung before restaurants along Fifty-fifth Street.

"Do you think we can convince either of them that any restaurant with a table is fine?" Kathleen asked.

"I doubt it. Do you think there are two more rigid women anywhere in the world?" was Susan's answer. "Oh, look. I think they've made a decision."

Kathleen murmured something about "one a day" as they hurried out of the cold and into their choice. . . .

"Bobby says Japanese food is very good for you," Claire announced.

"He should know," Kathleen said. "He's a nutritionist, isn't he?"

"Podiatrist. We'd like a table for four," Claire said to the waiter.

"Podiatrist? Isn't that feet?" Susan asked.

Kathleen was too busy wondering how they had gotten a table so quickly to worry about Dr. Barr's medical background.

"He studied nutrition in Europe before starting his business," Claire explained, sitting down at the table placed near the restaurant's one window. Evidently eating in a place with only one window bothered her less than her son and his family living in one. "He found being a podiatrist unfulfilling."

"I can see how that's possible," Kathleen said, accepting a seven-page menu from the waiter with a smile. The man didn't smile back.

"Too bad you didn't find anything that you thought Jerry would like for Christmas," her mother commiserated. "I thought that cashmere robe was lovely."

"So did I. I bought one almost like it for my husband the year Jeddy was born. It was a wonderful investment. In fact, it looked almost new when he died. He wore it in the hospital."

"I don't think Jerry needs a bathrobe," Kathleen said,

turning and looking out the window at the mobs hurrying along the sidewalk. "Why look! There's Rebecca!"

"Was it really?" Susan had to turn around in her chair to look.

"Yes. Definitely. I wonder why she's in the city."

"Probably shopping just like we are," her mother said from behind the menu.

"With Evan d—missing?" Susan looked at Kathleen.

"Interesting, isn't it?" Kathleen returned her look.

"Well, I don't see why you think it's so significant," Claire said, poohpoohing their concerns. "So she's in the city. She was here yesterday, too."

"She was?"

"Yes. She told me so herself," Claire insisted.

"When?" Susan asked.

"Last night. We ran into her at the inn."

"We?" Susan asked.

"Bobby and I. He's staying there, you know."

"So I heard."

"Did she say why she was in the city?" Kathleen asked.

"No, but she was in this part of town," Claire added. "Because she ran into Bobby at Rockefeller Center; his office is somewhere near there. That's how I know she was in the city. They did one of those 'fancy seeing you twice in one day' things in the lobby last night. Then Bobby explained about running into her earlier."

"That's interesting," Kathleen commented.

"Do you think it might mean something?" Susan asked as the waiter put her soup down in front of her.

"I think it's something to keep in mind," Kathleen said, picking up her spoon.

"Isn't this interesting? I don't think I've ever tasted anything quite like it," Dolores said, sipping.

"Bobby would approve. Not a bit of fat floating on top," Claire agreed.

"It is interesting." Kathleen put down her spoon after the first mouthful.

"Unique." Susan imitated her motion. "I don't think I've ever had bad soup in a Japanese restaurant before."

TWENTY-THREE

THEY WERE ON THEIR WAY HOME. FINALLY ON THEIR WAY home, Susan thought.

"My feet are killing me," Kathleen moaned, slipping her boots off and leaving them on the floor of the car. "You must be exhausted. The traffic has been horrible all the way in and out of the city."

"I am a little tired," Susan admitted. "I think that we should all eat at the inn tonight, Claire. The kids both like it. I can call Jed and have him meet us there. All right with you?" she asked, thinking that if that didn't suit her family, they would just have to put up with pizza—and hearing what Dr. Bobby Barr, the famous podiatrist/dietitian, would think about that.

"Good idea—" Kathleen began.

"We still have some of my pasta and calamari left over,"

her mother interrupted. "It will be fine heated up in the microwave. You and Jerry eat out an awful lot, you know. Some men don't like that."

"Jerry does."

Dolores shrugged.

Susan carefully maneuvered around a large chunk of ice in the middle of the highway and wondered briefly about the energy of the older generation. For six hours, Claire and Dolores had visited store after store, Christmas tree after Christmas tree, and restaurant after restaurant. They had criticized the traffic, the dirt, the rudeness, and the cold of New York City in the Christmas season. They had been offended by the prices of everything sold by everyone from the street vendors to Saks Fifth Avenue to Cartier. They had walked for miles, been bumped by fellow pedestrians, and yelled at by impatient cabdrivers. They had had a wonderful time. And they still had energy left. Susan and Kathleen were worn out.

"I wonder why Rebecca's been in the city so frequently," Kathleen said.

"It does seem a little unusual. With Evan missing and all." Susan was so tired she could hardly get the words out.

"She could just be doing the last of her Christmas shopping. We don't want to make too much of this," Kathleen said.

"Yes. She might also be working, I suppose. Even without Evan, the business has to go on."

"His business was located in New York?"

"Yes."

"You're sure?"

"Of course; he and our husbands commute in and out of the city together. Why? Do you think it's significant?"

"Just interesting. I wonder what Rebecca's exact function at his office is."

"Doesn't she describe herself as his partner?"

"Yes, but is she actually doing half the work—or does that simply mean that he turned over half of the assets of his business to her?"

"Good questions," Susan muttered.

The women in the car were silent for a few moments.

"So what time do we have to be at the high school?" Claire broke the mood.

"Where?" Susan asked before she remembered. "The Christmas concert! I'd forgotten all about it!"

"Are you going to spend a lot of time getting ready for it?" Kathleen asked. "Remember, we were going to try having a talk with Thomas and Travis this afternoon."

"Damn. Yes, I did forget. They'll be at the concert, though."

"They will?"

"Yes, they're part of the high school chorus; they came around caroling at our house a few nights ago," Susan answered. She wasn't paying much attention to what was going on in the car; she was too busy worrying about what she was going to serve tonight now that a leisurely dinner at the inn was ruled out.

"Do you suppose we'll be able to find Thomas and Travis after the concert?" Kathleen asked.

"Well, Rebecca will be around, too," Susan said. Maybe there was chili stashed somewhere in the back of the freezer in the basement—but enough for five people? "Do you want to talk with them alone or with her?"

"Alone. Definitely."

"You think that they're covering up for her?" Susan asked quickly, sighing with relief as she turned the car off the highway onto the country lane that led into Hancock.

"Possibly."

"But she couldn't have killed him. She was busy at the party," Susan protested.

"Everyone thought that Evan was busy at his party, too, remember."

"True. But that would mean that the whole thing was planned well in advance."

"It probably was," Kathleen mused aloud. "The cover-up alone would suggest careful planning. Think of it. Not only was Kelly's living room carefully set up, but the backyard was trampled down. Then the body was taken, the blood was cleaned up, and the living room was redecorated."

"Maybe not. The blood had fallen on his shirtfront," Susan said. "I don't think there would have been much to clean up."

"Still," Kathleen continued, "it must have all been done in a matter of minutes. I don't see how one person could have accomplished all that."

"Of course," Susan agreed. "And it must have meant a lot of passing through the shed . . . at least if it was done by someone at the party."

"I think it was," Kathleen said. "I've thought about that a lot. If Evan didn't get a phone call—and we think that he didn't—then he wouldn't have left the party with an outsider; it had to be one of the guests."

"Or a member of his new family," Susan added.

"Unless he made an appointment with someone during the party intentionally—to cover up maybe."

"That doesn't sound like Evan. He took his job as a host seriously. He might give a party for business reasons, but he wouldn't neglect his guests to do something else. I don't think he would, at least."

"So someone present at the party probably killed him," Kathleen said. "Unless it was Kelly, of course."

"But she was in the hospital when he was killed—or on the way home from the hospital in my car," Susan protested.

"Maybe. I only hope that the police will believe that."

"They haven't even found the body," Susan answered.

"Yes, but—"

"What are you two talking about?" The question came from the backseat.

Susan and Kathleen abruptly stopped talking and glanced at each other.

"I thought you had given up worrying about murders and missing people, Kathleen."

"I run a security company, Mother. Sometimes—"

"You're talking about Evan Knowlson, the man who disappeared in the middle of his own party the other night, aren't you?" Claire asked. "I thought that was very strange. And Bob said he's never heard of anything like it."

"I don't think Evan planned on disappearing in the middle of his Christmas party," Susan insisted, feeling odd about defending someone she knew was dead to her mother-in-law. But she was tired of hearing Dr. Bobby Barr's opinion of everything she or any of her neighbors did.

Susan was pressing the button on her automatic garage door opener, and Kathleen was pulling on her boots, when another thought hit her. "Is there any way to find out if Evan really got a call during the party?"

"Well, the phone company has records, but it takes a court order to get at them, and even then . . . The computer system! Susan, you're a genius. Of course we can find out if there were any calls. The information will be stored on Evan's hard disk—unless it's been intentionally erased."

"Do you think Rebecca would give us access?" Susan asked, getting out of the car.

"It would be simple to ask her. And it certainly would be interesting to find out. If no one called in, then it appears that one of us is the murderer." Kathleen winced at her own words. Her mother wasn't going to let that lie.

"We're going to have to hurry, if I'm going to feed the kids dinner before the concert," Susan said, trying to end the discussion.

"I'll find out about the computer and give you a call," Kathleen whispered to Susan as Claire and Dolores pulled their many packages from the trunk.

"Are you going to try to talk to the twins?" Susan asked.

"Yes. Grab them after the concert, if you have a chance."

"We usually take the kids out for ice cream after—"

"Let Jed take them. Find out how long those kids are claiming they were in the shed," Kathleen urged, and then, turning back, she added, "Dr. Barr won't approve of the ice cream anyway."

Susan rolled her eyes, ground her teeth, and smiled. "Can I help you with some of that, Claire?"

"No. Bobby would say that it's good exercise for the back." She draped herself with four large bags from Saks and an even larger box labeled F.A.O. Schwarz. "I'll take these up to my room."

"We won't leave for dinner for another hour, if you'd like to take a short rest," Susan offered, picking up a few boxes of her own. "Oh, I think I have something here that belongs to Dolores. I'd better call her . . ."

"I'll take it. I know what it is." Claire reached out a finger, and Susan draped the tiny Tiffany's bag over it. "It may as well stay here."

"Here?"

"It's her gift to you and Jed," Claire explained, starting for the door to the house.

"For us? Why is she giving us a present?"

"You invited her for Christmas Day. You didn't expect her to show up empty-handed, did you?"

"Well, she certainly didn't have to bring a gift—" Susan began to the back of her departing mother-in-law. She sighed and followed her, realizing that now she would have to buy something for Dolores.

But there was no time to think about that now. Chad was demanding her attention before she had taken off her coat.

"I don't have black slacks," he announced, standing in the middle of the kitchen floor munching on a cookie.

"You're going to spoil your appetite for dinner. No more cookies," Susan said automatically.

"I need black slacks tonight," Chad repeated, continuing to eat. "I told you last week."

Susan stared at her son. "I don't remember a conversation about black slacks. What do you need them for?"

"For the concert. The boys have to wear black or navy slacks and yellow, blue, or pink button-down dress shirts. No sneakers or basketball shoes; only leather dress shoes. The girls have to wear—"

"I'll see what the girls are wearing tonight. That's not my problem. You don't have black or navy slacks. You have gray wool and two pairs of chinos."

"I need black or navy. Although I'd rather have black. We have to have them, Mom. I can't be in the chorus unless we're dressed properly. I told you last week," he repeated.

"I don't remember, Chad. I don't remember you saying anything about needing new clothes for the chorus—but that isn't going to help anything now. Get in the car. Thank goodness the stores are open late this week."

Susan called up the stairs to Chrissy—asking her to tell her grandmother about the unexpected shopping trip—and returned to the garage. She hoped the chorus and orchestra planned on playing quiet music tonight. She was in serious need of a nap.

TWENTY-FOUR

THE FAMILIAR LYRICS OF "SILENT NIGHT" PEALED OVER the attentive audience—as well as over the less attentive.

"Jed, I think your wife is asleep."

"Susan? Honey? Wake up."

"Shh. Tell your mother to be quiet. I'm not asleep. I was just resting my eyes. Aren't the kids cute?"

"Which ones? The boy on the end with the diamond earring in his left ear? Or maybe the girl with the crew cut?"

"Jed! Shh! They're teenagers; they're expressing their individuality. Remember how your parents hated your long hair?"

"I remember." Claire leaned around her to assure Susan.

"Shh!" came an order from the seats behind them. Susan just hoped that it didn't come from a parent of one of the children whose appearance Jed had criticized.

Actually the concert was going well. Most of the children were adorable and the music was charming. Susan crossed her legs, placed her hands in her lap, and prepared for an uninterrupted half hour of time to think.

It took less than a minute for her to decide to pick up a large bottle of bath salts for her cleaning woman. She also reminded herself that she had to get Claire's Christmas present tomorrow morning. With her mental chores completed, she settled down to think about the murder. It had occurred to her, waiting outside the dressing room where Chad was trying on and complaining about every pair of navy slacks the men's shop in Hancock had for sale, that one of the Stevensons or the St. Johns was probably the murderer. Well, at least right now they appeared to be the most likely suspects. They had been at the party, and they could have planned a murder and carried it out more easily than someone working alone. No matter which one of them did it, the other partner of the couple could cover up while they were absent from the room. What was more likely than for a husband to explain that his wife was in the bathroom? Or for a wife to say that her husband was on the phone? Two perfect suburban alibis.

But why? Motive seemed to be the problem here. What exactly did she know about each couple and their relationships with Evan Knowlson? She decided to consider Elizabeth and Derek Stevenson first—mainly because they seemed the least likely of the two couples to be found murdering someone. Anyone.

Elizabeth was, of course, Kelly's best friend, but that was no way to start. She should think of them as individuals and then in relation to the others around them. What she thought of first with Elizabeth was her appearance.

Elizabeth Stevenson was a buyer for a large consortium of department stores: the Asian buyer. She had a fabulous wardrobe of leather and embroidered silk clothing that she wore with remarkable casualness for everyday. In the evening and on more formal occasions, she usually had on one of her many antique kimonos or a handwoven sari picked up on an occasional detour into India. Her hair was prematurely gray (she was two years younger than Susan, and Susan certainly didn't expect to have gray hair soon!), and she wore it swept up off her neck and into a chignon. On her, the style seemed ageless. She and Derek had two children, but they had sent them off to boarding school so young, and kept them busy with camp and European ski trips during vacations, that they managed to lead the life of a childless couple. Except, naturally, during graduation ceremonies and on parents' weekends. As Derek would say, One had one's obligations.

If that sounded pompous, it was probably because she thought of him as pompous. Now, wait, Susan reminded herself. This wasn't a popularity contest. It didn't matter if she liked Derek. But did Elizabeth like her husband? And did either of them like Evan? (Although Susan remembered his admonition to his wife that they shouldn't speak poorly of their host the night that Evan had died, she didn't know what he really felt. Such a statement could have just been more pomposity.)

Actually, if Susan thought of Elizabeth's clothes first, her immediate impression of the husband was his bossiness. Derek was always telling people what to do—followed by how it should be done. His relations with his wife followed form. Susan had more than once over the years watched Elizabeth leap when he said leap and, for some reason, she always seemed to do it happily. Susan had wondered about a woman independent enough to travel into exotic corners of the world, succeeding in a highly competitive business, and developing an independent image for herself, who was apparently content to follow her husband's instructions when they were together. The contradictions in a person's life always interested her.

Of course, both Elizabeth and Derek had spoken of the difference in their backgrounds. Derek came from an upper-class family and had spent his entire life moving in various prescribed paths between such places as Bar Harbor and Palm Beach, between Hancock, Connecticut, and Madison Avenue. He had gone to the right prep schools, the right colleges, and was settled happily into the right Wall Street brokerage house. Elizabeth had been born and raised in New Jersey. Not Princeton, not Bernardsville, just a tiny town in the middle of a state without cachet. She had worked her way from a scholarship at a state teachers college, to a masters in marketing at NYU by commuting into the city five days a week for one and a half years. Then on to a beginning job in the basement of Macy's, to stores further uptown, and from assistant buyer to buyer, to where she was today. She had made the most of every opportunity.

Susan had once heard Derek Stevenson describe his wife as looking as if she had been born with a million. It wasn't a look achieved by accident.

Susan didn't know much about Derek and Elizabeth as a couple. Elizabeth had told her that they had met through mutual friends and had gotten married almost immediately. Their two children had followed shortly thereafter. Elizabeth continued working, and a succession of nannies and au pairs had preceded the children's boarding school years. It was Elizabeth's work that was important, not her family. And it was Elizabeth's looks and her work that her husband bragged about—when he wasn't correcting her social skills. But, if Susan hadn't always thought of the Stevensons as a typically happy suburban couple, she hadn't thought of them as unhappy, either.

In some ways, the St. Johns were the opposite of the Stevensons. Not just because they were always quibbling and bitching at each other. But because, despite Elizabeth's high-powered career, she thought of Derek as the dominant force in the marriage. At the St. John house, the wife ruled.

Or so it seemed. Certainly Barbara St. John was the most verbal member of the duet. And a lot of her words were aimed at explaining the superiority of herself over her husband. Like the Stevensons, the St. Johns had come from different classes. Barbara St. John spent a fair amount of time telling everyone about it. She was the one who knew all the best places to eat and what to eat there. She also picked out their vacation destinations: Cambridge Beaches in Bermuda last spring, the Hassler in Rome in the fall, and everyone had been informed that they were on their way to Little Dix just as soon as the New Year's rush was over. Susan thought of Barbara as a person whose label consciousness extended beyond the way she dressed. She bought and did what was the best and the most expensive, and she made sure that it showed. No small discreet getaways for the St. Johns; their destination had to be well known—otherwise how would everyone know it was exclusive and expensive? Jeffrey St. John was different. Susan had always thought of him as a man unprepared for his own success. His small business selling rustic furnishings from the Minnesota lake area had grown to encompass crafts from the South, Southwest, and Northwest (the middle of the country apparently unable to produce anything sufficiently chic), and had bulged from one small store to almost fifty outlets in various fashionable shopping areas around the country. Jeffrey, who had dropped out of art college because it was too restricting and too bourgeois, had accomplished the miracle of accidentally becoming a successful businessman. Susan had always gotten the impression that it embarrassed him.

Or maybe it was the way his wife talked about his success that he found so embarrassing. Barbara adored broadcasting the opening of each new shop almost as much as she deplored (loudly) their increasingly high tax bill. She courted publicity, and there were frequently articles in local papers about her husband and his shops, with her own picture prominently displayed. Her husband never appeared comfortable with all the fuss. Jeffrey St. John, Susan had noticed, was beginning to drink too much.

So which of the four had a close connection to Evan? Derek

had gone to prep school with Kelly, which implied a long relationship with the family. Maybe Evan had some financial dealings with Jeffrey. Possibly Jeffrey had been financed by Evan? Barbara had become good friends with Rebecca almost as soon as she arrived in Hancock. Was there another reason for the relationship other than similarity of temperament? Well, here she was with more questions than answers—again.

Susan looked up at the stage as the junior high chorus made their noisy entrance onto the wooden risers placed upon one side of the stage. Chad, short for his age, was one of the first boys to take his place in the front row. Then he and a blond boy that Susan didn't recognize started whispering and giggling together. Well, there was nothing she could do about it from this distance. The high school chorus was mounting risers on the other side of the stage, and Susan was distracted by the appearance of Thomas—or was it Travis?

It must be interesting being identical twins, Susan had always thought. Of course, she'd heard stories of fooling teachers and friends. Even Rebecca admitted that sometimes, from a distance, she couldn't tell her own sons apart. Had the twins planned on that? Had they even used it to get away and kill their stepfather? Had one boy pretended to be both of them while the other was luring Evan to Kelly's house and shooting him in the head? But what was the motive? Something simple and oedipal? Did Thomas and Travis get along with Evan? Was the reason that Evan was always looking for employment for them just to get them out of the house? And what sort of trouble had they been in with the police, if that rumor was true? Or did that even make a difference when it came to Evan's death? Had Kathleen gotten a chance to talk to the boys? she wondered.

These questions kept Susan occupied throughout the chorus' performance. On the final note of a medley of rock Christmas carols, she decided that the more she thought, the more questions she had. She had a feeling that Kathleen would say something about that being a beginning, at least. She didn't want to hear it. Applause woke her up at the end of the concert, and she joined in enthusiastically. She felt remarkably refreshed.

After one last bow, the students broke ranks, hurrying off the stage to join their families and friends. In the rush, Susan lost track of Chad, but found someone else.

"Kathleen, what in the world are you doing here? There can't be another person in this audience who isn't a relative of one of the performers—except the teachers."

"I'm meeting Thomas and Travis. They were busy before the show, but offered to talk to me afterward. Besides, it was a nice performance. I enjoyed it. And I see Chad got new pants—"

"Susan, thank goodness I found you so quickly. Do you mind if Chrissy joins Jeffrey, Seth, and me for hot chocolate at the club?" Barbara St. John asked, appearing behind Kathleen.

"No, it's nice of you to include her," Susan agreed at once.

"We'll get her home before eleven," Barbara promised. "I love Chad's new pants," she added, hurrying off.

"New . . . ?"

"I'd love it if you'd talk to Travis and Thomas with me," Kathleen added. "Couldn't you make some sort of excuse to stay here? They're helping take down the lights; I told them I'd wait around until they were done."

"Sure, I guess so. Why does everyone ask me about . . . ? Chad, honey. You were wonderful!"

"I think you forgot something, Mom."

"Forgot . . . ?"

"Oh, there's Sean. Mom, can I spend the night at his house? I know it's a school night, but we're not doing any work these days and we'll go to bed early. Please. His mom said it was okay. Please!?''

"It is a school night . . ." Susan began as her husband joined her. "Why don't you ask your father?" she continued. "If he agrees, it's fine with me."

"Moving up to a higher authority?" Jed kidded his son. "What do you want now?"

"I want to spend the night with Sean. I know it's a school night, but none of our teachers are giving us any work, and we'll go to bed right away, and it's vacation in just two days, and . . ."

"Why don't we find Sean and his parents and talk with them," Jed suggested, putting his arm around his son's shoulders.

"Great, they were right over by the stage . . ."

Susan was watching them walk off when she realized that she had left all the tags on the rear pocket of her son's new slacks. "No wonder everyone's been kidding me about his new clothes," she commented to Kathleen.

"There's Thomas—or Travis. Come on. I'd better remind them that I want to talk." Kathleen hurried off through the thinning crowd.

Susan followed, wondering if Rebecca was around somewhere. Or if she was still in the city.

"Mrs. Gordon? Travis is still in the light booth, but he'll be done in a few minutes. Do you want to go up there? It's pretty private, and Mr. Amato—he's the history teacher who runs the stage crew—won't mind."

"Good idea. Mrs. Henshaw is going to join us."

"Fine. Follow me."

He led them around dozens of parents standing chatting in small groups at the back of the room and through a small door built into the wood paneling.

"The stairs are kind of narrow," he called back over his shoulder.

"We're fine," Kathleen assured him, pulling her short, straight skirt up higher.

"Trav!" Thomas called ahead of them.

It was almost a warning of their presence, Susan thought.

And a needed one, she decided a second later. As they entered the dark room, two people were scrambling up from the floor, rather embarrassedly straightening out and tucking in clothing as they went.

"Hello, Mrs. Henshaw."

"Hello, Amelia."

"My parents will be waiting for me," the girl said to Travis, who was standing there with his hands in his pockets, looking embarrassed.

"See you tomorrow," he mumbled, and turned back to the projector.

"We said we would answer some of Mrs. Gordon's questions—about the night that Evan disappeared." Thomas was trying to bring his brother back to the present.

"I can answer while I wind these wires," Travis mumbled.

"Fine." Kathleen took control of the situation. "I wonder if one of you could just review the whole evening from the time the first guest arrived."

"Why don't you start with Kelly bringing the salad to your house?" Susan suggested quickly.

"We weren't there when she came; that is, we were upstairs in our room," Travis said, pulling apart one of the large lights hanging from the ceiling.

"The first we heard about it was when Mom called upstairs and asked if one of us would sweep off the front steps," his brother explained.

"So you didn't know when the doorbell rang?" Susan asked.

"No. It had been ringing for hours—delivery men, and caterers, and everything."

"I went down and swept off the steps," Thomas said. "They were a mess. I didn't know it was a salad, though, not until later. I thought the florist had dropped something, there were a lot of flowers—and even some of those strange little white berries that everyone uses at Christmastime."

"Berries? You mean mistletoe?" Susan asked.

"Yeah, if that's the stuff that people kiss under," Thomas agreed. Travis looked up at the ceiling of the booth. It was empty.

Kathleen was smiling as she asked the next question. "When did you two join your parents for the party?"

"Mom had told us to be around to greet the guests, so we came down when the St. Johns arrived," Thomas said.

"They were the first guests?"

"Yeah. Mom and Mrs. St. John are pretty good friends." Travis shrugged. "You know how it is."

"And you stayed around talking to guests for the whole party until Evan vanished?"

The twins exchanged looks.

"Look, is this confidential or anything?" Thomas asked finally.

"We're not here to find out if you were doing anything wrong," Susan assured him. "We just want to find out exactly what happened that night."

"Well . . ." Thomas paused, then plunged in. "We were planning on relaxing in the shed. We had a supply of booze, and we added to it throughout the evening. So sometimes one of us was out of the house for a few minutes. But not for long at the beginning of the party. Then, as the party got going, we decided that we wouldn't be missed and we went out to the shed and had a little party of our own."

"And that's all we know—until you and the policeman and Kelly Knowlson showed up," Travis added.

"You—" Susan started, but Kathleen interrupted, kicking her in the shin at the same time.

"When did you hear that Evan had disappeared?"

"That night Mom said that he had some sort of emergency and had to go in to the office. The next day after school she said he had been called out of town. The first we heard about his disappearing was when Mom told us she had hired you to find him. Yesterday."

"Did you get along with your stepfather?" Kathleen asked. Twin shrugs.

"All right," Thomas answered.

"Do you have any idea where he is right now?"

"None." It was Thomas who answered, Travis having resumed his examination of the ceiling.

"How are you two guys going to get home?" Kathleen asked.

"Amelia was going to drive us—" Travis started.

"There's always someone around to go home with," his brother interrupted.

"Why don't you come with me?" Kathleen suggested. "Then we can talk some more."

To her relief, the boys agreed. But she didn't get much more information on the drive to their house, and she had to push to get invited in. There weren't many lights on, and she was afraid that their mother had gone to bed. But, to her surprise, Rebecca Knowlson came to the door, still in the clothes she had been wearing for the concert.

"I was hoping you'd still be up."

Rebecca walked back to the desk she had been sitting at before Kathleen arrived. "I'm trying to finish this pile of Christmas cards tonight." She sat down.

"You send a lot of cards," Kathleen said, taking a seat without waiting to be asked.

"It's mainly business. That's why I'm so busy. It's important that people don't think we've forgotten them—or their investments."

"Really? I don't send cards to my clients," Kathleen said.

"You should think about it. It's important to some people." She put down the pen she had just picked up. "But you didn't come here to talk to me about Christmas cards. Do you have any information about Evan?" Rebecca got right to the point.

"No, but I wanted to talk with you, if you don't mind. I know it's late, but since Thomas and Travis needed a ride home, I thought I could give them a lift and then speak to you. There are one or two points that I'd like to clear up."

"Of course. Do you mind if I stuff envelopes while we talk?"

Kathleen would have preferred Rebecca's full attention— as well as a chance to see her face—but she couldn't very well say so.

"Fine. Did you get finished in the city today?" It was a trick that sometimes worked: surprise the suspect. This time it didn't.

"Yes. In fact, one of the reasons I went in to the office was to pick up the list of cards that were sent out last year to check them against the list of cards that we mailed last week. And I had to drop off some Christmas gifts as well." True to her word, she began stuffing envelopes.

"And yesterday?" If at first you don't succeed, try, try again.

"Christmas shopping. You know how it is; I thought I had everything done, but then some last minute errands came up. I was hoping it would be easier to get it all done at one time in the city."

"Did you find anything at the office that might be a clue to why Evan vanished?"

Rebecca turned and looked at Kathleen. "Nothing. And I spent a lot of time there. I went through all the mail twice, through records of the work he was doing last week, through his notes on projects coming up. I spent a few hours in his private office, and I didn't find anything."

"It sounds like hard work," Kathleen said.

"I went through all his records," Rebecca repeated.

"There are a few more things I need to talk to you about." Kathleen was hesitant.

"Anything, if it will help us find Evan."

"I was wondering if I could go through the hard disk on your computer and see if it recorded who called Evan the night of your party. I seem to remember that it was programmed to record all calls." Kathleen looked at Rebecca carefully. How would she react to this request?

Apparently calmly.

"I erased that program yesterday morning when I was looking for something else. That's why I had to go in to the office today." Rebecca looked her straight in the eye.

So why shouldn't she be calm? If there had been something to hide, it was gone now.

"There is something else," Kathleen said, trying to hide her disappointment. "Thomas and Travis are lying to me about the night of your party."

"What are you talking about specifically?"

Kathleen thought Rebecca sounded wary. "They claim they were in the shed between your property and Kelly's house for a lot longer than they possibly could have been there."

"They're probably just not sure of the time." Did she sound relieved? "They're teenagers. They have no idea what's going on around them. And, to be honest, they were drinking that night, so their reporting is probably less reliable than usual—and usually it's not very good.

"I have to admit," Rebecca continued, "those two boys have been a big worry to me ever since their father and I divorced. They were at a difficult age when we broke up, and they started having trouble in school . . . I'm sure you don't have to know about that. It's all in the past now."

"How did they react when you married Evan?" Kathleen wanted to keep her talking.

"Fine. They like him." It was the standard answer.

"Susan told me that Evan was trying to help them get jobs out on the Island this summer; it's nice to hear about a concerned stepfather." Kathleen hoped Rebecca would talk more.

It didn't work.

"Yes. Evan is like that."

"Then they're upset by his disappearance."

Rebecca seemed startled by the thought. "I guess they are," she said slowly. "I've been so busy that I haven't worried about them very much. I guess I'm not a very good parent."

Kathleen left the house thinking that Rebecca's last statement might have been the only honest one.

TWENTY-FIVE

"I'M SO GLAD TO FIND YOU UP." KATHLEEN THREW HER coat over a kitchen chair.

Susan glanced around the room. "I won't be leaving this

place before Friday night—unless it's to do some last minute shopping and wrapping."

"Jed's busy, too?"

"He's finishing up the Christmas cards and worrying about his mother. She's out with Dr. Barr again. He picked her up at the concert." Susan pressed the button that turned on the light in her oven and glanced inside before she looked up at Kathleen. "Jed's daughter is out tonight, too, but it's his mother that he's worried about. I think he's going crazy."

"Can you believe that Dr. Barr's a podiatrist?" Kathleen asked, momentarily distracted.

"No. Claire claims that he studied nutrition in Europe, and maybe he did—"

"But maybe he didn't," Kathleen finished for her. "Or maybe he didn't study at an accredited university."

"Or at any university at all. He might have spent a year or so developing a business with a quack dietician."

"Did you ask any specific questions?"

"No, but I'm pretty sure Jed isn't going to keep quiet much longer. He—"

The kitchen door opened, and both women turned around. Kathleen spoke first. "Mother! What are you going here?"

"I was upstairs in the bathr—"

"Didn't you know Dolores was here? I thought you'd come to pick her up," Susan said, looking from mother to daughter in amazement.

"Is that smoke?" Dolores asked, opening the oven door and looking inside.

Susan grabbed her pot holders and tried to salvage the mushroom turnovers before they turned from dark brown to black.

"I heard what you were saying about Bob," Dolores commented, reaching out and taking the worst turnovers off the pan. She picked up a knife and scraped the darkest dough into the sink. "If we sprinkle these with some Parmesan cheese, it will add a nice glaze and cover up some of the burn," she suggested.

Parmesan and mushrooms? Well, it was better than throwing them away and starting from scratch. Susan got the cheese from the refrigerator.

"What are you doing here?" Kathleen repeated, a little impatiently.

"Helping Susan. She's been talking about how busy she is this week and I had some free time . . ."

"And she's been wonderful. You never told me that your mother was a great cook," Susan said enthusiastically.

"Why are you so surprised?"

"Well, you know you've never made any secret of your own lack of interest in things domestic, my dear," Dolores answered, sprinkling cheese energetically. "Your friends don't know how far this apple fell from the tree, that's all."

"My father was a policeman," was Kathleen's stubborn response.

"Well, yes. But most people expect a daughter to be like her mother, don't you think?"

It was said sweetly, but you didn't need to be Willard Scott to know a storm was approaching. Susan decided to try heading it off. "Maybe your mother can help us with your detecting as well as my cooking."

"You have questions to ask me about Evan's disappearance?" Dolores lost interest in the domestic side of life more quickly than Susan would have expected.

"We—"

"Kathleen's father always talked over his cases with me."

"Mother! I don't remember that!" Kathleen's tone was accusatory.

"You didn't know everything about our relationship. Now what can I help you with?" The question was directed at Susan.

Susan thought quickly. Just what had she gotten herself

into? "Well . . . Did Dr. Barr tell you that he's a podiatrist? The night of the party, I mean."

"We didn't really have all that much time to talk—just a few minutes before you and Kelly came running into the room half dressed."

"Now, Mother. The first rule of investigation is not to exaggerate. Father must have taught you something in all those years."

"I spoke with Dr. Barr for only a few minutes and Kelly, at least, was dressed for bed and not for a party."

"And did he tell you anything about his background?" Susan asked. "Anything at all?"

"He went to medical school in Philadelphia. He told me that." Dolores looked at her daughter.

"The University of Pennsylvania?" Kathleen asked.

"There are many medical schools in Philadelphia. I wouldn't like to exaggerate my knowledge. All I know is that he told me he had attended medical school in Philadelphia. He volunteered the information after I told him where I live. Is that accurate and clear?"

"Mother!"

"Isn't it funny how mothers and daughters argue and act like they don't get along? I've even seen books on the subject." Susan had decided that the time had come to get straight to the point.

And it worked. Both women smiled, and Kathleen even went so far as to chuckle a little. "I guess we're typical then."

"Why don't you two talk and I'll wrap up the rest of these things," Dolores offered. "I really am a better cook than a detective."

"There isn't that much to talk about. I came over here wanting Susan's opinion on some things."

"I'm getting tired of opinions. What we need are some

facts.'' Susan sighed and poured herself a cup of tea. ''If there are any.''

''Well, I couldn't prove it, but I think we can say that Rebecca knows Evan is dead.''

''What? She admitted it to you? That means she's seen the body!''

''Not necessarily. And maybe I'm jumping to conclusions.''

Dolores smirked at the puff pastry but remained silent.

''But—'' Kathleen raised her voice, after a quick glance at her mother ''—but I just went to see her and she didn't act the way I expected her to act.''

''You *are* going to explain?'' Susan took a sip of her tea.

''If Jed was missing and you hired someone to find him, wouldn't you ask that person if they had succeeded first thing every time you saw them?''

''Well, I certainly wouldn't waste any time talking about the weather,'' Susan agreed. ''When did you talk to Rebecca?''

''Just now. I drove the twins home. Rebecca was up writing Christmas cards.''

''And she didn't ask about Evan?''

''Of course she did, but only after a bit of polite chitchat about Christmas. It didn't feel right. She should have asked me immediately—that is, she should have if she were worried about him.''

''That's what you call a fact?''

''Mother!'' Kathleen ground her teeth. ''What would you call it?''

''Well, I don't know what I would call that. All I would call factual in your story is that Rebecca was sending out Christmas cards to her friends.''

''To business associates of her's and Evan's,'' Kathleen corrected, thinking that she had scored a point.

"Well, if she knows that he's dead, how come she's continuing their business as if he's alive?"

"She—" Kathleen stopped and looked from her mother to Susan.

"Because she needs the money that the business earns to live on," Susan suggested. "And Evan is the founder and president—or whatever—of the business, and his clients might get very nervous if they knew he were missing, so it is in her interest if no one knows what's going on."

"You're probably right," Kathleen said, picking up her cup of lukewarm tea.

"On the other hand," Susan continued, "doesn't the business have some assets? If Evan were dead, wouldn't there be something to sell or profit from in some way?"

"Am I interrupting a secret discussion about my Christmas present?" Jed appeared in the open kitchen doorway.

"There's an ink smudge on your face," Susan commented, ignoring his question.

"And I have writer's cramp. Why don't we have our cards printed like other people do?" Jed asked, sitting down in a chair next to his wife and peering over her shoulder to look at his face reflected in the toaster oven. "I do seem a bit inky; I wonder if that pen was leaking."

"Now I know what to get you for Christmas," Susan said, getting up and pulling a paper towel from the rack near the sink. "Would you prefer Paper Mate or Bic?"

"Anything that doesn't leak," Jed answered, taking the towel from her and wetting it with his tongue.

"Jed, what do you know about Evan's business?" Susan asked, looking into the teapot before pouring him another cup.

"Probably not much more than you do. He's a venture cap—"

"But what is his business worth? Is there anything to sell if he's dead?" Susan interrupted.

"I don't know for sure, but I would think so. He invests money . . . and certainly he expects to be paid back with either interest or equity in the project. There would be a certain amount of capital value."

"You mean, his investments in business could be bought or sold, just like stocks or bonds?"

"Sure, just like the bank could sell our mortgage; we'd still owe the money, and whoever held the mortgage would collect the interest. Why do you ask?"

"So, if he's dead—or just missing, for that matter—his business is worth the same as if he were alive."

"I didn't say that," Jed said, working hard on the smudges of ink as he talked. "I would imagine that his reputation has an intrinsic worth that it would be difficult to place an exact dollar value on, but which, if it were eliminated, could cause the company a substantial loss."

Susan looked at the other two women. "We do hope you're going to explain that."

"Well, my guess is that no matter how desperately a company wants investment capital, where—or who—the money comes from is always a factor. After all, it's better to get the money with as few strings attached as possible. An interfering investor wouldn't be as popular as one with a hands-off attitude." He looked around at three blank faces. "Think of it this way: You might need money to buy a house, but you wouldn't want the bank that loaned it to you to tell you what color to paint that house.

"On the other hand," he continued, "the situation with Evan might have been the exact opposite; he might have possessed business experience and acumen that helped the businesses he invested in, and people might have come to him for money, hoping that they could profit in other ways as well." He glanced around to see how they were taking that. "Like if a bank not only gives you a loan, but also does an appraisal of the house and neighborhood to assure you that this particular property is a good investment. Am I making any sense?''

"Then Rebecca may have a good reason to want everyone in the company to think that things are normal—that Evan is still alive.''

"Certainly.'' Jed smiled, thinking that he was at last being understood.

"So it might not be that she killed him, it might be that she's just protecting her money.'' Susan sighed. "So much for a clue.''

"A clue?'' Jed repeated, finishing his cleaning process and putting the towel on the counter.

"We thought that Rebecca was hiding the fact that Evan was killed because she killed him, not that his business would be worth less without him,'' Susan explained.

"Why not both reasons?'' her husband asked sensibly. "Aren't two motives better than one?''

"That's a good point—'' Susan began, stopping almost immediately as more people arrived in her kitchen. "Claire! Dr. Barr! I didn't hear your car.''

"We left it down by the curb so we didn't block anyone in,'' Claire explained. "I invited Bobby in for a cup of herb tea, Susan. I hope you don't mind.''

"Of course not. I'll just boil some water.'' Susan leapt into the role of hostess.

"You do have bottled water, don't you?'' Dr. Barr asked as he helped Claire remove her coat.

"Yes, yes. We do.'' Susan removed the bottle from the refrigerator and noted, with relief, that it wasn't carbonated. She poured it into the teapot, realizing as she did so that she should have poured out whatever water was left in it first. She looked around the room guiltily. As no one seemed to have noticed, she shrugged and put the pot on the burner. Claire was speaking.

". . . just driving around looking at Christmas decorations. Downtown is just beautiful at night with all the tiny white lights outlining each building and all the trees. Hancock has done a remarkable job.''

''Then we toured through the residential sections of town; there are some extraordinary decorations—so unusual,'' Dr. Barr added.

''Did you see the cutouts of Evan and Rebecca in front of their home?'' Susan asked.

''Heavens, yes. What did you think of them?'' Kathleen asked.

''They reminded me of those pictures of Nixon and Bush that you can have your picture taken with,'' Claire said. ''Do you think that's where they got the idea?'' she asked her son.

''How would I know?'' came the huffy reply.

Susan was getting disgusted. He was her own husband; when was he going to grow up? The water was boiling. ''Maybe they were going to use them in that way,'' she suggested. ''Maybe we were all going to get to have our pictures taken with those cutouts the night of the party and then be given the photo to take home.''

''Now that sounds like Evan,'' Jed agreed. ''He used to like to give unusual favors at his parties. Remember the small baskets filled with freesia and splits of champagne that everyone who attended his wedding to Rebecca was given at the door?''

''But that isn't the same thing as having your picture taken with a cutout. Why have a cutout prepared?'' Dolores asked. ''It's not as though they knew Evan was going to disappear, right?''

Susan opened her mouth and nothing came out. Just how much of a coincidence was having the cutouts made right before Evan's death? Was someone planning some sort of strange setup? Was the cutout a stand-in for a dead man?

TWENTY-SIX

Susan COULD SEE THEM ALL LAID OUT UNDER A LARGE balsam standing in the living room bay window; there were dozens of presents, each one happily chosen during the leisurely summer months, each one artfully wrapped while nibbling leftover turkey the first week of December. On the coffee table between the couch and the fireplace stood a magnificent Dickensian plum pudding, a piece of holly sprouting from its shiny crown. It had been aging in brandy since Halloween. On the couch were pillows on which she had embroidered gold angels during cool autumn evenings in Maine, when the stars shimmered in the sky and waves splashed against boulders on the shore. . . .

The grinding wrench of metal hitting metal jarred Susan from her daydreams. In her rearview mirror, she watched a woman in a red Volvo back away from the light pole that had just impaled her car. The accident reminded her that reality was very different. Some of her presents weren't even bought, to say nothing of wrapped, and she could look around the mall parking lot and see that she wasn't alone. A couple of dozen cars sat nearby, their occupants busily checking lists, reading newspapers, or absently drumming polished finger-nails on expensive dashboards and leather-covered steering wheels. These were the early birds, the women who were out to start their shopping the very moment the stores opened.

Or finish their shopping, Susan corrected herself. This one last gift and she would be done until next Christmas. Except that next year was going to be different; next year would match the vision she had just had. But didn't she plan some-thing like this every year? And here she was again, hitting the stores three days before Christmas. A uniformed security guard, busy releasing the lock on the front door of Saks Fifth Avenue, interrupted her reverie and her resolutions. She dropped the newspaper on the floor of the car and got out.

Christmas carols, playing in the same order as on the day after Thanksgiving, greeted her entrance to the store. She headed for the lingerie department. Fifteen minutes, she would give herself just fifteen minutes to pick out a warm robe for Claire and then she would be done.

Twenty minutes later, a dark green cashmere robe folded into a bright red box at the bottom of the large shopping bag she carried, she was ready to leave the store. And she would have made it, if she hadn't remembered Dolores. Kathleen and Jerry were bringing her along to the Henshaws' house for Christmas dinner. Certainly she needed a gift to open while Kathleen and Jerry were opening theirs. Susan looked around at the displays of gifts, some already wrapped, pre-sumably to make them easier to give. What about gloves? she wondered, walking over to an unoccupied counter. She picked up a pair of pale, creamy suede-lined with some sort of fur. Were gloves too unoriginal? She turned over the tags idly in her hands. What was printed on the other side made her decision for her. Two hundred dollars a pair? A hundred dollars apiece? She backed away, smiling tentatively at the salesperson who was heading in her direction.

"Oh, I'm sorry!" Susan turned to apologize to the person whose foot she had stepped on. "Kathleen! Are you hurt?"

Kathleen looked down at her foot. "Everything in its place, nothing to worry about."

"I'm so sorry. I'm glad to see you, though. I need your help."

"What do you need?"

"A suggestion. I want to get Dolores a small gift, but I can't think of anything."

"I can. She's been admiring those large silk bows on barrettes, and one would look nice in her hair," Kathleen suggested. "I was thinking about picking up one myself."

"Don't. I'll get it," Susan said. "It's the last thing I have to buy."

"I still haven't found anything for Jerry," Kathleen said. "I was having an impossible time before he gave me the Jaguar, now it's worse."

"Worse?"

"You know. Now I want to get him something just as special, just as clever; something he's wanted just as much. Except that I don't know what he wants, and whenever I ask, he says that he has everything he wants. You know, I was wondering if he ever wanted to fly. I've been thinking about giving him an ultralight or maybe—"

"I thought Jerry got nervous on those little island hoppers you two took around Barbados last spring," Susan reminded her.

"You're right. I'd forgotten that." Kathleen stared off into space.

"How about some coffee?" Susan suggested. "There's a deli out in the mall."

"I'd like some tea," Kathleen said. "I still feel stuffed from all that food I scarfed down in your kitchen last night."

"Your mother is some cook," Susan observed.

"Definitely. She's spoiling Jerry and I'm gaining weight—

and now she's working on filling my freezer so I won't have to do any cooking after she leaves. To be honest, she's driving me crazy."

"Claire is making Jed a little nuts, too," Susan said, following Kathleen out into the enclosed mall. "She treats him like he was still her little boy, and he treats her as if she's so senile that she needs watching every minute. Every time she leaves the house with Dr. Barr, he paces around and worries until she returns."

"I noticed that last night."

"So Merry Christmas," Susan sighed, opening the door to the deli. "Why are these family celebrations such a strain?"

"Good question." Kathleen followed her to a booth at the back of the room. "You know, I've been thinking about families a lot these days."

"Me, too. Because we were talking about the St. Johns and the Stevensons, you know."

"No, I don't know." Kathleen had been thinking about her mother and her husband.

"Well, it occurred to me that—"

"Kathleen, Susan. It's like a miracle. I was thinking about you both—thinking that you were the only people who could solve my problem. And I looked up and there you were—not just one of you, but both of you."

"Kelly." Kathleen spoke first. "Sit down."

Susan didn't say anything—couldn't say anything. Kelly Knowlson looked as if she hadn't slept all week; her eyes were red, her skin patchy and dry, her lips chapped, her hair only slightly controlled by a terry elastic. Her clothing was a mess, unkempt and unclean, and she was gripping the table as though afraid she might fall over without its dubious support. What was happening? Susan took a deep breath and got up. "Yes, Kelly. Sit down here. In my seat." And she shoved her rather roughly onto the bench.

"Do you want something to eat? Some coffee?" Kathleen asked, moving over so Susan could share her side of the booth.

"No. Nothing. I can't eat. I think I should, but then I can't force myself to put it in my mouth. Just the thought of chewing makes me gag." Kelly wiped her hand across her mouth as she spoke.

"Another cup." Kathleen gave the order to the waitress who had appeared with their order. "And another pot of tea."

"Just something to drink," Susan urged, removing the tea bag and adding two teaspoons of sugar to Kathleen's cup before pushing it across the table at Kelly. "Try it. Just try it."

Kelly stared at the liquid, but didn't move.

"Just try it. If you start feeling sick, we'll go to the ladies' room. When was the last time you ate a meal?" Susan asked.

"I don't remember. The day of Evan's party, I guess. You and I had hot chocolate that night before we found him . . . remember? I may have had some of that," Kelly answered uncertainly. "And I've nibbled on some cookies left over from the cookie exchange, but the thought of a full meal makes me queasy."

"You didn't eat anything for lunch the day after that when I was at your house," Kathleen reminded her.

"I told you . . . It makes me feel sick to even think about eating," Kelly repeated.

Susan pushed the tea closer to her. "Just a small sip. Then I won't say anything else. Please. I'm worried about you."

"Okay. Just a little sip," Kelly agreed. "As soon as it gets cooler." She put her hands around the cup as if to warm them.

Susan noticed that she had bitten all her nails almost down to the cuticle.

"Maybe we should leave here and find someplace better

to talk,'' Kathleen suggested as the room began to fill up with harried shoppers carrying full bags.

"No, I feel comfortable here," Kelly insisted. "Here, I'll try the tea," she offered, like a small child anxious to please.

"Fine," Susan said urging her on. "It will be good for you."

"I guess so." Kelly sipped, swallowed audibly, and looked up at the two women, tears in her eyes. "I'm going to be arrested, aren't I?"

"Arrested?"

"For Evan's death. Even though I didn't do it, of course. He wasn't poisoned." She scrunched up a paper napkin and dabbed at her tears.

"Poisoned? Who said anything about poisoning?" Kathleen asked quickly.

"Evan was shot," Susan insisted. "Why are you talking about poison?"

Kelly took another sip of tea before answering. "It's in the *New York Times* today," she said obliquely.

"What is in the *Times* today?" Susan asked gently, wondering if the strain had driven Kelly mad.

"It's in the gardening column," Kelly said, and started to cry.

"The gardening column?" Kathleen repeated.

Susan, who was sitting where she could see the door of the deli, got up. "Just a sec," she said, hurrying off.

Kelly sat and sipped the tea. Kathleen wondered if everyone was going crazy.

"Here. There was a stand just outside the door. This is today's paper. It's this issue you're talking about, isn't it?" Susan asked Kelly.

Kelly looked at the front page and nodded her head. "Yes. That's it."

Susan pulled the third section from the middle of the pile and opened it from the back. "It's usually . . ." She stopped and began reading as soon as she found the column that Kelly had described. It took a few minutes and, when done, she looked up at Kelly and bit her lip. "Rebecca said they were daffodils," she said.

"Narcissus," came the one-word reply.

"And mistletoe," Susan said.

"And English yew, and the tiny leaves of poinsettias, and lettuce, and mushrooms—"

"Mushrooms?" Susan interrupted to ask.

"From the Grand Union," Kelly explained. "Everything else was just normal salad ingredients."

"Except for the narcissus, and mistletoe, and poinsettia, and English yew," Susan enumerated.

"Yes. They're all Christmas plants, you see," Kelly said, calmer now.

"And the dressing?" Susan asked.

"Oil and vinegar and . . ." Kelly hesitated.

"And?" Susan prompted.

"And a little dribble of Christmas tree preservative—you know, the stuff you buy to put in the tree stand to help the tree stay fresh. I had a bottle around the house and it said it was poisonous." She shrugged. "I didn't add too much. I was afraid it would taste awful."

"You're talking about the salad you brought to Rebecca's house before the party, aren't you?" Kathleen asked, catching on.

"Yes," Kelly answered.

Susan just nodded.

"Can I see the paper?" Kathleen asked.

Susan handed it to her, opening it to the relevant place. Kathleen read it quickly.

"It says these things, these plants, might kill household pets if they were eaten, not people," Kathleen said to Kelly, putting the paper down on the table between them.

"Well, it says they're poisonous," Susan pointed out. "If enough of each plant was eaten . . ."

"But wouldn't the salad taste terrible?" Kathleen asked, thinking of the English yew mixed with tree preservative.

"Probably," Susan agreed.

"I don't know if anyone would have eaten the salad," Kelly said. "I just made it and brought it over to Rebecca's house."

"Well, what did you think would happen to it?" Kathleen asked.

"I didn't think about it at all," Kelly answered. "I just did it."

Susan looked at her curiously. She was beginning to have an idea of what had happened the night Evan died, but she didn't see how it could possibly be true.

TWENTY-SEVEN

THE HENSHAWS' PARTY WAS A SUCCESS.

"Merry Christmas! I can't decide which I like more, the eggnog or that punch of Jed's. What does he call it again?"

"Ivy League Punch," Susan answered, swerving to keep

the two large trays she was holding from being knocked from her hands by a guest too preoccupied with celebrating to notice what he was backing into. "It a secret recipe from his club in college."

"Does that mean you're not going to tell me what's in it?" the questioner wailed.

"Believe me, you don't want to know. Just make sure someone else drives if you have more than two," Susan suggested.

"Not to worry. John Armstrong is driving. He's allergic to evergreens, so this time of year is murder on his sinuses; he's taking so many decongestants that he wouldn't dare touch alcohol."

"Great." Susan smiled and moved on to the kitchen, planning to replenish her buffet table. But she was to hear more about Jed's Ivy League Punch before her errand was accomplished.

"Susan!" Claire grabbed her arm tightly, stopping her progress. "I must talk to you immediately. Dr. Barr says you are poisoning all these people."

"What . . . ?" Susan glanced around to see how her guests were taking this loud accusation. "For God's sake. Watch what you say. Let's go to the kitchen!" Susan grabbed her mother-in-law's arm and pushed her in that direction. "Now what are you talking about?" she asked, twirling around as the kitchen door swung closed behind them.

"That awful punch that Jed makes every year. I was telling Dr. Barr some of the ingredients, and he says it's the same thing as serving your guests poison."

"I—"

"All that fruit and maple syrup and brandy . . ."

"How do you know what's in it?" Susan asked, putting the trays down on the counter and moving over to the table, where full platters awaited her.

"You don't believe that old story about the recipe being a secret from his school club, do you?"

"I . . ." Susan seemed unable to complete a sentence.

"He got that recipe from the first girl he dated after graduating from Yale, and she got it from some old Vermont cookbook of her mother's. Is there any place else in the universe where people would put maple syrup in a drink?"

"But . . ."

"Dr. Barr says that the combination of all those fruit sugars and alcohol is lethal. I didn't want to embarrass Jed by talking about it in front of his friends, but—"

Susan took a deep breath and let her have it. "Claire, Dr. Barr is a guest in our home, not our family physician. I don't expect to get medical advice at a party I'm giving—if it *is* real medical advice and not just some sort of health food garbage," she added angrily.

"Susan . . ." Now Claire appeared to be speechless.

Good thing, Susan thought. But, like many unexpected blessings, it didn't last for long. Claire inhaled and expelled the air noisily. "You are speaking of the man I love," she announced, whirling around toward the door. "And" she paused on the threshold to add, "the man who is going to be your new father-in-law." The door swung shut behind her.

"Oh, no!" Susan slumped against the counter. How was she going to tell Jed? What was he going to say? To do? And could she keep him from finding out about this until after her party? "Oh, damn," she added.

"Pardon?"

Susan turned around to find Kathleen right behind her. "Anything I can do?" she offered.

"What?"

"Are you okay?" Kathleen asked.

"Fine. No, that's not right," Susan said, correcting herself. "I'm awful, and it's going to get worse."

"What can I do?" Kathleen asked again.

"Keep Claire and Dr. Barr away from Jed," Susan suggested, thinking quickly.

"What?" Kathleen looked at Susan curiously. "I came in here to offer to help with the food. What are you talking about?"

"Claire just told me that she and Dr. Barr are going to get married—only that's not the way she put it."

"What did she say?" Kathleen asked.

"She said that I was going to have a new father-in-law. Kathleen, Jed will die."

"Well, he certainly won't be happy about it," Kathleen conceded. "I gather she hasn't said anything to Jed."

"Not that I know of. I can't believe that Jed would keep me in the dark about it. I think if he knew, I would know; we'd probably all hear the yelling."

"You heard us. I thought we were being so quiet!" Kathleen and Susan spun around to find Elizabeth Stevenson behind them, dabbing at her eyes with a linen handkerchief. "Oh, Susan, I'm so sorry. I never meant to have a fight with my husband at your party."

"You— We— Elizabeth. I didn't hear you come in." Susan stopped for a second to figure out what was going on. "We were talking about Jed and me arguing, not you and Derek. But what's wrong? Anything we can help with?" Susan volunteered quickly, hoping to avoid questions about her own marital problems. And it worked.

"Oh, I don't know." Elizabeth flung herself down into a chair, moving aside a tray of vegetables and spinach dip so she would have more space. "Derek is in one of his moods— and you know what that can be like."

"No, I don't," Susan said honestly.

"He criticizes everything I do. I wave my arms around too much; I forget people's names and call them *dear*; I call them *dear* just because I like them; I don't act blasé enough when people are telling me about their most recent purchases; I act too blasé when people tell me about their week at some western fat farm; I forget that it isn't chic to eat a lot at parties; and, of course, I didn't buy the Duchess the right Christmas present. I never do.''

"Duchess?" Susan asked, thinking about a golden retriever she had known by that name.

"My mother-in-law. Everyone calls her the Duchess." Elizabeth picked up a raw mushroom and popped it in her mouth. "The witch is more like it."

"Christmas can be hard on families," Susan muttered tactfully. "We were talking about it the other day, in fact."

"Hard! It's impossible!" Elizabeth chose broccoli this time. "I thought it was difficult when we first got married—you know, adapting my family's holiday traditions to fit Derek's family's. . . . I guess everyone goes through that. But it seems to me that it's gotten worse over the years, not better."

"Worse?" Susan asked.

"Well, at first I just tried to cook all his mother's traditional recipes—and that was terrible because they all took forever. The Duchess has always had someone to cook for her, you see, so it didn't matter if even the tiniest sugar cookie took hours to make. Derek expected that I would follow the same traditions—despite the fact that I didn't have any help! And Christmas gifts were the worst. I would pick up some fabulous material on one of my buying trips and give that to her for a gift. She had this incredible dressmaker who used to make it up. That seemed to work for about four years and then, we were all opening our gifts after the traditional dinner at the house Derek was born in, and his mother told Derek that his wife must think she couldn't pick out her own clothes. And I had given her the most fabulous piece of antique Chinese silk that was still in its box sitting under the tree, I almost died."

"And Derek?" Kathleen asked.

"He was horrible. Just horrible. He actually apologized to her for the choice—and it really was museum quality—and he nagged at me all the way home. The next year he made a big point about how important it was that I buy his mother just the right present—not clothing or fabric, of course, but something personal."

"So?"

"So I brought an antique tea set back from China—that was when Americans were first allowed into the country and some fabulous things were available."

"And?"

"And she hated it. No, that's not true. What she said was that she already had a tea set—a Coalsport one that had been in the family for generations. That she thought of the great traditions of the Stevensons every time she drank from it. You would have thought that I was robbing her life of all its traditions instead of giving her a gift."

"And things haven't gotten a lot better since then," Susan guessed.

"True. It's not just that I buy the wrong thing, it's that I spend hours and hours, and days and days, trying to find just the right thing, and then she hates it."

"Well, if that's the only thing wrong with the holidays," Kathleen began, "why don't you ask Derek to buy his mother's present himself?"

"Because in the Stevenson family, the gift buying is done by the wife," Elizabeth answered unreasonably. "Besides, that's not all that's wrong with Christmas. For me, Christmas is just one long series of pits that I have to jump over instead of fall into."

"I don't understand," Kathleen said. Susan, who had known Elizabeth longer, thought that she did.

"There are a lot of things. Take this party, for instance."

"This party?" Susan repeated.

"Oh, no, Susan. You give a wonderful party," Elizabeth

said, protesting the unasked question. "It's just what happens at parties around Hancock. Everyone knows how to act, what to do. I always seem to be making mistakes."

"Like not acting blasé enough," Kathleen suggested, remembering how this conversation had begun.

"Yes."

"When I first came to Hancock I never knew quite what to wear to parties, or the club," Kathleen said, thinking that she was catching on.

"Oh, clothing is my field. I don't worry about that," Elizabeth said. "In fact, I think Derek married me because he knew I would always wear the right thing. Too bad I wasn't deaf and dumb as well—then he'd still think I'm perfect."

"Elizabeth . . ." Susan couldn't think of anything else to say. What a sad feeling.

Elizabeth Stevenson bit the top off a large blossom of cauliflower and chewed it thoughtfully. "Sometimes you can't win, no matter how much you try."

"Maybe you should stop trying," Kathleen said. "After all, if Derek's mother isn't going to like what you give her anyway . . ."

"And if Derek isn't going to like what I do, no matter how hard I try to do the right thing . . ." Elizabeth sounded pensive. She picked up a thin spear of asparagus and snapped off the head. "Maybe I should do what I want. Shouldn't I?" she appealed to Susan and Kathleen.

"I would," Kathleen said promptly.

"I . . ." Susan thought for a moment that she might be causing an eruption in the Stevenson's marriage—and it might start at her party. Well, what the hell. Maybe Elizabeth would be better off without the Duchess's little boy. "I would, too." Her tone was emphatic.

"Then why am I eating these raw vegetables when there are bowls full of eggnog and punch in the other room?"

Elizabeth asked, standing up with a determined look in her eye.

"I . . ." Susan began, wondering what she had started and why it had to begin at her party. But she didn't have a chance to say anything; Elizabeth was headed out the kitchen door.

"Maybe this year the only thing the Duchess will get for Christmas will be an empty box. A big, beautiful empty box!" Elizabeth elaborated as the door closed behind her.

"I'll keep an eye on her," Kathleen said, following quickly. "And I'll see if anything is happening between Jed and Claire, too."

"Jed and—" Listening to Elizabeth's problem, she had forgotten her own. "Do that," she called after Kathleen. "Please do that," she repeated, picking up two trays of food to bring to her guests. But a stray thought struck her as she followed the other women out the door.

An empty box. Why did that ring a bell?

TWENTY-EIGHT

"OF COURSE, IF SHE KEEPS MARRYING LAWYERS, WHAT can she expect?"

"It's the Merger and Acquisition men who have all the fun these days."

"They were roasting chestnuts in the fireplace—just like in the song—and the chimney caught on fire. Well, eight thousand dollars' worth of repair work had to be done to fix the damage, and he's allergic to nuts anyway."

"He applied for early admission to Tufts and he didn't get in, but we're hoping . . ."

"Our caretaker in the Hamptons died and it turned out he was a millionaire. He invested in the companies of the people he worked for and then, when they stopped paying his bills on time, he would sell at a profit—right before they went bankrupt. He found an infallible system!"

"So this short, fat, bald guy with the pinkest skin I've ever seen stood in front of the room and told us we've got to be lean and mean!"

"Well, it's obvious to me that Kelly kidnapped him. What else could . . ."

So much for small talk. Susan hurried over to the large oval dining room table where she had set up a buffet dinner. She glanced at the table quickly; everything seemed to be in order. The party had begun less than an hour ago and most guests had confined their dignified grazing to the appetizer trays scattered throughout the living room and study. It was these trays that she should be checking. And, she reminded herself, on Jed. And Claire.

But the first person who commanded her attention was Dr. Barr.

"Susan . . ." He touched her shoulder.

"Dr. Barr . . ." If he said something—anything—about the food she was serving . . .

"Wonderful party, my dear. A wonderful, wonderful party. I thank you for inviting me."

"I— You're welcome." How nice that he was being so cordial. Of course, if he was expecting to become a member of the family, how else would he be acting? Well, now was no time to deal with it. She looked around for a distraction and spied Dan Hallard, her next-door neighbor. "Have you met Dan Hallard? You two might have a lot in common. Dan is a doctor, too." A gynecologist is not a podiatrist, but it could be considered the same end of the body, she reminded herself as, smiling at them both, she hurried off to the den to find Jed.

The Henshaws had given this party for almost ten years and they had worked the bugs out of the system. The bar's location had changed a couple of times in the first few years, coming to rest in the corner of Jed's study. As usual, there were a dozen or so men standing around and talking. She greeted a number of them on the way to her husband.

"Well, here comes your beautiful wife," said one of their more avuncular neighbors, moving back to allow her access to Jed, who was busy pouring Ivy League Punch into small round glasses.

"Have you had some of the punch this year? I think it's better than ever." Jed smiled at his wife.

"Your mother and I were just talking about the recipe," Susan replied, matching his smile. "I—"

"My mother . . . ?" Jed's eyes asked the question that he didn't want anyone to hear.

Susan decided that one of her Christmas presents to her husband would be not revealing his tradition as a fraud. "Yes," she answered. "She thinks your punch is a lethal combination. And Dr. Barr—"

"Dr. Barr loves it," Jed interrupted, looking relieved. "I think he's had three or four glasses already."

"He has?" Susan picked up a glass of red wine and sipped. "That's interesting."

"Why?"

"Well, it isn't exactly health food."

"Maybe he's turning over a new leaf. I saw him eating shrimp a few minutes ago."

"Dr. Barr?" Susan repeated. This personality change was really remarkable.

"Yes, Dr. Barr. I looked twice," her husband assured her.

Susan sipped her wine as another guest stopped to chat with Jed. Dr. Bobby Barr was certainly acting strange—or could he have a twin brother who was taking his place tonight? He certainly wasn't acting in character, or like the character that he was, to be more exact. Or the character that he was pretending to be, she thought suddenly. Maybe Dr. Barr wasn't who he said he was and all his strong likes and dislikes were just an act. Why hadn't she and Kathleen looked up his credentials at the library? Or had Kathleen? Susan walked away from her husband's group without a word.

She found Kathleen just where the other woman had said

she would be—talking with Claire and keeping her from announcing her engagement to Jed.

Except that her impending marriage didn't seem to be on Claire's mind. She was more interested in the gardening section of yesterday's *Times*.

". . . I met a woman on the cruise who was talking about that same thing. She had a grandchild—a boy I believe—who ate the leaves—because they're really leaves on the poinsettia, not flowers, you know—and he was very sick. I think she said he was in the hospital for weeks and there was some possibility of brain damage—or was it liver damage? Well, we only have one of each so it's serious no matter which one it was."

"I think they're called bracts." Susan hadn't noticed that Dolores had joined the group.

"What are, Mother?"

"The leaves on the poinsettias."

"I—" Claire seemed anxious to retain control of the conversation.

"But I didn't know that they were poisonous," Dolores interrupted.

"Yes, very. I was just telling your daughter about the woman on my cruise whose grandson—"

"We were given a beautiful poinsettia plant by one of the men that Jed works with, Claire. And two of the guests brought white poinsettias as hostess gifts." Susan's suggestion that maybe this conversation might offend someone was blithely ignored.

"I heard that Kelly brought a salad to Evan's party that was full of poinsettia leaves—bracts," Claire announced. "We all could have been killed if it had been served."

"I had some salad at that party . . ." Dolores seemed concerned.

"So did I." Claire rubbed her stomach as though looking for a protruding piece of poison.

"The salad Kelly brought wasn't served," Susan assured the woman. "It—it was spilled before it got to the table. How did you hear about it anyway? I mean what the salad was made from?"

"Susan, everyone is talking about it. There was something in one of the papers about poisonous plants. Rebecca is saying that Kelly tried to kill Evan and all their guests, and that she should be locked up," Claire explained.

"I don't think they can arrest her for intent to kill," Dolores said. "Especially since nothing happened; the salad wasn't even served."

"I think— Oh, hello, Kelly. I didn't know you were here," Susan said loudly, hoping her mother-in-law would forgive the kick in the shins once she knew the reason. Kelly, wearing a full-length kilt and dark green silk blouse, looked neater than Susan had seen her since the cookie party. She smiled sincerely. "You haven't met Jed's mother yet, have you? And Kathleen's mother, either?"

"Yes, I've been wanting to get you two together," Kathleen added. "Remember, I was telling you about the minestrone that my mother makes? And I know she would love to hear how you make those wonderful little Italian rolls."

Dolores looked a little startled, possibly at the thought of sharing recipes with someone whose favorite ingredients included toxic plants, but she had never been completely successful with bread. "Do you let it rise once or twice? I've tried both, but never been able to tell the difference. I never get a really crunchy crust."

"Oh, I have an easy way to get a really crunchy crust; I glaze the loaf all over with a mixture of yeast and water," Kelly started enthusiastically.

"If you'll excuse me," Susan said. "I have some errands in the kitchen. Will you help me, Kath?"

"Of course, of course. Be sure to have my mother tell you about the soup." She squeezed Kelly's arm in parting.

"Do you want me to help you carry things or what?" Kathleen asked as they passed through the swinging door into the kitchen.

"Neither," Susan whispered. "I just wanted to talk to you someplace private."

"Fine."

"Don't sit down. This isn't going to take very long," Susan said. "Kath, did you look up Dr. Barr's credentials in that book at the library?"

"Is that all you want? Yes, I did. There weren't any real surprises and he didn't lie about anything. He graduated from an accredited medical school in Philadelphia; he did his internship at a hospital out on Long Island; he's a certified podiatrist. There was no mention of any study in nutrition, but there probably wouldn't be. He's not doing anything illegal. He represents himself as a medical doctor and he gives advice about nutrition. Fair enough. The information I got anyone can get. It's printed yearly in one or two medical reference books—almost all libraries have them. Why all the interest now?"

"He's out there eating seafood and drinking Jed's punch."

"Not part of his usual creed, is it?" Kathleen asked thoughtfully.

"No. You know, for a moment I wondered if his identical twin was attending this party for him."

"That's an interesting thought," Kathleen said.

"I'm having a lot of interesting thoughts these days," Susan replied smugly. "And I know if I could just attach them all together, I'd get a complete picture of what happened." She frowned and licked the last of her lipstick off her mouth. "Well," she sighed, "I'd better get back to my guests."

"Do that," Kathleen urged. "I'm going to sit at your kitchen table and put my feet up for a few minutes. These shoes are killing me."

"Can I bring you anything?" Susan asked.

"No, I'll be out soon. Shouldn't you be carrying a dish of food or something? You did say you were going to the kitchen for a reason, remember."

"That's right." Susan hurried to the refrigerator and grabbed a large pitcher of foamy eggnog. "I'll go fill up the bowl in the living room."

"Great." Kathleen had reached under the chair where she had stuffed her purse earlier in the evening and was rummaging through it. Finding what she wanted, she pulled out a small, half-filled notebook and a gold pen. She ruffled through the sheets to the page labeled BARR in capital letters and, picking up the pen, she added a few words to her notes on the subject: family? twins? look-alikes? She skimmed through the rest of the notebook smiling. It was just like the old days when she was investigating for the police. Every answer seemed to lead to two more questions. Sometimes three.

But the question of twins was something to consider, and she leafed through the notebook for Thomas and Travis's page. Was it significant that they shared one page—that they were not listed as individual suspects, but as a team? She would have considered the question in more detail, but the kitchen door opened suddenly, and half a dozen women came dashing into the room.

TWENTY-NINE

THE PARTY WAS OVER. THE BEDS WERE NO LONGER COVERED with coats and scarves; the street was no longer lined with parked cars; the windows were open to let out the accumulated scents of perfume and cigarette smoke. And the Henshaws were still washing the carpet.

"Will it stain?" Claire asked anxiously.

"It's so wet, I really can't tell. But I keep thinking about all those eggs and heavy cream that have probably seeped through to the padding. I don't want the living room to smell like rotten eggs." Susan scrubbed harder as she spoke.

"Maybe the bourbon will act as a preservative," Jed suggested, entering the room. "Are you going to need this?" He indicated the bucket of fresh soapy water he was carrying.

"Maybe one more rinse, just to make sure," Susan answered.

"This is going to be the best-washed carpet in Connecticut," Claire commented as Susan took the water from Jed. "After all, one or another of your neighbors was busy cleaning it for the last few hours or so." She moved a pillow

227

behind the small of her back. "That was some spill, I must say," she added.

Jed chuckled. "I'm sorry I missed it. From what I heard, the moment of impact between the glass pitcher and the punch bowl was only slightly less than extraordinary."

"I still don't understand why you threw the pitch—" Claire began.

"I didn't throw anything," Susan insisted, not for the first time. "The pitcher slipped from my hands; it's just unfortunate that it fell into the punch bowl."

"And that they were both crystal," Claire added. "You know, there are some attractive plastics on the market these days. Maybe you should look into that when you get around to replacing what you broke tonight." She yawned.

"Mother, why don't you go to bed? Susan and I can finish up here by ourselves," Jed said quickly, understanding that his wife didn't need any more questions or suggestions right now.

"That's a good idea," Susan chimed in enthusiastically. "Why don't you go up, too, Jed? It's almost two A.M., and I'm going to quit. This can dry, and we'll see what it looks like in the morning."

"When—" Jed started, helping his mother to stand.

"In just a few minutes," his wife answered his unasked question. "There are some things I want to do. Go up and turn on the electric blanket. I'll be in bed before it has time to warm up," she added, knowing he would be asleep the moment he got into bed and wouldn't notice if she was lying. She dropped the sponge into the bucket and stood up.

"You do look tired, Jeddy."

"Well," he said, hesitantly, "I do have some shopping to finish up tomorrow, and it would be easier if I got to the stores early."

"You'd better. Everyone and his cousin will be shopping the last Saturday before Christmas," Susan reminded him.

"You should have shopped earlier. After all, it isn't as though you didn't know Christmas was coming. You've always been one for putting things off. I remember how you used to study for tests at the last minute. And you were always up late the night before your term papers were due."

"Why don't we go upstairs like Susan suggested?" Jed reminded himself that this was the season of peace and goodwill toward men—and that probably included mothers.

Susan left mother and son to squabble their way to bed, and, picking up her buckets and sponges, she headed to the kitchen. Once there, she dumped the buckets into the sink, squeezing out the sponges before throwing them into the trash compactor. She left the now-empty buckets at the head of the basement stairs, and left, heading for the study and, not incidentally, to the bar, where she helped herself to a large goblet of burgundy.

She loved the time after a party. Especially a successful party, like this one had been. Although, she smiled to herself, there had been moments when she worried. She sipped her wine and remembered. Kelly's entrance had upset a lot of people; conversation had stopped, one or two snide comments had been made, Rebecca had looked as if she was barely resisting an urge to kill. Her second urge to kill? Susan mused, pulling candle stubs from their holders and throwing them into the embers of the fireplace. She watched them flare up and took another sip from her glass. Maybe her accident with the eggnog had been an unconscious inspiration after all. It had certainly given everyone something to think about, and anyone who wanted could keep busy by offering to help. She smiled again, remembering how many women had mopped and sponged down the coffee table and the rug. Luckily no one had been cut on slivers of glass. Too bad about the pitcher, but she had hated that punch bowl since they had gotten it as a wedding present.

She put down her glass and checked around the rest of the

room. Ashtrays had been dumped in the fireplace, extra Ivy League Punch had been returned to the refrigerator in the basement. She reached into the straw pot holding a large red poinsettia, pulled out some napkins a guest had stashed there, and threw them into the wastebasket. Then she walked around the room once more, switching off lights as she went. Glass in hand, she left the study and circled the first floor of the house, straightening and thinking. Until getting to the kitchen.

Usually a complete mess, the commotion of her accident had mobilized a number of women, some of whom appeared to have cleaned counters, emptied trays, and rewrapped leftovers. Jed had carried numerous bags of garbage to the garage along with all the broken glass. Her dishwasher was humming through its third load of glasses, with one last pile of odds and ends waiting their turn. Susan put her glass on the table and sat down to pull off her shoes and stockings. Then she raided the refrigerator. Shrimp and crab legs, smoked salmon and caviar on crackers, pâté and spinach dip; she loaded a large plate. Desserts filled another. She grabbed some silverware and sat back down at the table. Any other time, she would have feasted and enjoyed herself. Tonight she had work to do. Kathleen had left the notebook she was keeping on the case, and Susan had promised to read it and add anything she thought pertinent.

She picked up a shrimp, dipped it in sauce, opened the book, and started to read. Was it surprising that Kelly's name was on the first page?

THIRTY

THE PHONE HAD BEEN RINGING SINCE EIGHT A.M.

"Do you always get so many calls on Saturday mornings?" Claire asked, handing Susan another Santa-and-elf covered package.

"Always on the morning after a party," Susan answered, removing the paper. "Another bottle of Irish Cream! There must have been a sale at the store!" The import of Claire's question hit her as she put the liquor on a tray with half a dozen twins. "Why do you ask? Did the phone wake you this morning?"

"It's just that Bobby said he would call early and I don't see how he's going to get through." The phone rang as she spoke.

Susan answered and then passed the receiver to Claire. "It's for you. The call you've been waiting for."

Claire beamed and took it. "Hello? Bobby . . . Yes. I know. Susan's friends have been tying up the line all morning."

Susan decided to open the rest of her hostess gifts later

and left the room just as Jed came downstairs, a notebook in his hand.

"I gather this is what you were reading in bed last night."

"I thought you were asleep. I'm sorry if I bothered you. It's Kathleen's. She asked me to go through it and add any ideas I had—"

"Mother!" Chrissy appeared in her father's wake. "Seth said he was going to call this morning—early this morning. And I don't see how he's going to get through. Can't you ask your friends to call some other time? Can't—"

"Your grandmother is on the phone with Dr. Barr," her mother interrupted. "Why don't you wait until she's off, then call Seth before the next call comes through?"

"But he's supposed to call me!" Chrissy wailed.

Susan shrugged. She couldn't handle her family's romantic problems. "Then I don't know what I can do about it." She turned to her husband. "I thought you were going to get up early and hit the malls?"

"Best laid plans." He laughed. "But I'm on my way out the door."

"What about breakfast?"

"I'll get something while I shop. Don't worry about me."

"If you're sure." Susan looked around the hall. Chrissy had vanished and Chad had yet to appear. "Are you going to be able to pick up the stuff at the ski shop? They promised everything would be wrapped and ready for you. But, if you're in a hurry, I could do it."

"Would you mind? I really could use the time."

Christmas was tomorrow. She wouldn't kill him. "No problem. Have a nice time."

He didn't even pause long enough for her to grab a kiss. Susan shrugged again and glanced down at the notebook Jed had handed her. She could return it to Kathleen when she dropped the skis off at her house. She could hear her mother-in-law and her daughter chatting in the kitchen. Let them take care of each other she decided, and headed upstairs to tell her son that she was going out.

Twenty minutes later she was standing in line at the ski shop. Sure enough, she'd been right when she told Jed that the stores were going to be jammed; this place was packed with shoppers. Cranky shoppers, Susan found out to her embarrassment when she asked one of the people behind the counter if she had to wait in line just to pick up a purchase. Half of the people in line frowned at her; the other group made audible comments. She resumed her place in line (had that woman with the ugly brown coat cut in front of her?) and, feeling like hiding, opened Kathleen's notebook. Maybe she'd go through the names of the suspects one last time . . .

"What is my name—and my husband's name—doing there? What are you reading?"

Susan snapped the book shut and spun around to face Barbara St. John.

"Well, what's my name doing there? You can't deny it; it's written down in block letters and I had ample time to see it."

"I—um . . . Barbara, what are you doing here? Last night you were saying that you were finished with your Christmas shopping!" Susan evaded the subject, trying desperately to think of an answer.

"You're not answering my question, Susan. Don't try to put me off by babbling about Christmas gifts."

That was the answer. "Then you've probably guessed," Susan said, working to place a smile on her face. "You were looking over my shoulder at my Christmas gift list—the list of people I bought presents for this year," she explained.

"Christmas gifts . . ." Susan watched as the look on Barbara's face changed from anger to embarrassment and then to something resembling irritation as she realized she was going to have to return the favor—that her Christmas shopping wasn't finished after all. "You didn't have to do that," she said sincerely.

"Well, we've seen so much more of each other this year. With the kids dating and all." Susan tried to explain this sudden closeness with the St. John family. "I just thought . . ."

"But it's so nice of you, Susan. So thoughtful." Barbara seemed to be thinking about something.

"So what are you doing here?" Susan asked, more to keep the conversation going than because she was interested.

"Waiting for Rebecca. She asked me to meet her here. She's buying new boots for the boys for Christmas. I got here early and decided to wait in line. To save her a place.

"That was a nice party last night. I was a little surprised that you had invited both Kelly and Rebecca, though. It was very embarrassing for Rebecca, you know. You really should have altered your guest list—especially after Evan's disappearance."

If she had bought this woman a gift, she'd never give it to her now, Susan decided. Just why did Barbara think she could censor the guests Susan had in her home? How rude. And this was the woman who was always claiming to be so au courant about manners and social customs. She almost, but not quite, sniffed aloud her disapproval. "I sent out the invitations before Evan disappeared, and I certainly couldn't change them when he vanished. Besides, how was I to know that he wasn't going to return from this business trip . . . or whatever it is that Rebecca says he's taken?"

"Are you accusing me of lying?"

Susan didn't have to turn around to find out who was talking this time. "Rebecca." She paused. "I wasn't accusing you of anything. I was just explaining to Barbara why Kelly was invited to the party last night." She had to face her. She turned slowly.

"You know, Susan, you're beginning to believe this silly little game you play. You're not a real detective, you know.

Aren't you going to move up?" she continued before Susan could think of something to say. "Everyone ahead of you appears to have been waited on."

"Oh, yes, Susan. You'd better move," Barbara agreed.

Susan recognized that they had closed ranks; she wouldn't learn more. She handed the receipt she had been clutching in her hand to a tired-looking salesman and, collecting a note to take around to the loading dock, she said her farewells and departed. A quick glance behind her as she opened the door for an elderly woman juggling a gigantic pair of Muk Luks and a snowboard revealed Barbara and Rebecca deep in conversation.

Fortunately the line at the loading dock moved more quickly than the previous one, and she was done and out of the parking lot in minutes. Knowing she would never get such large packages into the house undetected, Susan had arranged to drop them off at Kathleen's. She drove over to her house immediately.

And almost ran into her friend's car backing out of the driveway.

"I'll be home in about fifteen minutes," Kathleen called, slowing down for just a minute. "I have one quick errand. My mother's home. She knows where to put the skis. Wait for me; I want to talk to you!" She waved out the window of the long sports car and sped off down the road.

Susan didn't think she had any choice but to do what Kathleen asked. She and Kathleen had to decide how to get these gifts to the Henshaw house before tomorrow morning. Besides, she wanted to return the notebook in person. "Hello?" she called out, opening the front door.

"I'm in the kitchen."

"Hi. Would you like some company? I'm going to wait for Kathleen to return. Or maybe you could use some help?" Susan leaned the skis against the wall and looked around the room. Dolores seemed to have filled the kitchen with tomato sauce. There were copper pans of it, ceramic bowls of it, even a large enameled stockpot bubbling over with crushed tomatoes and little bits of herbs.

"I'm just getting the gravy ready for tonight." Dolores stirred as she spoke.

"Gravy?"

"That's what we call tomato sauce in my family. This is a traditional recipe; I brought some of the ingredients from the market in Philadelphia. I wasn't sure I could find fresh oregano and fennel in Connecticut."

"You can probably buy it at that wonderful herb shop up near Kent." Susan continued to expound on her adopted state's resources—until she realized no one was listening. She shut up, took off her coat, and dropped it across a chair.

"Watch where you put that. Kathleen was sitting there when she chopped the onions and garlic for me," Dolores warned, stirring the pot vigorously.

"I see what you mean." Susan laughed, flicking yellow onion skins off the seat and sitting down. "Is there anything I can do to help?' she offered again.

"Just keep me company. I can't imagine how Kathleen manages to cook on this terrible electric stove; I keep having to stir, stir, stir. If I leave it for a minute, it starts to scorch on the bottom."

"Maybe the pan—"

"I brought this pan from home. I've been making gravy in it for years. Years," she repeated, stirring away, "and I've never had any trouble with burning." She sighed and changed the subject. "Who do you think killed Evan Knowlson?"

"I wish I knew. I think the police suspect Kelly," Susan answered.

"Kelly didn't do it."

"She— How can you be so positive?" Susan asked. But, if she was hoping for proof, she certainly wasn't getting any.

"She loved that man— No, she was obsessed by him,"

Dolores corrected herself. "She would kill for him, but she wouldn't kill him. At least, that's the way I read it."

"I—" Susan began.

"I know Kathleen thinks I'm nothing more than a domestic, but my husband used to depend on my intuition. I don't know anything about law enforcement, but I have a lot of feminine intuition . . . . Damn this stove." She stirred vigorously.

"But you don't have any proof that Kelly didn't do it—or that someone else did?"

"I just know she couldn't have done it."

"Me, too," Susan agreed. "But our combined intuition won't hold up as a defense."

"I think Rebecca did it. Prove that and Kelly won't have to worry."

"But Rebecca loved him, too—apparently," Susan added, interested that Dolores had happened on her favorite suspect.

"Maybe. Or maybe not. But she gets all the money, doesn't she?"

"The money?" Susan repeated.

"Yes. She was his wife at the time he died; she gets his estate. She profits. Kelly, on the other hand, loses. After all, you can't collect alimony from a dead ex-husband."

"No, that's not true," Susan said, and explained about the two-million-dollar insurance policy.

"But Rebecca? How large an insurance policy did he take out in her name?" Dolores wasn't as willing to give up.

"None."

"None? That doesn't make any sense. Maybe that means he didn't love her . . . Maybe that's the reason she killed him—revenge for taking better care of his ex-wife than of her." Dolores was ready to change her theory to fit new facts—just as long as the same party was guilty.

"It doesn't mean that. Evan tried to get another policy right after he got married," Kathleen explained, entering the room. "He couldn't find an insurance company that would sell to him."

"Why not?" Susan asked. She hadn't heard this before.

"Not even Lloyd's of London would sell two large life insurance policies to a slightly overweight, definitely over-stressed man in his late forties, Susan."

"So who gets the houses? The business?" Dolores asked.

"The houses are both mortgaged and the business recently seems to have been collecting massive debt. There isn't any estate. Evan hadn't even paid the bill I sent him for security for the new house."

"I guess you've run into another dead end," Dolores said smugly.

"Maybe not," Kathleen insisted, with a slight smile at her mother.

"Would you kindly explain instead of making these abstract statements?" Dolores asked, and turned to Susan. "She was just like this when she was a little girl. Totally unwilling to admit that she'd made a mistake."

"I think—" Susan began.

"I didn't make a mistake, Mother. You did."

"I was just explaining what I thought were possible motives. You appear to be taking this the wrong way. After all, I was a great help to your father in his investigations. You could have merely said something if you wanted me to mind my own business. I was just trying to help, you know." She stirred so energetically that tomato sauce spurted out of the stockpot and over the stove top. "There, look what you made me do. This wouldn't have happened if you had bought a proper gas stove. How do you ever expect to learn to cook on this thing?"

"I am doing just fine," Kathleen said angrily, grabbing a sponge and dabbing furiously at the mess. "Jerry is very happy with my cooking."

"Why, Kathleen!" Her mother stepped back and looked

at her in surprise. "Just last night he was saying that he had gained five pounds since I arrived! Now if that isn't a sign that he prefers my cooking, I don't know what it is."

"Jerry doesn't need to gain weight." Kathleen talked and ground her teeth at the same time.

Susan was impressed with this talent, but didn't feel the need to witness it for long. "Isn't that nice? But Jerry is always talking about what an inventive cook Kathleen is; she even makes sushi!"

"And I know why. If I had to use this stove, I'd serve raw food, too," Dolores muttered, moving the pot off the hot burner. "You and Susan had better leave me alone, if I'm going to get this meal ready before tonight."

"I—"

"We will. I know how good cooks like to be left alone in the kitchen," Susan said loudly, drowning out Kathleen's voice and pushing her out of the room in front of her.

"I—" Kathleen began again.

"Shut up!" Susan insisted as the door swung shut behind them. "How are we going to solve this murder if you spend your time fighting with your mother?"

"It keeps us busy when you're not worrying about your mother-in-law!" Kathleen hissed back.

Susan opened and shut her mouth without saying a word. What was there to say?

THIRTY-ONE

It was a topic that was tiring Susan. "Jed and his mother," she said pensively. "You know, it's worse than you think. He's talking about hiring a detective to find out what's going on there."

"Well, that *is* ridiculous. She's a grown woman; no matter what she might be doing with Dr. Barr, it's certainly her own business."

"He's not worried about what they're doing—at least that's not what he's telling me. He's talking about hiring someone to look into Dr. Barr's finances . . . His diet food company and all. He's acting like Dr. Barr is a fortune hunter of some sort and his mother is an heiress. It's crazy."

"Well, maybe not so crazy. I thought the same thing for a while. In fact, I had a friend of mine get hold of all the information he could on Dr. Barr's Diet Plan and it's on the up-and-up. I mean, I don't know if it works, if it will actually help anyone lose weight, but the company is solvent—and growing. He recently got a contract from a chain of health food stores. It's not millions of dollars, but it's pretty good

240

for a business that's only a few years old. I don't think Jed has anything to worry about. Unless he objects to a rich doctor being his new stepfather.''

"Maybe he just objects to having a stepfather.''

"Susan, do you really think Jed is like that? Don't you think he would be happy for his mother to find someone to spend the rest of her life with?''

"Well, I would have thought that until she appeared with this particular someone. But Jed doesn't seem to be able to cope.''

"This being the man, not the situation,'' Kathleen said gently.

"Yes. I guess you're right. He really is an awful man, isn't he?''

"Yes. Do you know how they met?''

"Sure. Claire told me about it the other night. She evidently considers it to be a romantic story.''

"So tell me,'' Kathleen urged.

"Well, you know Claire had been on this cruise since Thanksgiving . . .''

"Yes, it was just a normal vacation, right?''

"Right. In fact, from the postcards she was sending, we were even beginning to worry that she was finding the whole trip a little boring. On one of them she said that she had run into the Jeffersons—you know, Marge and Donald from over on Spring Court—and they had spent hours together talking about Christmas in Hancock. What a way to spend an evening in Istanbul! Anyway, after she told us about that, Jed and I got the idea that she was anxious to get off the boat and come home to celebrate. In fact, that was my first thought when she appeared a week earlier than expected. Who thought she was here to be with Dr. Barr, not us?''

"No one. So tell me how they met.''

"Oh, well; it sounds like a rather tacky shipboard pickup if you ask me, which, fortunately, Claire didn't. According to her, she was standing at the rail of the boat late one night, watching the reflection of the full moon on the water, when he came up to her from behind and introduced himself, confessing to admiring her for the entire journey but only now getting up the courage to speak. I ask you!'' Susan rolled her eyes. ''That man is making her act like a teenager!''

''So it wasn't until late in the trip that he introduced himself?'' Kathleen asked.

''Yes. The tour went from Athens, around the Aegean Sea, and out to Egypt. They spent three nights in Istanbul, and then headed back out in the Mediterranean. It was before they got to Egypt that he spoke to her.''

''And then they came home early.''

''Yes, the ship was scheduled to spend five days going down the Nile, but she and Dr. Barr decided to skip that and rush home to tell her loved ones about their engagement.''

''That's not right, Susan.''

''Huh?''

''You're jumping the gun. They weren't engaged when they arrived.''

Susan thought about that for a moment. ''No, I guess you're right; they weren't. Although Claire was obviously ready to say yes to anything he suggested. I suppose Jed should be happy Dr. Barr suggested marriage instead of running off to a commune in New Mexico.''

Kathleen allowed herself a chuckle before getting serious again. ''So why did they come home early?''

Susan opened her mouth to answer before realizing that she didn't have an answer. ''I don't know. I really don't know.''

''But she must have offered some explanation. She didn't just call and say she was coming early, did she?''

''You know,'' Susan began slowly, ''that's exactly what she did do. I was so busy cleaning and getting ready that I didn't think about why.''

"And you haven't asked since then?"

"No." Susan shrugged. "She was here, the house was cleaned, her damn diet food was filling up the kitchen. I really didn't worry about anything else." If she sounded a little defensive, it was because she felt slightly guilty. She had been letting a lot just pass over her; she had to admit it.

"Why should you have?" Kathleen soothed her. She had stood up and was staring out the window. The phone on the coffee table rang, and she reached over to answer it.

Susan got up, planning on going to the kitchen to talk with Kathleen's mother and, at the same time, give Kathleen some privacy. But the call ended before she was out the door.

"Where are you going?"

Susan turned around and discovered that a look of complete happiness had supplanted the musing look on her friend's face.

"I was going . . ." She gave up the thought as unimportant. "What are you looking so thrilled about?"

"Oh . . ." Kathleen paused—as if to remember what had given her so much joy. "That call," she explained. "It was about Jerry's Christmas present."

"What are you getting him?" Susan asked, thinking that the sheepskin coat she had ordered for Jed, while appropriate, wasn't going to give anyone the happiness that the thought of this particular gift was evidently giving Kathleen.

"It's a surprise," Kathleen answered. "Now what were we talking about?"

"The murder. How could you forget? Kathleen, was that call really about Jerry's present?" She couldn't believe that Kathleen's mind had wandered so far and so fast. And where to?

"Oh, yes. Well, I've given it all a lot of thought and I certainly haven't come to any conclusions." Kathleen fiddled with the cord of the phone while speaking.

Susan stared at her friend. She'd just been given the brush-off. She blinked twice and opened her mouth once before anything came out. "I'll say good-bye to your mother before I leave. By the way, what time do you want us for dinner?"

"I—I'm not sure. Ask my mother."

"I'll do that." She hesitated again. "Bye?" It was almost a question.

"Bye." It was automatic. Susan headed for the kitchen. Maybe Dolores had some ideas about this present that was so remarkable even its giver was struck dumb.

But Dolores professed to know nothing and, after a perfunctory conversation about plans for the evening, Susan found herself back in her car with absolutely no idea where to go or what to do. It was Christmas Eve. After running around all week, her shopping was done, most of the meal for tomorrow prepared, everything was wrapped and decorated. Since the family's traditional oyster stew feast had been replaced by Dolores's dinner tonight, Susan found herself uniquely unoccupied. She wanted to do something Christmassy, but wondered if she was bound to go on investigating the murder. After all, as soon as the body was found, Kelly probably would be arrested and—

The answer was staring her in the face. She would go home, collect one of the half dozen fruitcakes that had been aging in the back of her linen closet, and take it to Kelly. Two birds with one stone. She smiled to herself.

She was still smiling when she walked up the path to Kelly's house, beribboned fruitcake in her hands. The door chime played the first four notes of "Silent Night," an innovation she hadn't noticed at the cookie party, and she waited for Kelly happily. Then the door opened.

It was probably a good thing Rebecca had abstained from alcohol last night, because Kelly appeared to have drunk her share and another person's besides. She was obviously hung over—or possibly in the later stages of a fatal illness.

"That damn bell," she stated, feebly pulling open the

door and leaning against it. "Oh, Susan. Good to see you. Come on in."

Susan had to push Kelly aside gently to carry out her wishes, and, once inside, she had to turn around and pull the door closed after her. Kelly appeared unable to move.

"I think I have the flu—or something." Kelly leaned against the wall and closed her eyes.

" 'Or something,' I believe. How much did you have to drink last night?" Susan asked, taking her hostess gently by the arm and leading her into the living room.

"Drink? I don't drink," Kelly protested, sitting down in one of the plaid chairs in front of the fireplace.

"Maybe you had some eggnog last night?" Susan suggested quietly, remembering the quarts of bourbon that had gone into that white, fluffy beverage.

"Yes, and it was delicious, Susan. You must give me your recipe. But I didn't have more than a few cups of eggnog. I have to admit, though"—she giggled as girlishly as a woman over forty can—"that I fell for Jed's punch. I must have had five glasses. I asked him what was in it, and he told me the secret ingredient. I don't think I've ever had maple syrup in a drink before."

Or so much alcohol, Susan thought, giving up trying to figure out just how many pints of eighty proof Kelly had consumed. No wonder she was feeling terrible. "What did you think about the food?"

"Food! I didn't have any food. I was much too upset to eat anything." Kelly closed her eyes after this protest.

Susan, left on her own, looked around the room. A large white pine stood before the bay window, perfectly decorated and surrounded by wrapped presents. A large one at the front of the pile was topped with an unusual and gigantic gold star. Susan glanced at Kelly and then, deciding she was asleep, got up to take a closer look. It appeared to be some sort of complicated origami. She was just wondering if Kelly had

made it herself when she noticed the gift tag on the present:
TO EVAN. WITH LOVE FROM KELLY.

Susan sat back on her heels and stared at the words. Wasn't
it a little unusual to have a gift for your ex-husband under
your Christmas tree? Especially if he was dead? She opened
her mouth to say something when the long box next to it
caught her eye. The gift was obviously a tie; the tag was
identical to that on the first gift she had looked at.

Susan carefully shuffled through the gifts under the tree.
One and all, absolutely, positively, each one, was from Kelly
and for Evan. What could it mean? Was Barbara right in
suggesting that Kelly was crazy?

"Susan?"

She spun around, knocking a tiny tin angel off the tree. "I
was just admiring your tree." Susan picked up the ornament
and rehung it while speaking. "I love these bows; they're
made out of paper or something, aren't they? Or origami?"
she added, when Kelly didn't answer.

"No," Kelly said finally. "They're not origami. They're
German. I learned how to make them in Europe a few years
ago. Why were you going through my gifts?"

"They're all from you to Evan," Susan said, wondering
if she would get a response.

"Yes. I've been buying them ever since last fall. Well, not
quite that early. Since a little before Thanksgiving, though."

"Why?"

"Why?" Kelly seemed surprised by the question. "Because I love him. I always buy him a lot of presents. Don't
you buy things for Jed?"

"Yes, but . . ." Well, what would she do if, God forbid,
Jed died right before Christmas? Pull his gifts out from under
the tree? But she was married to Jed, she reminded herself,
before she accepted Kelly's actions as normal. And, if Jed
had left her for another woman, she certainly wouldn't give

him a colored paper clip for Christmas, to say nothing of this extraordinary haul!

Kelly seemed able to read her mind. ''I told you that he was going to come back to me, didn't I? I thought it would be before Christmas.''

''But—but you saw his body in this room. You were with me. You know that he's dead.'' Susan insisted on some sort of sanity.

Kelly's eyes filled with tears. ''That wasn't supposed to happen, Susan. I didn't know what to do. So I just continued on with the way everything was planned. I even bought gifts for all Evan's business acquaintances. He insisted on nice gifts for everyone who did business with him and he always trusted me to buy them for him. Look!'' She leapt up with more energy than Susan would have thought she had and opened a large built-in cupboard next to the fireplace. ''Look!''

And Susan looked. There must have been thirty brightly wrapped gifts, stacked carefully in the space, each one labeled, each one tied with that distinct star-bow. But there was something unusual here. ''Kelly, I didn't know—'' she started to say when the front door opened and Elizabeth and Barbara walked into the house, arguing as they entered.

THIRTY-TWO

THEY STOPPED ARGUING LONG ENOUGH TO ATTEMPT TO draw Susan into the fray.

"Susan, thank heavens you're here. This woman and Rebecca have gone completely crazy. They are talking about filing some sort of police report charging Kelly with kidnapping Evan! You have to stop them!" Elizabeth insisted, pushing her silvery hair out of her face as she spoke.

"I . . . ? How could I . . ." Susan began, then her glance caught Kelly's face and she stopped. "Watch out! I think she's going to faint!"

"No. No." Kelly put out a hand and leaned against the mantle. "I'm okay. It's just this damn flu."

"Flu!" Barbara hooted loudly. "You're hung over. I saw you slurping up Jed's punch last night. The way you were drinking, you're lucky you're not dead."

Elizabeth did not rush to her friend's aid as quickly as Susan would have expected. In fact, that last comment seemed to have stopped her in her tracks.

"Dead?" Kelly repeated, pushing her headband back slightly. "Who said anything about dead?"

"No one. No one said anything about anyone being dead," Elizabeth insisted, loudly and unconvincingly. She looked around the room. Susan was still sitting on the floor near the tree, Kelly was clutching the mantel with one hand and her head with the other, Barbara was standing in the doorway with her mouth open, staring at Elizabeth.

"You know, don't you?" Barbara asked. "How did you find out?"

"Find out?" Elizabeth repeated the phrase.

"Find out that Evan's dead," Barbara elaborated.

"That Evan's—" Susan started. "Hey! How do you know?"

"Why don't you ask her how she knows?" Barbara countered the question.

"How do you know that I know?" Elizabeth asked, smiling.

"Oh, Evan!" Kelly wailed, threw herself down in a chair, and began to sob. "Oh! It hurts my head to cry!" She did so anyway.

Susan sighed and got up from the floor. "So how does everybody know?" she asked, picking a piece of tinsel from her slacks.

"Well, I don't know about everyone else, but Rebecca told me," Barbara said, coming into the room and sitting down.

"And who told Rebecca?" Elizabeth asked. "The night of the party she and Evan gave, she was swearing loudly that Evan was called out of town on business."

"Well, I only know what Rebecca told me," Barbara began. "But she didn't have any reason to lie. She was very upset. Remember, she loved Evan. She was married to him."

"Not as long as I was. And they weren't going to stay married very long. I know Evan and I would have gotten together again if someone—if someone hadn't killed him,"

Kelly perked up long enough to add before again melting into tears.

"Let's go back to the beginning," Susan urged, sitting down in a chair and waving Barbara and Elizabeth to do the same. "I gather you both know that Evan is dead. Right? Right. So how did you find out—and how did the people who told you find out?" She had expected Barbara to answer first, but Kelly surprised her by speaking up.

"I told her about it. Elizabeth, I mean. I needed someone to talk to yesterday, and it just burst out. I know I wasn't supposed to say anything to anyone, but I couldn't bear it alone anymore." Her crying continued.

"Is she going to cry all day? She'll dehydrate," Barbara said unsympathetically.

"She'll be fine. After all, she's had more than a week to get used to the idea of losing her ex-husband. Not that he was even hers to lose," came a voice from the doorway. Rebecca followed it.

"To continue this little expose, I told Barbara about Evan's death." Rebecca sat down.

"Who told you?" Susan asked quickly.

Rebecca looked at her appraisingly. "Very good. You've been keeping track of what's going on, haven't you?"

Susan was more than a little offended by the surprise in the other woman's voice, but she worked not to show it. "So who *did* tell you?"

Rebecca sighed. "The twins. According to them, they saw the body before you and Kelly found it. I'm afraid they broke into Kelly's house looking for something to drink after the bartender shooed them away from his supply. They said Evan was sitting in the chair, shot, and, when they saw him, they panicked and took off. Thomas suggested that they run around in circles in the backyard to obliterate the tracks from the shed to the house."

"Why?" Susan asked.

"I asked that, too. They claim that they were trying to protect me, that they thought tracks from one house to the other might implicate me in the crime, but my guess is that the excuse came to them later. They were probably afraid someone would accuse them of murdering Evan." She shrugged. "Neither of them is very honest, I'm afraid. And they really didn't get along with Evan very well."

"Why not? Evan always seemed to be trying to help them—looking for summer jobs for them and all that . . ." Susan ended her question lamely.

"They felt that he was just trying to get them out of the way," Rebecca answered.

"He probably was," Kelly said. "After all, Evan never wanted to have any children of his own. He always said they were a distraction and ruined any chance for a decent lifestyle."

"I'm sure they didn't kill him," Rebecca insisted. "And he did love my boys," she added, with less conviction.

"When did they tell you about—about finding him?" Susan asked.

"Late that night—long after the guests had left. Oh, I really didn't believe my own tale about him dashing off to a business emergency," she said, seeing the look on Susan's face. "But I really had no idea of how to account for Evan's disappearance. The last I saw of him, he told me that he was going to the bedroom to make a quick business call, that some sort of emergency had come up, and that he would tell me about it later. He told me everything about his business," she went on, almost sneering at Kelly. "We were business partners, you know."

"We were partners in life," Kelly answered smugly.

Susan would have leapt between them to avoid some sort of hair-pulling, face-scratching contest, but there was something more important on her mind. "Is that exactly what happened? Evan didn't get a call from the office or anything? He said he had to make a call?"

"Yes, exactly." Rebecca shrugged, seeming to think the distinction was unimportant.

"And you didn't see him after that?" Susan asked.

"Are you accusing Rebecca of luring him over to Kelly's house, shooting him, then dashing back through the snow to continue to play hostess at her party?" Barbara asked.

"Well, she could have done it, couldn't she?" Elizabeth argued. "After all, her own sons thought it was a possibility."

"You didn't see him again after that?" Susan repeated her question, glaring at the two women. "You never saw him dead?"

"I—"

"You don't have to answer that." Barbara rushed to her friend's defense. "What right does she have to ask you questions about this?"

"What reason does she have not to answer?" Susan slashed back.

"There's no reason to hide this anymore. The truth might as well come out now," Rebecca said quietly.

"Rebecca . . ." Barbara started in a warning tone of voice.

"Good, it's about time. Poor Kelly has been just miserable, knowing that Evan was dead, but not knowing who killed him—not even knowing where the body was!" Elizabeth jumped in.

"I don't know who killed him! And I don't know where the body is—not anymore, that is," Rebecca admitted.

"She means that she knew where he was killed—in your living room, Kelly Knowlson," Barbara added.

"In his favorite chair," Kelly elaborated.

"Now wait!" Susan almost had to shout to be heard over the rising voices. "Let's start at the beginning." She turned to Rebecca. "When did you see Evan dead? You did see him, didn't you?"

"She—"

"Barbara, shut up! I'm going to tell Susan the whole story. Then she can figure out what to do with it!"

"It's about time," Kelly had the energy to say.

Rebecca just glared at her and began. "I was talking to your mother-in-law at the party when Evan came over to me and said that he had to make a call—a business call—and would be in the bedroom for a few minutes—"

"If you were so important to Evan's business, why didn't he tell you what the emergency was about? How come—" Elizabeth interrupted.

"Maybe because that would have been rude to our guests," Rebecca shot back.

"Evan was never rude to guests in his house," Kelly agreed, but Rebecca glared at her anyway.

"As I was saying! He left the room, and I was busy, and I didn't think anything about him being gone until Kelly and you came back to the house, Susan. Well, think about it," she continued, guessing that no one believed her, "I was giving a party. I was busy, and, it wasn't as though I thought Evan was missing; I didn't think about him at all. If I had thought about him, I would have assumed that he was in the media room, or someplace else with one of our guests. I had no idea that he was shot, after all."

"Of course not," Susan said, hoping everyone else would have the sense to shut up and let her continue. They did.

"Well, we all went through the shed and over to Kelly's house. You were there, Susan. You know I'm telling the truth."

"Thomas and Travis were drinking in the shed, and had already discovered the body and done heaven knows what with it," Elizabeth added.

"Now wait. Just who discovered the body first? Kelly and I, or the boys?" Susan asked.

"You and Kelly must have," Rebecca said sadly. "And I'm afraid they were the ones who moved it. They thought that I had something to do with his death and they decided to hide the body."

"Why?"

"Well, what else could they do?" Rebecca responded to Susan's shrill exclamation. "They were trying to protect me. I thought it was sweet of them, actually."

"Where did they hide it?" Susan asked, not wanting to get into a discussion of the twins' behavior.

Rebecca smiled. "I think you almost guessed where, Susan."

"I did?" Susan gasped, then slapped her forehead. "Oh, no. The punching bag! It was hidden in the punching bag! I knew there was something odd about that! Rebecca, did the twins hide Evan in my garage?"

Kelly started to wail, and Barbara and Elizabeth stared at her with shocked looks on their faces.

"No, they didn't. They put a punching bag in your garage, just like they said they were going to. What sort of children do you think they are? At first, they just stuffed his body in the trunk of our Mercedes—until the party was over and they could tell me about finding him. I was furious with them for stealing all that liquor and planning their own private party. With Evan disappearing and all, I was ready to explode when the last guest went home and the caterers left. But they looked so upset—much more upset than I had ever seen them. I insisted that they tell me what was going on." She paused a moment. "And they did. They were terrified, of course. They hadn't had anything to do with Evan's death, but who was going to believe them? So the three of us decided to keep the body hidden. Later that night, we all moved Evan's body into the box that the punching bag had come in, wrapped it up in a half-dozen rolls of metallic wrapping paper, and left it standing in the corner of our garage. We thought it should be in the cold, you know," she added, with a quick look to see what response that got from Kelly.

Kelly only sniffed loudly.

"So, anyway," Rebecca continued, "that's where it stayed from that night until he—it—was stolen . . . taken—well, it vanished," she concluded.

"It what?" Elizabeth asked.

"When?" Susan asked.

"Oh, I thought we were going to get to have a proper funeral at last," Kelly wailed. "Everyone in town would have come, and heaven knows how many others would have sent flowers. And there would have been so many speakers and tributes . . . Evan knew some really famous people, you know. We could have had a large reception at the house afterward. Something tasteful, but creative, you know. Evan would have loved having a large funeral!"

"I doubt that," Rebecca said ruefully. "And I don't know when it vanished. I suppose it could have been right away. I just found out this morning myself."

"You'd better explain," Susan suggested.

"Well, when I ran into you at the ski shop, it occurred to me that, as of tomorrow, our wonderful hiding place wouldn't be so wonderful anymore. After all, no one expects to see large wrapped presents around the house the day after Christmas, and I decided to figure out what to do with it—him. Anyway, the—the box was in the back corner of the garage, behind Evan's Porsche. I had been ignoring it as much as possible. You can imagine."

"Yes, I can," Susan agreed.

"Well, I thought it might, well, it might smell a little by now and I approached it pretty slowly, but imagine my surprise when I found that the wrapping paper had been altered slightly and some of the tape was loose. And when I went to look more closely, it toppled to the floor—and bounced!''

''It was empty,'' Susan concluded.

''Yes.''

''And you have no idea when this happened?''

''None. It could have been right after the twins and I put it—him—there. I avoided looking at it as much as possible. And they did, too.''

''You checked with them about that?''

''Yes. Right away. I could tell by the looks on their faces that they were as surprised as I was.''

''Did anyone else get into the garage?''

''No one that I know of.''

''Could anyone else get into the garage without an alarm going off?'' Susan asked.

''Oh, yes. The alarm system that Evan had put into the house is broken in the garage. I smashed one of the connections or electrodes or something when I was setting up those cutouts that Evan had made for the front yard. It hadn't been fixed yet.''

''So where is Evan now?'' cried Kelly, getting back to the point.

THIRTY-THREE

THE GORDONS' HOUSE SMELLED DELICIOUSLY OF BALSAM and garlic when the Henshaws arrived to spend Christmas Eve with them.

"You're still thinking about the murder?" Kathleen asked, taking Susan's coat from her.

"Yes, because I think I'm getting close to solving the problem. I thought that whoever murdered Evan must be the person who moved his body, who was trying to cover up, but I don't think the twins killed him, do you?"

"It doesn't seem likely," Kathleen agreed, turning the rest of Susan's family over to her husband to entertain.

"Do you think he was killed at Kelly's house?" Susan asked.

"Probably. You said that the blood was on his body, right?"

"Yes, it had flowed out of his head and straight down his shirtfront." She shuddered and went on. "I don't think any of it got on the chair or anything else. I know there wasn't any blood around after the body disappeared. Why?"

257

"Well, we know he went into the kitchen—supposedly to make a phone call—but we don't know where he went after that. He could have gone straight out the back door, through the shed, and to Kelly's house."

"And been shot," Susan added quickly.

"But why?" Kathleen persisted. "Why did he go to Kelly's house unless he was planning to meet Kelly?"

"Who was at the hospital by that time."

"But he didn't know that, did he? And, even if he knew she was at the hospital, why would he go to her house?"

"To get something that he had left there? Something she wouldn't give him?"

"Susan, can you imagine Kelly refusing Evan anything?"

"That's true, but there must be some reason for Kelly's house to be involved in this." Susan bit her lip.

"Why was he killed during his own party? That's a pretty risky time to murder someone," Kathleen continued. "In my mind, this all seems just a little unplanned. There must have been other opportunities to kill him."

"Maybe the timing was critical," Susan suggested. "Maybe he was killed to prevent something from happening."

Kathleen looked at her friend in surprise. "You've learned a thing or two about crime, haven't you?"

"Since I was just a minor officer in the PTA? You bet I have. Why do you think I've been hanging around you so much for three years?" Susan asked in a kidding tone of voice.

"Well, we're going to have the chance to see what I've learned from you in your own field of expertise," Kathleen said enigmatically.

"What do you mean?"

"You'll see. Isn't that Jed calling you from the kitchen?"

"Sounds like it. Are we starting our meal in there?"

"Yes. Do you like mussels?"

"Love them."

"Good. Follow me." She turned and looked Susan in the eye. "Have you ever been to an Italian Christmas Eve dinner before?"

"No. I'm not terribly hungry, though. Do you think your mother would be offended if I just pick?"

"Yes. Eat. It's good for you."

"Hey!" cried Chad, appearing in the hall with a plate in each hand. "You sound just like your mother. That's what she said to me," he told Kathleen, and then turned to Susan. "Dad told me to look for you. He says that you'd better hurry if you want some clams. He's eating them by the handful."

"We'd better get in there," Kathleen said, pushing her friend before her.

Susan had spent a lot of time in Kathleen's kitchen, but it had never been so filled with good food. Pots were bubbling or steaming on the stove, both ovens were on and full, baskets of bread sat on the table flanked by a dozen bottles of gleaming Amarone wine, and laid out across the counter were two huge pans. One turned out to be brimming with mussels marinara and the other contained clams casino. "Seafood!" Susan cried.

"Didn't Kathleen tell you? It's traditional to have only fish on Christmas Eve. Eat. It's good for you!"

"Mother was just telling us that Dr. Barr is planning on stopping over later," Jed said to his wife, a smile fixed on his face.

"How nice."

"Yes, I called Dolores earlier and she said it was just fine," Claire chirped up. She was sitting at the kitchen table, apparently not eating.

"This is a case of the more the merrier," Kathleen insisted quickly. "In fact, I've invited a few more people for dessert later. Mother has made enough for an army, as usual."

"Well, if some people aren't going to eat anything," Dolores said, pouring a little more sauce over the mussels and glancing at the glass of water Claire was clutching.

"Kathleen said I could invite Seth. You don't mind, do you?" Chrissy asked her mother.

"Of course not."

"Why don't you call him from the phone in the living room," Kathleen suggested. "I'll show you where it is."

Susan was standing between Kathleen and the door, and Kathleen took the chance to grab a few words with her. "Go on to the living room, Chrissy. I need to talk to your mother for just a minute."

"Don't worry, Mrs. Gordon. I don't mind when people keep secrets this time of the year!"

"Is this about Chr—"

"No, but it just occurred to me that you've been inviting all the suspects in—in Evan's disappearance," Susan whispered.

"I just wanted to get one last look. I keep thinking that I know—"

"I do!" Susan interrupted. "I know who the murderer is! I just figured who went into the bedroom to call—but he didn't call from the bedroom! He called from Kelly's house!"

"Where? Who?"

"What did you say, dear?" Dolores called.

"Nothing. We're just discussing Christmas gifts . . . and things," she called out, then turned back to Susan. "Now, did you say what I think you said?"

"I think Evan must have called the police about his own murder; remember *someone* called them. And I really do think I know who the murderer is, but I have to know a few more things to be absolutely sure," Susan insisted. "Listen, did you invite everybody who was at the party over for dessert?"

"Everyone except Kelly."

"No. Kelly is important. It's essential that Kelly be here. Give her a call."

"What am I going to say to Rebecca? I promised her specifically that Kelly wouldn't be here."

"She asked?"

"Yes, she did. I promised her that, if she came over for dessert, she wouldn't run into Kelly."

"Okay. Then let me take care of that," Susan suggested.

"It's more important to solve this crime than to make Rebecca happy," Kathleen said. "Especially if she did it. Susan . . . ?"

"No, not a word. I have to be sure—"

"And you have to get back to your guests. Your mother is wondering out loud what has happened to you," Jerry said, appearing in the hall. "Hey, Susan. Like my Christmas attire? My secretary gave these to me." He held up one foot and displayed a tiny Santa face woven into navy socks.

"Cute," Susan replied absently. "Jerry, I have to talk to Chrissy in the living room. I'll be back in a second."

She found Chrissy just hanging up.

"Seth says he'll come on over with his parents, but do we have to hang around long, Mom? Couldn't we go for a walk and look at the lights or something?"

"Wonderful idea!" Susan surprised her daughter by agreeing. "You better get back to the kitchen now. I have to make a phone call or two."

"Fine, Mom. Thanks."

Susan acknowledged her daughter and picked up the phone for a quick call. In a few minutes she was munching her way through the appetizers.

Half an hour later, everyone except Kathleen and Dolores were in the dining room hungrily eyeing six gigantic platters of food. More was on the way.

Two hours later, platters empty except for the shell collection that a meal like this always produces, Susan and Kathleen met in the kitchen. "I told your mother she had done enough and she was not to move from that couch until espresso was made and the desserts were on the table. But, you know," she added to Kathleen, "you're the one that looks exhausted. Are you all right?"

"Fine. Just tired." She glanced around the room. "But look at this mess. If I know my mother, she won't even think about going to bed until it's cleaned completely."

"Well, let's get to work. What time did you ask everyone else to get here?" Susan asked, rolling up the sleeves of her silk dress and pulling on rubber gloves.

Kathleen fiddled with the knobs on the espresso maker. "I said nine o'clock. It's almost eight-thirty now. You know, I've been very patient, Susan. Aren't you going to at least tell me what you're looking for tonight?"

"Kathleen, have you ever thought that this crime depends on people lying? Or maybe any crime depends on people's lies. What makes this one different is that it's the lies of the person who was murdered that are covering up for the murderer."

"How much wine did you have with your dinner?"

"I'm not making sense?"

"Not much. What do you think Evan lied about?"

"Almost everything. And it's been going on for a long time," Susan announced, dropping a pan full of silver into the soapy water in the sink. "It took me a long time to catch on, but I really think I have the whole story."

"So who did it?" Kathleen asked, taking Saran Wrap off a plate of cookies.

"Susan knows who killed Evan?"

"She probably just *thinks* she knows who killed him," a second voice said, correcting the first speaker.

Susan kept washing, and Kathleen hurried to greet her guests.

"Rebecca! Barbara! I didn't know you'd arrived. I'm so sorry. I hope Jerry let you in and took your coats."

"We're fine—" Barbara, always the polite social comment ready, began.

But Rebecca interrupted. "Who do you think killed my husband?"

"I—"

"And you had better be careful about what you say. I know a lot about the law and slander charges."

"You know a lot about a lot of laws, don't you?" Susan murmured. "But don't worry, I won't slander anyone."

Rebecca looked at her curiously. "You *do* know something, don't you?"

"I think so, but I also want to wait until everyone is here. Why don't you go on into the living room with everyone else? We'll be serving dessert soon. There's no reason for you to worry, is there? Not now, at least," Susan said.

But Rebecca had recovered her poise. "Sure. Why not? Coming, Barb?"

"I— In a minute. I want to talk to Susan for a second. Go ahead."

Rebecca shrugged her indifference. "Fine. See you out there."

Barbara waited until the door had swung closed behind her friend before speaking. When she did it was in a hiss. "You think you know what's going on, don't you?"

"I think I know who killed Evan—and why."

"Why can't you leave well enough alone? Evan is gone. Kelly is near a breakdown. No one could pin anything on someone as unstable as she is. She won't go to jail; she'll go to some expensive hospital and be cured of this stupid obsession with Evan. You don't know what you're meddling in."

"I do, you know," Susan replied gently. "But I'm not

going to let Kelly take the fall for a murder she didn't commit. I know the solution to this crime and, in a while, everyone is going to know it.''

Kathleen got up quickly and stood behind her friend as Barbara moved forward menacingly. ''Susan's right, you know,'' Kathleen added.

Barbara gave them both a nasty look before spinning around and almost flying out the door.

''She'll leave . . .'' Kathleen started.

''No, I don't think so,'' Susan disagreed. ''She'll want to stay to the end. This has gone on long enough. We all need to know the truth now.''

THIRTY-FOUR

KATHLEEN WAS SURPRISED WHEN HER BACK DOOR OPENED, and Kelly Knowlson hurried into the room.

''Good timing,'' Susan commented.

''Susan told me not to ring,'' Kelly said, apologizing to Kathleen for her lack of manners. ''Oh, Susan,'' she continued, without waiting for an answer, ''is it really going to be over tonight?''

"I think so. I hope so. Do you mind staying in the kitchen until—"

"I don't mind doing anything, just as long as I find out who killed Evan." She sat down in a chair and stared at the espresso maker for a minute before saying, "I don't know why, but I feel that once the murderer is exposed, everything will be over and I'll be able to sleep again." She looked up at Susan. "The worst part has been not understanding. Surely this wasn't supposed to happen. Evan couldn't have wanted this!"

"No, of course not," Susan agreed.

Kathleen looked at them both and then at the desserts she had accumulated on the table. "Are we ready to start?"

"Yes. Just be sure that only you or I enter the kitchen. We don't want the wrong person to know that Kelly is here."

"I assume you mean Rebecca. Don't worry. I'll keep everyone in the living room. Can you handle that espresso machine? Or Jerry . . ."

"I can do it. Don't worry. Just get out there and start passing around cookies. Ho. Ho. Ho. Merry Christmas."

Kathleen smiled at her friend. "Maybe it will be a better Christmas than any of us are expecting," she said, leaving with a plate of pastries in one hand and a tray piled with pignoli macaroons in the other.

Susan issued some last-minute instructions to Kelly, then followed Kathleen to the dining room.

"Everyone seems to be here. They're gathered in the living room listening to Dr. Barr babble on and on about how terrible the meal they just ate is for their health. Keep that espresso machine away from my mother; she looks as if she might pick it up and throw it at him. We don't want another murder."

"Definitely not. On the other hand, at least your mother isn't pining away for him."

"True. How do you want to handle this? Are you going to let everyone eat dessert and then reveal all or—"

"Reveal all?" Susan quoted. "You make this sound like some sort of game. I do know who the murderer is. I was just going to tell you what I wanted you to do. Kelly arrived a little early or I would have told you sooner." She hurriedly gave Kathleen a few directions, ending as Dolores entered the room.

"I was going to—"

"You're not to do anything. We have one more load of stuff to bring out, and then you can call everyone to come and have dessert," Susan said, knowing that Dolores would listen to her orders rather than those given by her own daughter. "Besides, that meal was so stupendous that if we let you do any more work, Jerry and Jed will think we've become ungrateful beasts. You must give me the recipe for that scampi. It was heaven," she added, hoping to soft-soap her orders.

And it worked! "Whatever you say. But, if you want my recipes, you're going to have to come and watch me cook. I just guess at amounts. That's the way my grandmother taught me."

"Fine," Susan agreed, as Kathleen reappeared with the last load of goodies. "Why don't you tell everyone we're ready?"

But they had heard. The teenagers appeared first, ignoring the coffee and filling their plates with cookies and cake. The twins, both tall and thin, had gigantic appetites, and Seth and Chad weren't far behind. Chrissy was more careful of her figure. Her mother grabbed a word with her before she left the room.

"Why don't you take Chad with you and Seth when you go for that walk?" she suggested. "I know it's not what you want to do, but it *is* Christmas Eve," she added before her daughter had time to protest.

"Okay," the girl said, surprising her by agreeing. "We'll leave as soon as possible, if you don't mind."

"Great." Susan was anxious that her kids be out of the way before they started talking about the murder. Although she wanted the twins to hang around.

"We already asked Thomas and Travis if they wanted to come with us, but they refused," Chrissy continued, as if reading her mother's mind.

"Fine." Susan walked around the table, picking out a selection of desserts that she certainly didn't want, and followed the other guests into the living room.

"So, you're going to solve the puzzle of Evan's disappearance?" Barbara St. John asked sarcastically.

"I think we can wait to talk about this until the kids leave, Barb." Her husband amazed everyone by correcting her in public for the first time.

"We were just on our way out the door." Her son popped out of his chair. "Coming, Chrissy?"

"Sure," she said. "Chad?"

"I just got all this food!" the boy cried, looking greedily at his full plate.

"You can fill your parka pockets," his mother suggested, anxious that her children should leave.

"And we'll save you a nice big plateful," Dolores added. "My, how that boy does like to eat." She appeared to think this was the greatest compliment she could pay anyone.

"I don't understand," Dr. Barr was heard to say. He had moved while everyone else was getting dessert and now had the best seat in the room. "I thought we were here to socialize. Now everyone is talking about murder. I thought that man was just missing anyway." He looked around the room, obviously disgruntled.

"Oh, Bobby. I'm so sorry. We could leave, of course. I'm sure we're not needed here."

"I'm sure you are, Claire. In fact, you hold an important

clue to who the murderer is. Please don't talk about leaving.
I need everyone who was at Evan's party," Susan said. "I'm
sorry . . . and I know this isn't a pleasant way to spend
Christmas Eve, but I think we'll all have a better Christmas
if we know which one of us killed Evan Knowlson."

"I didn't know that we all knew that Evan was dead,"
came the sulky response from Thomas—or Travis.

"I . . ." Jed began.

"I think everyone except for possibly Claire and Jed, and
maybe Jerry . . ."

"No, Susan. Kathleen told me about it," Jerry Gordon
explained.

"Look, we're not going to get anywhere if Susan keeps
being interrupted," Elizabeth Stevenson said. "And I, for
one, would like to get home tonight. Could you just go on
with your story, Susan? I suppose it can't take very long since
Evan's only been dead—and in case any of you are wondering, Kelly told me about finding him—for a week."

"If everyone will just sit down and eat their dessert, I'll
explain. But we have to go back more than a week." As
Susan spoke, Kathleen got up and left the room. "We have
to go back to when Kelly and Evan broke up."

"What?" Rebecca was the only person to speak, although
everyone else's looks indicated their surprise. Everyone in
the room, Susan noted. Everyone.

"Let me tell you what I know," Susan began. "Some of
the story is just conjecture, but a lot of it is pieced together
from what's happened and what everyone has said—or didn't
say.

"I don't know why Evan left Kelly and married Rebecca.
I suppose he really could have fallen out of love with Kelly
and fallen in love with Rebecca. Or maybe he never was in
love with Kelly; maybe he just enjoyed the fact that Kelly so
obviously worshiped him and would be his slave. Anyway,
whatever happened when Evan left and married Rebecca, it's

important to realize that Kelly never really left him. She was still in love with him, she would still subjugate her own needs to his, she would still do anything he asked her to do. Anything.''

"Even murder him?" Rebecca asked sarcastically.

"No, but she helped cover up for the person who did kill him."

"Susan, give me a break," Barbara interjected. "Evan told Kelly to cover up for the person who murdered him? Why would he want to protect his own murderer?"

"It doesn't make much sense, hon," Susan's husband agreed.

"If you'll all just let me go on with my story? Fine. Well, Evan and Kelly got divorced and Evan married Rebecca and, in some ways, set out to duplicate his old life-style. He built a house in a different design, but for the same purpose: to impress and entertain business acquaintances. He gave the same parties and lived the same life as much as he was able. The twins were a slight problem, but one that could be dealt with by getting rid of them for the summer and finding them jobs."

"He hated us. Wanted us to get out of the house. But we got kicked out of every boarding school on the East Coast, so he had to let us live with him," one of the twins spoke up.

"True," the other agreed. "We bought him the punching bag for Christmas because we knew he'd have loved to punch us out—not that he could have."

Susan smiled weakly. "Anyway, there were two things different about his life now—the first is that he had a former wife living almost in his backyard who was ready, willing, and able to do his bidding."

"And the second?" Rebecca asked sarcastically.

"That you were involved in his business—as a partner, as

you so often remind us—and as a wife who couldn't be forced to testify against him if he were doing anything illegal."

"That condo deal over the old Baxter property!" Jeffrey St. John exclaimed. "I heard that Evan was involved in that. Isn't that where you and the twins lived when you first came to town, Rebecca? Was Evan making some sort of deal that involved the property that long ago?"

Rebecca opened her mouth and then shut it again.

"There's no reason for you to say anything," Susan said. "Remember, you're protected. Anyway, when I realized the legal ramifications of being married to a man you're in business with, I realized for the first time just how clever Evan was, just how good he was at taking care of himself by surrounding himself with people who would do things for him. Both you and Kelly have been pretty busy in the past few weeks, haven't you?"

"If they've been so busy helping Evan, how come he's dead?" Barbara asked, rolling her eyes to show how preposterous this whole story was to her. "What sort of help have they been?"

"We'll get to that later. First we have to consider a few other things about Evan's life right before the murder."

"Such as?" Barbara continued her goading.

"Insurance. Life insurance, to be more precise. Kathleen found out something very interesting. Part of Evan's divorce settlement was a two-million-dollar policy, payable to Kelly."

"Well, that gives her a motive—"

"Barbara, would you just shut up and let Susan finish a sentence?" her husband insisted.

"I—"

"Shut up!" he roared. And it worked.

"As I was saying, Evan had this huge life insurance policy and, like Barbara"—Susan smiled at her, feeling embarrassed at the other woman's public humiliation, no matter how justified—"I thought it gave Kelly a motive. Or, to be more precise, a motive for Rebecca to want to keep Evan alive. You see, Evan couldn't buy another policy at his age, so her only financial security would have to be found elsewhere. Kathleen's research turned up the facts that both houses were mortgaged and Evan's business had been acquiring debts rather than profits for the last year or so. It was beginning to look more and more like Kelly had the only motive for killing Evan—or, more to the point, that Rebecca had every reason in the world to want him to stay alive. Because as his second wife and business partner, she was going to be saddled with massive debt after his death.

"Then I discovered the answer to something that had been bothering me all along. Why did the body disappear? The twins admitted to moving it. They claimed they were trying to protect their mother. But why keep it around? Why not dispose of it in the ocean or someplace? Why did Rebecca continue to insist that Evan was on a business trip? If Rebecca really believed that Kelly had killed him—"

"I did, and I do!"

"Then why did you keep the body hidden? It made absolutely no sense to me for a long time. Until I remembered something else—that you had been to New York City two days in a row after the murder, probably at Evan's office.

Once I connected this unexpected flurry of business activity—unexpected because Evan told me the night he was killed that he and Rebecca were taking a break from work for a full week—the answer occurred to me. You wanted the body hidden so you could do some quick financial maneuvering before Evan was discovered missing—before all his assets, such as they were—were frozen while his will was probated.

"I assume you have everything like that taken care of now?"

"It's as right as can be." Rebecca shrugged. "All the capital has been removed from ongoing projects. It's enough to cover my personal expenses for a while. And I didn't do anything illegal; all I needed was a few extra days. But now''—this time the shrug seemed to indicate despair—''now I sure wish I knew where the body was.''

''You've really only proved that Rebecca had better reasons to want Evan alive than dead,'' Barbara insisted, glaring at her husband.

''True. But eliminating Rebecca and her kids as murder suspects helped me think this mystery through.''

''You mean you think Kelly did it?'' Elizabeth cried, horrified. ''Susan, I thought you were trying to help Kelly!''

''I am. One of the biggest problems I was having doing that is that Kelly's lies were hiding the truth that might help her.''

On cue, the kitchen door opened and Kelly, followed by Kathleen, entered the room.

''You're right, Susan,'' Kelly admitted, sitting down in the armchair that Jed had hastily vacated for her. ''But I wasn't lying for myself. I was doing it for Evan.''

THIRTY-FIVE

"You were doing just what he told you to do, weren't you?" Susan said gently. "You see," she explained to the rest of the room, "Kelly told me that very thing more than once, but I wasn't listening.

"The first time she said something was right after we found Evan. I, of course, ran to the phone to call for help, but the line had been cut. I was surprised and more than a little distressed, and then Kelly made a strange comment. She said, 'We're not supposed to call anyone.' At the time, I assumed that she was merely referring to the phone line, but later I realized it was fitting in too well with other things she was saying."

"Such as?" Elizabeth asked, thinking she was defending Kelly.

"That she knew what to do, that her actions that night were part of a plan—Evan's plan. Kelly almost told me that much on the way home from the hospital emergency room that night. When I suggested she visit her mother out of town for the holidays, she told me she was 'needed' here in Hancock. By whom? By Evan. And after the murder, she told me that what was happening 'wasn't making any sense,' implying that a different outcome had been planned—that, in fact, there had been a plan. In my kitchen the other day, Kelly said that Evan made all the plans in her life. And that she hadn't been told what to do since the night he died.''

"You're right, Susan. But it doesn't make any sense. It was Evan's plan, but something must have gone wrong. Surely Evan wasn't planning his own murder!'' Kelly cried out and then, covering her face with her hands, began to cry in earnest.

Susan took a sip of her now-cold espresso and sat back to wait until Kelly could speak.

"Susan's right,'' Kelly began, sniffing. "Being in Hancock with all my friends and neighbors giving parties and going on with their lives was painful for me, very painful. I had, in fact, been planning on going away this year, just like I did last Christmas. But on the day before Thanksgiving—I remember I was busy in the kitchen making Evan's favorite cranberry sauce with Grand Marnier in it—Evan knocked on the back door and asked to come in. Well, of course, I let him''—she shot Rebecca a defiant glance—"and we had some Stilton and some crackers and a little Moët that I always keep in the refrigerator in case—''

"Oh, get on with it!'' Barbara could control herself no longer. She glared at her husband, who didn't speak.

"He asked me to do him a favor. He had a plan, and he said it was very important, and that he couldn't possibly carry it off without my help. I was essential, he said. Absolutely essential.'' She smiled at the memory.

"And the plan?'' Susan prodded. "What was this plan?''

"Well, he told me that he and Rebecca were going to give a Christmas party. Of course, he assured me that he wouldn't even think of giving a party so much like the ones we gave each year, except for the fact that giving this party was necessary for his plan to be carried out.

"Anyway, there were some things he wanted me to do that day—before, during, and after the party. Although, actually, he wasn't that specific about what he wanted done after the party."

Susan remembered the bedroom set up for two and wondered if Kelly had been making a few plans of her own, despite what she claimed.

"But the first thing he wanted me to do was supposed to happen the day before the party. Evan wanted me to call Kathleen and convince her that I believed someone was trying to kill me. Does that make sense?" She looked around the room.

"As much as anything," Barbara said a little sarcastically.

"And that was the only thing you were to do until the day of the party?" Susan prompted.

"Yes. On the day of the party, he wanted me to make a salad and deliver it to Rebecca in the afternoon. You can imagine how surprised I was when he suggested that. After all, I would have thought that even an incompetent cook can manage a salad."

"But this wasn't an ordinary salad, was it?"

"No." She took a breath before continuing. "It was a Christmas salad."

"Red and green?" Rebecca asked sarcastically.

"Made with Christmas ingredients," Kelly said, correcting her. "Mistletoe, poinsettia, narcissus, yew needles, and berries."

"All poisonous," Susan added. "Including the tree preservative in the dressing."

"But no one was going to eat it. No one was supposed to and no one did!"

"Then why did you bring it to my house? What reason did

Evan give you?'' Rebecca looked disconcerted for the first
time.

"I didn't ask him why. I just did what he asked me to do,"
Kelly answered, appearing proud of the fact.

"But there were other things that Evan asked you to do,"
Susan continued.

"Yes. He told me to fake a minor auto accident and to call
him for help.'' She seemed confused. "But the policeman
who found me wouldn't take me home to make the call—and
I had everything set up: eggnog, cookies—he insisted on
taking me to the hospital. Then, when I finally got a chance
to call Evan's business number, someone else answered—
and he had told me he would . . . and that I was to talk to
no one else—and my car was wrecked, so I called Susan's
house. I knew her kids would be home and could get in touch
with her. I had to get home from the hospital." She stopped
again and took a deep breath, remembering that night.

"But then . . .'' Susan prompted.

"Then, when Susan and I got home, there was Evan's
body in the living room—in the chair that he had asked me
to set up."

"For him?'' Kathleen asked.

"He didn't tell me who it was for."

"But later—after Evan's body had disappeared—did you
change the whole arrangement and put out tea and lemons?''
Susan asked.

'Yes. Evan had given me very specific directions, and I
had prepared everything ahead of time, because Evan said
there might only be a few minutes to do it. I had to stuff the
old cookies and eggnog down the garbage disposal and put
out the fresh refreshments. But I did that, yes.''

"You didn't think it was all a little strange? You didn't
think about giving up on the plan once Evan was dead?''
Susan asked.

"No. You see, Evan told me to disregard anything unusual that happened that night. So I did."

Rebecca stared at Kelly with her mouth open. "You're crazy, you know that?"

"I just did exactly what Evan told me to do. He said that the most important thing was that I tell nobody about it. And I haven't—at least, not until now." Kelly folded her hands in her lap and looked around at her neighbors.

"So he was killed while you were at the hospital," Barbara said.

"So Kelly didn't do it, either," Elizabeth added triumphantly.

"So who did? And who called the police?" Jerry Gordon asked, looking puzzled.

"Evan called the police. Remember he said he had to make a phone call from the bedroom? Well, he didn't then, of course, but he must have called from Kelly's house right before the murderer got there," Susan announced. "And the person who killed Evan was the person that Evan was planning to kill." She paused. "It took me awhile to figure it out. Of course, it didn't make sense that Evan would make such elaborate plans for his own murder. But I couldn't even begin to figure this out until I put together what he had been asking Kelly to do—to behave in a manner that would make her appear unbalanced and then have an accident. We were all talking about Kelly's supposed mental problems; it had become common knowledge that she wasn't always acting in a balanced manner. Calling Kathleen was supposed to make her sound paranoid, and making the salad out of poisonous ingredients certainly wasn't normal behavior. So what would Evan do if he was called upon to help his ex-wife in this situation?"

"Call a doctor!" Claire cried, looking at her fiancé with a shocked expression and yanking her hand from his clasp.

Dr. Barr responded by jumping up. "So what?" he exclaimed. "Who would have thought a middle-aged suburban housewife could figure it out." He glared at Susan. "Yes, Evan was going to call on me to help his poor little crazy ex-wife, and then he was going to kill me—to save himself and his business. Evan loaned me the start-up capital for my company. And to make sure he would make a profit if I died (because my company is almost entirely dependent upon my selling ability—anyone can figure out how to package vitamins and vegetable protein), he insisted that I take out a very expensive life insurance policy on myself. With Evan, of course, as the primary beneficiary. Thus, I'm afraid, I became the answer to all his financial needs—which were considerable, I understand. And, besides, with me dead, he didn't have to worry about the exposure of some of his shoddier business deals. Such as that Baxter property thing. So he decided to kill me."

"Evan planned to kill you?" Kelly was incredulous.

"Yes, he even told me so just before I shot him. How stupid he was to think that I would meet him alone without a weapon. I knew how much I was worth to him dead. And I knew how much he wanted to keep his sleazy business deals to himself."

"You—you used me as an excuse to see Evan socially . . . to get to that party," Claire cried out.

"No, my dear, I didn't. Evan knew I was going to be in New York City over the holidays and had invited me himself. He was planning to kill me, remember. But, when I heard you talking on the ship with that couple from Hancock that evening in Istanbul, I decided that I could use some allies in town."

"You were still using your relationship with my mother," Jed said angrily. "You convinced her to end her vacation early and come back here. You made her think that you were serious about your relationship! We accepted you at our house and as our friend."

"I had no choice," Dr. Barr responded. "I was fighting for my business, for my life."

"Why didn't you just stay out of his way? Why did you ever come to Hancock?" Jed asked a little more calmly.

"I had to kill him. Don't you see? One of the conditions of Evan's investment was that I keep up the payments on that damn insurance policy. I couldn't go through the rest of my life looking over my shoulder, hoping Evan was solvent!" He turned to Susan. "But you had connected me with Evan in some way, hadn't you?"

"Yes. Kelly showed me the gifts she had bought and wrapped and labeled for all Evan's business associates. There was one for you."

"An alpaca scarf!" Kelly cried out. "I shopped for hours to find just the right one. Then you killed him!"

"And you're not going to get away with it! You're a miserable man," Claire cried.

"So what are you going to do?" Barr said, with a sneer, and Susan thought that they were all seeing his true personality for the first time. "Believe me, I'm not afraid of a bunch of beef-fed, cholesterol-clogged, heavy-drinking suburbanites. Especially since I have this." He pulled a gun from his jacket.

Maybe it was their cholesterol levels or maybe it was the gun, but no one moved toward the man who, aiming his weapon at Jed in a way that made Susan's heart miss more than one beat, moved backward toward the front door. What he didn't know was that the doorway was filled with a half a dozen unsmiling, similarly armed policemen. Two grabbed his arms, one grabbed him around the neck, and one spoke.

"We've got him. And, thanks to whoever called, we heard everything. My chief needs someone to make a statement, and he also wants to talk to the Henshaws."

"He . . . ? Why?" Susan spoke up.

"Seems a United Parcel man was making a last-minute

Christmas delivery at about five-thirty this afternoon and he found a strange package leaning against your front door—a package containing the dead body of a Mr. Evan Knowlson. The chief thinks you may know something about it.''

THIRTY-SIX

THE PRESENTS UNDER THE TREE HAD BEEN OPENED, THE wrapping paper was sizzling in the fireplace, and the Henshaw family was happily entertaining the Gordons on this Christmas Day. Susan was in the kitchen putting what is known as the finishing touches on their dinner. Kathleen was with her.

"Dr. Barr explained to the police that he left the body in front of our door on his way to your house," Susan explained.

"Assuming it would be found when you got home?"

"Yes. It was in one of those gigantic plastic bags that are sold to wrap large gifts in; this one was embossed with thousands of tiny candy canes. Luckily it had ripped and a hand was sticking out—otherwise it probably would have been there waiting for our return, just like Dr. Barr planned." Susan opened her oven door and pulled out a large brown goose as she spoke.

"The UPS man must have been surprised," Kathleen commented, leaning on the counter and watching Susan baste the bird.

"I suppose so. All the police said was that he called them from next door and then returned here to wait for them."

Kathleen reached across the counter and snatched a cube of stuffing. "I cannot believe that we're going to sit down and eat another big meal after the one my mother prepared last night. I didn't think I'd ever be hungry again and here I am . . ."

"Watch out, it's hot," Susan warned, returning their dinner to the oven and checking the timer. "The police must have had some day. Didn't they think it was a little unusual when you called and asked for armed officers to wait in case a murderer confessed?"

"Who knows what they thought? They did it."

"So I guess it's all over."

"Except for Kelly's and Rebecca's grief," Kathleen reminded her.

"It really is horrible," Susan answered. "It's true we all said that Kelly would do anything for Evan, but who would have thought that the lies he wanted her to tell would eventually provide a cover-up for his own murderer?"

"And, with Rebecca hiding the body for her own reasons, it was incredible that Barr was ever discovered. Then she lied about how successful the business was as well. It's amazing that we found out the truth, with so many people committed to keeping it hidden. You did some good detecting there, Susan."

"Kathleen, did it ever occur to you who Evan expected to be convicted of Dr. Barr's murder?"

"Kelly," she answered slowly and sadly. "I know. He was setting her up for two purposes: first so he'd have an excuse to get Dr. Barr away from the party and to her house and then, probably so he could claim that she was crazy and killed him. I assume that was the reason that he wanted her to change the setting after the body was originally found. Involving her in a cover-up, no matter how inadequate, would definitely help convince the police of her guilt. It really is sick, isn't it?''

''Well, I'm not going to waste any time regretting his death, if that's what you mean.'' Susan slammed down the lid on a copper casserole and turned to Kathleen. ''I'm not terribly sympathetic to Dr. Barr, either, of course. To kill another person in self-defense is one thing, but he appeared to think so highly of himself and the business he created that he had no scruples about using Claire and us—and everybody, in fact, to protect himself.''

''How did he discover the body in the garage?'' Kathleen asked.

''Jed gave that away,'' Susan admitted ruefully. He got angry at Dr. Barr's bragging about his strength and mentioned the punching bag. Barr realized that there was a box as well as a bag involved.''

''And Claire? How's she taking all this?''

''She's holding up well—better than I would have thought. In fact, last night she made some comments along the lines of 'There's no fool like an old fool' and then asked to go to the midnight carol service at church.'' Susan turned off the oven. ''When she woke up this morning, she was ready to help us celebrate Christmas. I must admit, I'm impressed.''

''Me, too.''

''Although—'' Susan paused and grinned—''she's been on a real eating binge. But then, so have we all.'' She looked at the warm Parker House roll that Kathleen was munching. ''Everything can sit here for another half an hour. Why don't we join the others in front of the tree?''

''Great. I promised Chad I'd look at his new tape deck.''

''Just don't ask him to demonstrate the volume. He turned it up all the way first thing this morning and the ornaments on the tree are still shaking.''

They were greeted by a chorus of "Grandma got run over by a reindeer" on the stereo as they entered the living room. Chrissy was sitting in a window seat, reading a new book; Chad was lying under the Christmas tree, playing with the dials on his new tape deck; Jerry, Dolores, and Claire were seated around a cheerful fire. Jed appeared behind them, a tray of crystal flutes in his hands.

"I have anticipated your every need," he announced, putting the tray on the coffee table beside two sweating bottles of Moët.

"Wow! Especially if this turns out to be a cold winter," Kathleen agreed, picking up a full-length, spruce green sheepskin coat from the back of the sofa. "Some gift."

"Yes," Susan agreed, laughing. "And there's my gift to him." She pointed to a larger, shorter brown version of the same coat lying on a chair across the room.

"They even came from the same Madison Avenue store," Claire pointed out.

"Just another example—"

"Of great minds thinking alike." Everyone chorused the ending for Jed.

Jed chuckled, poured, and passed out the champagne. "We all saw that fabulous car you bought Kathleen," he said, handing Jerry a glass. "What did she give you?"

Jerry smiled at his wife. "Do you want to tell them or should I?"

"She's pregnant!" Dolores blurted out, preempting everyone else.

But, in the congratulations that followed, everyone forgot everything except the good news. As Jed told his wife that night as the two of them sat in front of the fireplace in their bedroom, it really was a perfect Christmas. All the problems of the past had been cleared away, the future was sure to bring much happiness and joy, and the present was perfect.

Susan just nibbled a *lebkuchen* and smiled happily.

ABOUT THE AUTHOR

Valerie Wolzien lives in Tenafly, New Jersey. She is also the author of *Murder at the PTA Luncheon* and *The Fortieth Birthday Body*.